'Til Death

Do Us Part

TAMMY CAPRI

'Til Death Do Us Part
Copyright © 2014 TAMMY CAPRI

Til Death Do Us Part is a work of fiction. The events and characters that are described are imaginary and are not intended to refer to specific places or living persons.

ISBN 13: 978-0989134279
ISBN 10: 098913427x

Nu Class Publications
P.O Box 23662
Phila, Pa, 19143

www.NuClassPub.com

This Book is dedicated to all the women who have become a victim of falling in love with the wrong man.

Attachment

A ten letter word that I vowed to never let consume my life, again. I've learned a long time ago that getting too attached to someone never worked in my favor; especially when it came to the men in my life. They were all trifling ass nothings; every single one of them. None of them ever did right by me, even when I was too young to realize it. First, there was my dad, Gary Odoms. He was the first nigga to ever hit me with the bulshit and the okie-doke. He set the tone for the rest of the lames. I should have known better, though. Those tears that my mom used to shed weren't for nothing. I was just too young, too naive to believe that a man like Gary would one day just abandon the one thing that was supposed to be his pride and joy. *Me*. Gary mutha-fuckin Odom. I didn't understand it. How could a loving, caring, just outright most amazing man a girl could ever know just up and leave her life. He was my playmate when I didn't have any friends to play with, my patient when I pretended to be a 7-year-old, world class surgeon, my audience when I learned a new magic trick, and the one who scared away all of the monsters who seemed to move into my closets without my permission. Yeah, he was my dad. The best dad from what I remember. That was until my 10th birthday party. Little did I know that would be the last time I would see him. I remember that day as if it just happened. It wasn't a regular encounter by far. From the moment he walked into my mom's house his aura was so thick it nearly choked all of my party guest. His stern expression, the way he drug his feet, and his late arrival were all dead giveaways. He wasn't the same old, happy, playful Gary. He didn't even bother to speak to my mother. He came straight to me.

Without words, Gary grabbed my hand and pulled me away from my friends and into the kitchen. My mother didn't offer a word either. She watched from the stairs as we disappeared into the back. When we were alone he lifted me into the air and hugged me tightly. The embrace lasted longer than usual. He hugged me so tight that I swore I could feel the beat of his heart. It was rapid; as if he had ran a marathon and holding me would help clam its pace. I didn't think much of it then. When he finally pulled away our eyes met.

"Daddy, what's wrong?" Were my exact words when I noticed his glassy eyes staring back at me. His big hands began to tremble as he lowered me back down to the floor. Something was wrong, and it was obvious he wasn't going to tell me a damn thing.

Gary kneeled down and straightened out my light blue tutu dress just before he kissed me on the cheek.

"Zayda," he finally spoke. Even the way he said my name was off. It wasn't the soothing tone he'd normally used, it was dry—unenthused. I couldn't help but to wonder if I had upset him.

"Do you love me?" He asked.

Reluctantly, I nodded.

"And you know your daddy loves you, right?"

"Yes, daddy."

"No matter what happens, I want you to always remember that, okay?" He stroked my cheek with the back of his hand before returning to his feet. He looked over at my mom who was now leaning at the threshold of the dining room.

If looks could kill…God damn! Gary's jaw clenched so tight I could hear the grinding of his teeth. He looked at her like she was the grim reaper there to collect his soul.

He looked back down at me. "Remember what I said."

I watched him walk passed my mom and back out of the front door. The next few days went by without a trace of him. Hoping he would soon return only led to anxiety. No explanations, no phone calls… nothing. My mother went on with her life as if nothing had changed. Like it was normal for a man, your man, to leave and never come back. Anytime I would ask about him, the answer was always *he'll be home soon*. Well, I'm twenty-eight now and *soon* still haven't come.

Then, there was my best friend, Tony. He was the first guy friend that I had, or any friend for that matter. We met in junior high. The most common factor that we shared was that no one else knew we existed. Well, they knew who I was. It wasn't hard to miss a two-hundred pound, fourteen-year-old walking the halls of the school. Truth be told, I wished they would have missed me. It would have made junior high a lot easier without the fat jokes and teasing every damn day. Tony, on the other hand, was invisible. He could walk down the hall and not be the center of attention, unless he was walking with me. No one even noticed when he wore the same outfit three days in one week. Money was a major issue in his household. He lived with his grandmother who was on a fixed income. His mom died when he was born, and he never met his dad. I was his only friend. We weren't considered to be one of the popular kids, so we formed our own alliance. Just him and me.

The summer after we graduated eighth grade, Tony got a job cleaning up my uncle's barbershop. He spent just about all of his summer days there; from the time the shop opened in the morning until the very last customer left. Anytime I wanted hang out with him, it was always "I have to work today." I was a bit bored for a while, but I didn't mind. I knew how much he really needed to make money. I could survive the three summer months, and then we would be back together hanging out like always. High school was our next journey, and we were going to take it together.

A week before school started, I called Tony to go school shopping. I knew he would be excited to go. He would finally be able to afford clothes he wasn't ashamed to wear. I hadn't heard from him in a few weeks, and I was missing my friend. His grandma told me that he was outside on the front porch and asked if I could call his cell phone. *Cell phone?* I didn't know he had one. He never even bothered to call me and give me the number.

I decided to just go visit him. He lived two blocks away from me, which wasn't far at all. Philadelphia wasn't known for long streets. Tony was right where his grandmother said he was. I spotted him as I walked down his block. He was sitting on the concrete porch step and he wasn't alone. As I got closer, I recognized who his companion was. Tiffany Myers. She was the last person on earth who I expected to see. She was like the Beyoncè of popular girls. Every guy wanted to date her, and the girls either hated her or wanted to be her. She was blessed with perfect genes and flawless features. From her perfect caramel complexion to her thick, long, jet black hair she was like a 14-year-old goddess. I had no idea she even knew Tony's name, let alone, be at his house.

Uneasily, I slowed my pace. I didn't know why I was so nervous. I had no reason to be. Tony was my friend and as far as I'm concerned she was the outsider. Maybe this was it. Maybe this was our new start that we had always hoped for. If she was cool with Tony, then she'd be cool with me; Tony would make sure of it. I don't know how he did it, but I'm almost glad he did. I mean, we are going to high school, right? If people knew that we were hanging out with Tiffany that would definitely give us some cool points. At that moment, I actually felt a bit excited for the new school year. Things were about to change for Tony and I. Hanging with the most popular girl in school was going to be one hell of an upgrade on the popularity food chain.

I saw Tiffany get up from the steps and walk into Tony's house. His eyes were glued to her; he hadn't even noticed I walked up on him.

"What's up?" I could tell that I startled him when he flinched. He looked at me as if he'd seen a ghost. "Tiffany Myers, huh?" I sarcastically mentioned.

"Yea, umm," he stood to his feet. "Her dad cuts hair at your uncle's barbershop. You didn't know that?" Periodically, Tony would peek back at his front door.

"Really? I wouldn't know; I hardly ever go there." I shrugged, taking a seat on the warm concrete step. "So, you got a new cell phone? Things must be nice at the shop." I noticed the fresh outfit he was sporting. A yellow Ralph Lauren pull-over, tan Cargo shorts, and a pair of white Air Maxes.

"Yea, things— things are pretty good there." He nodded, hesitantly.

Tony was acting strange. He wasn't his normal talkative self, and he purposely avoided making eye contact with me.

"So...?" I questioned.

"So, what?"

"When did you start hanging out with Tiffany Myers? How much did you have to pay her?" I laughed.

Tony didn't seem to find my joke funny. He shot his eyes at me. His piercing stare made me feel some type of way. I was ashamed for even saying it. "I didn't mean it like that. I was just wondering why—"

"All done," Tiffany announced as she returned to the porch. "Are you ready to go?"

Tony and I both looked up at her. A look of disgust overran her face when she saw me. See, I forgot to mention that Tiffany was a bitch; a young, beautiful, stone-cold bitch. She was the goddess of bitches. If bitch was an island, she would be the water that surrounded it.

She shifted her body to one side, put her hand on her boney hip, and slow rolled her eyes to Tony. "*Why* is this fat ass here? You're making friends with grizzly bears now? I know her ass is hungry?"

I wanted to say something…anything, but once again these damn butterflies horded my insides. They must have traveled to my throat and stopped anything from coming out because I just sat there like a mute.

"She was just leaving." Tony spoke. "And she's not my friend. She just got lost on the way to the zoo."

I swear my heart was about to pound out of my chest. His words felt like a lethal injection. They burned my lobed the moment the words left his lips. *What was he talking about? Why would he say some shit like that?*

"Come on," he reached for her. "We out."

She grabbed his hand and followed his lead, leaving me sitting on the step.

Did that just happen? I felt like I was in a bad dream. You know those dreams where you can't move or can't speak; like I was fighting a losing battle against gravity.

I replayed that moment in my mind about hundred times before I came to accept my reality. My best friend was gone and I had no answers as to why. He turned on me without any warning; not one sign. I felt so betrayed…so hurt, while all at the same time, a small part of me still cared. I wanted to hate him, wanted to hurt him like he hurt me, but I couldn't help but miss him. His smile, the way he'd sit on my porch railing waiting for me to come outside, and the way he'd always told me not to let the teasing at school get to me. That I was going to be successful when we grew up. I knew he cared; that's what I like about him the most. That was also what made this hurt so badly.

At first, I thought he would feel bad about what he did and come back to mend our friendship. I just knew the old Tony would eventually show up, but after our freshman year in high school, the old Tony was dead and gone. And Tone, the high school superstar, was born.

So you see nothing ever worked out in my favor. Ever since then, I, Zayda Marie Jones, made a promise to never get attached to anyone, again. I avoided that word like it was the plague. Or, at least I tried to.

Chapter One

"Germany?" I exclaimed. "Are you serious, babe?" Instantly, I stopped thumbing through my IPhone which held part of my attention during our usual morning talks. The shit my husband just tried to sneak in trumped me getting my social media updates. Putting the phone down on the bed, I looked up at Carl with my face completely scrunched up. "And they're just *now* telling you this?"

"Zay, you knew that there was always a possibility that I would get this partnership," he said adjusting his blue nylon tie in front the full body mirror in the corner of our bedroom. His baritone was deep and commanding.

Resting back against the cushioned headboard, I folded my arms across my chest. "The partnership… yes."

"And…relocating." Finished with his tie, he turned to face me. My eyes traveled the length of him eulogizing how the Brooks Brother's tailored suite hugged his masculine frame as he attuned his gold cufflinks. His shoulders were broad. His posture screamed boss, and oh yes…Carl Kinsley was exactly that.

"I agreed to move but not out of the god damn country. Cherish is only four-months-old, and I know you don't expect me to be okay with moving our daughter to Germany." Climbing off the bed, I walked over to him. The floral-pattern silk robe dangling from my shoulders gently swayed around my voluptuous physique. "We're just *really* getting settled in here." I argued, yet in a soothing tone. "Maybe we could just… stay. I mean, you're making good money now at the firm." Reaching up to his shirt collar, I added my wifely touch to his tie adjustment. "We're good here."

"I know, Zay. But you know it's not about the money." He planted his strong hands on the slim of my waist, caressing as he spoke. "This is an opportunity for me to become a partner… a partner, Zay. A seat at the round table. Do you know the type of connections and deals that happen inside of that network? And," he leaned in and pressed his soft lips against mines before continuin g. "If I move into that position our lives are set. Trust me on this, Zay. It would only be for a year, two at the most. We can always come back to the states after I get the firm up and running over there. You never know, you may not want to come back."

He kissed me, again, this time on my neck slightly below my ear. Instantly, I melted into his affection. Carl had a way of persuading me. Just the very scent of that man had me weak in the knees and creamy between my thighs.

"Ok...." I moaned softly as a seductive grin eased on to my face. "I'll think about it."

I pulled his body closer, wanting him to have his way with me; just one good nut before he parts from me for the day. Besides, a man is always supposed to finish what he starts.

My fantasy was short lived when Carl kissed me once more and pulled back. "I have to go, or I'll be late."

Damn! I thought.

He turned to get one last look in the mirror. As I stood behind him and admired his reflection, it still amazed me that he was mine—all mine. He hadn't changed a bit since the day I first met him— well, aside from his neatly trim mustache and goatee. Carl was the epitome of a man. Confident. Handsome. Educated. His evenly chocolate complexion, dark wavy hair, and pearly white teeth often interjected any potential disputes I had towards his decision making.

"Who are you trying to impress?" I asked, jokingly. "You're going to make me put a tracker on your ass."

"I'm already covered." He smiled with a quick flash of his Colin Cowie black diamond edge wedding ring. "There's not another woman out there who can take your place— well Cherish, however, is giving you a run for your money."

Coos from the baby monitor on the dresser reverberated through the tiny speakers. I was as if she was summoned. My baby girl chimed in at the right moment.

"I see," I laughed.

Carl retrieved his wallet and keys from the dresser, and headed out of our bedroom.

"Oh," he turned back towards me just as he reached the door. "The brothers are coming over tonight. I forgot to tell you."

"Tell me what?"

"I offered to host the unofficial chapter committee meeting since Neil's basement flooded."

"Carl!" Dropping my head slightly to one side, I gave him that *give me a break* look, and he knew exactly what that look meant.

"I know, I know…we won't be long, I promise. We just need to get things in order for the Kappa Alpha Psi Gala."

I huffed. "So go to a damn Starbucks. When it comes to your fraternity, you are *always* long. Y'all will be here 'til 4 in the morning, I'll still have to cater to our infant… the noise…the smoke, and not to mention I'll end up doing all the cleaning the next day."

"Come on, Zay." He pleaded. "You know I wouldn't have offered if it wasn't important. And all you have to do is set the basement up for me. I'll make sure it's clean afterwards."

"No, Carl." I said, firmly. "Not tonight. It's too late of a notice."

He just stood there looked at me not offering any more words as if he was waiting for me to change my mind.

Opposingly, I returned the stare. It was a silent war of the eyes that didn't last too long. Once again, he captured me with his big brown eyes, and finished me off with the playful pout.

"Please?" He mouthed. "For me?"

I giggled, rolling my eyes at him. *You just can't say no, huh?* I thought, partly because the gesture was mutual. Carl rarely said no to me. If there was something I truly wanted, he made it happen; like this house for instance. The massive, three thousand square foot, five-bedroom home was my wedding gift. There was more space in my house than we could occupy. After completing the master bedroom, Cherish's room, and the guest bedroom, the remaining two were converted in an office and a small gym. At the time, I wasn't even sure if we could afford such a huge finical commitment because, after all, Carl had been the sole provider since I conceived the baby. I had to take a leave from my position as a case worker due to pregnancy complications. Carl didn't mind. His main priority was to make sure our daughter made an entrance into this world. I hadn't been back since. Luckily, Carl was excelling at the firm. I still can feel the butterflies dancing in my stomach the same as they had the day he told me that he had a surprise for me. We had just come from the farmer's market fulfilling my watermelon craving when he pulled up to the beautiful premises. I had no clue where we were until I realized it was the house I'd been looking at for months on the real estate website.

"What are we doing here?" I asked him as I ogled the masterpiece. It was much bigger in person. The photos on the site didn't do any justice. When I finally tore my eyes away and looked over at him, Carl had a pair of keys dangling from his finger.

"Welcome home." He said, a smile garnishing his face.

"Home?" I gasped in disbelief. "Stop pl— are you serious?" Excitement invaded my body and I couldn't control my vocals. The cheerful shrill leaving my mouth was piercing.

"Oh my God! Baby, for real? This is ours?"

"It's what you wanted, right?"

"Yes, yes, yes, yes, yes!" Grabbing him by the neck, I pulled him into my arms placing kisses everywhere.

Carl laughed. "Baby, calm down. You are seven months pregnant. You know what Dr. May said about staying calm. We need that bun to fully cook."

I released him from my grip, yet my smile was still as big as day. "With surprises like this, you'll be the reason I go into an active labor." I turned back to look at my new residence. "Oh my god! It's the best. Baby, I love you so much!"

"Only the best for my queen." He grabbed my hand and used the tip of his finger to turn my face back to him. The sincere look in his eyes made a wave of emotion inside of me. I was already hormonal and would cry at the drop of a dime.

"When I told you back in college that I want you to have to world, I meant it. Even if I have to fly to outer space and collect it myself, you will never go without. You or my seed. You are giving me more than any man could ask for. And for that, I am forever in debt to you. I love you, Zayda Kinsley."

That was him. My man. My king. Carl was all that I needed, and til this day, he still is. The same charm he put on me then still worked in his favor now.

"Fine…" I gave in. "You can have your meeting, but—"

He rushed back to me before I could finish my sentence and kissed me on my cheek. "That's why I love you."

"Oh don't think it's not coming with a price." I sassed. "You tell me this at the last minute, *and* you want me to set up?"

"I promise to take you on the best date you've ever gone on this weekend," Carl pouted and put his hand together in a praying position.

"You're gonna have to come a lot better than a date, Mr. Kinsley." I teased as I folded my arms across my chest.

"Ok, a date…with roses?"

"Uh-uh, better." I shook my head.

"You're not going to make this easy for me, are you?" He smiled.

Playfully, I giggled. "Oh, come on, Mr. Business Attorney. If you're bargaining this way for your clients, then you better start looking for a new profession."

"Oh, it's like that, huh?" He nodded, gently biting his bottom lip. "Okay, I'll tell you what… meet me at my office today around noon."

"I have a GYN appointment at 11:30."

"Well, afterwards. I promise to make it worth the trip." He winked before turning on his feet.

"It better be." I said as I watched him walk out of our bedroom.

Shortly after, I heard the buzzer from the alarm system indicating that Carl had left out, still managing to put a smile on my face before he departed.

That man, I thought walking out of my room and into the nursery. In the cherry wood crib, Cherish lay on her back googling and spontaneously moving her limbs.

"Is that mama's princess making all that noise?"

Cherish's eyes seemed to light up the moment she spotted me. I lifted my chocolate drop into my arms and held her tightly. It was something about the way her smooth skin against mine crated a tune that only she and I could hear. Never in life did I imagine loving someone as much as I did her. Now, don't get me wrong. I loved Carl with every being in my soul and wouldn't hesitate to lay my life down for his. But my baby girl, my daughter…she was my entire existence. Without her, there was no Zayda. And at such a young age, I could tell she was fully aware of our bond. Cherish was smart. And I vowed to be the woman she needs me to be to lead her through this life.

"Was mommy taking too long?" I continued my morning chat with her as if she verbally understood. Her gums flapped back as I took a seat on the rocker next to the window. Even with the huge oak tree conquering most of the view, the early morning sunrays still beamed through the pink sheer nursery curtains.

Pulling a clean flannel blanket from the straw basket beside the foot of the chair, I threw it over my left shoulder to prepare for our nursing session. With the tight and heavy sensation from the milk built up in my left breast, I was probably more excited than her. Hopefully, she's extra hungry and takes every drop of it.

I removed my breast from my bra and positioned my nipple atop her bottom lip. The moment she got on a good latch, my cell phone rang from the other room.

Dammit! Call me lazy, but I honestly did not feel like walking back to my room with my daughter clinging to me. *Whoever it is will have to just wait until I'm done.* Usually, my phone is glued to my hand since we didn't have a land line. With the unlimited features on our wireless devices, there was really no need for one.

Minutes later, it rang again. It had to have been my husband, or an emergency, because that's the only time I get back-to-back calls.

Sighing intensely, I pulled myself up from the rocker. Cherish didn't budge. My movement didn't interrupt her meal one bit.

By the time I walked the few feet across the hall to my room, the caller hung up. Snatching up my cell from the bed, I swiped my thumb across the screen to view the missed calls. Strangely, there were none. A quick chirp diverted my attention over to the dresser. There, sat my husband's cell phone.

"Daddy's always forgetting something," I said out loud as my hand gently stroked Cherish's silky jet-black hair. It wouldn't be the first time. Carl loses his mind when he is in reach of achieving another milestone. This partnership in Germany must be more important to him than I thought. I walked over to retrieve his phone. A notification displayed on the screen of the two missed calls and a text message; all of them, however, coming from the same unsaved number.

Briefly, I glared at the screen contemplating on whether or not I should open the message. During our entire two year marriage, Carl never once gave me any suspicion that he was unfaithful, and honestly, I had no clue as to why those uneasy feelings lightly pecked at my gut so quickly. Intuition…that's what it's called, right? Well, it was becoming annoying enough for me to address it. And so I did.

I tapped on the screen and the message popped up.

Are you almost here?

"Almost where?" I questioned as if the person could hear me. Carl is supposed to be on his way to work, so who and why would someone, besides the firm, be expecting him?

Who is this? I replied, already anticipating it to be a woman. A sense of cold emptiness cascaded over my heavy heart. *Was I over reacting? Carl has been nothing but good to me. He is the only person that I know, for sure, who would give me their last breath.* The thought of him betraying my trust was unbearable. Him touching another woman in the exact way his hands have pleased me, and giving her a satisfaction that a woman can only get from a man; especially a stallion like Carl.

"No." I exclaimed, shaking my head. "I am his wife. I swear to God if this is another bitch, I'll kill him. There are lines that should never be crossed once we said *I do.*"

Pulling Cherish away from her feeding, I lay her down on top of my black and crème striped comforter and took a seat on the edge of the bed. A few minutes had passed, and the person had yet to respond. That only heightened my eager suspicions.

"Her ass must know it's not him responding." I said. "If they had been talking previously, then there is no reason for him to be questioning her identity now. This bitch must know about me. My reply must have been her signal to shut the fuck up."

My heart pounded inside my chest and through my ears as I stared at the screen waiting for an answer. All types of scenarios played through my mind. As more time passed, guilt had to make its presence known as well.

Shit. Zayda, what are you doing? I asked myself in thought. *Carl is not cheating on you. When does he have time to cheat? If he's not at work, he's home. Everyone in the office knows who you are, so even if he was cheating, he wouldn't dare bring another woman there.*

How can one text message—four simple words coordinated in the perfect form have my mind all fucked up. The ringing phone interrupted my thoughts. When I saw the word *Office* flashing on the screen, I knew that my questions weren't about to be answered.

"Carl?" I said sounding a bit mustered. "Are you at work already?"

"Yea, I just got here and realized I left my phone. Are you Ok? You sound mad."

No. Who is this bitch texting your phone? I thought, rolling my eyes. As much as I wanted to bring up the questionable text, I didn't. I couldn't have him thinking that I go through his phone on a regular basis because I don't. Never have, and thought I never would. But you better believe I'm sure as hell turning into inspector gadget on his ass now.

"Um, yes." I cleared my throat of the dry knot that formed. "Yes, I'm good. I was just feeding the baby."

"Ok, well bring my phone with you when you come this afternoon. Just call the office for now if you need to get in touch with me."

The voice on the other end was one of a man in love; one who valued his marriage and contributed to the foundation that we built. Having no sense of urgency for his phone soothed all of my unwanted qualms. If Carl knew the possibilities of another woman calling him, he probably would have doubled back to get it. Instead, he didn't bother.

A message alert chimed in. I pulled the phone away from my ear to see if it was the mystery caller…it was.

"You heard me, Zay?" Carl said just as I put the call on speaker.

"Yes, baby. I'll have it later on." I agreed as I opened the text message.

It's Lance. Nigga you didn't save my new number yet? I thought you were going to stop by and bring the forms for me to look over before the meeting tonight.

How stupid did I feel? Lance was his fraternity brother and good friend. Shaking my head, I had to laugh at myself.

"…Ok, babe?" Carl inquired.

Sidetracked by the text message and my senseless actions, I didn't hear a single word that spilled from my husband's lips.

"Wait, what?"

"What, you got another man over there or something? You're all distracted and shit."

"Boy, please." I chuckled. "The phone was going in and out, and I didn't hear you."

"I was saying that I really appreciate you getting things together for me tonight. I won't spring it on you like that again."

"Anything for you. But listen, I have to get ready to drop Cherish off at my mom's. I'll see you later on."

Foolish. Just foolish of me to put blame on him from one misunderstanding. Here I am creating something that doesn't even exist, and worrying myself into a heart attack about it. There was no way I was going to let Carl find out about my moment of insecurity.

With the tap of a button, both messages were erased leaving behind no evidence that I was even in his phone. I turned to look over my shoulder at my baby. That quickly, she had gone back to sleep.

Figuring I'd better hurry and shower before she wakes back up, I stood from the bed, walked over to the dresser, and slid open my panty drawer. Pulling out a matching blue and white patterned set, I lay them down on the bed to fetch my outfit for the day.

As I walked passed the same full length mirror that my husband stood in front of earlier, I couldn't help but notice how much wider I looked in my night gown. I mean, I was always on the plus side of the scale, but after having Cherish, my body was out of control. I hadn't yet gone back down to my regular size sixteen jeans, and the unhealthy eating habits I picked up lately only added to my figure.

With both hands planted firmly on my hips, my eyes traveled down my body's reflection and back up. I wasn't too thrilled with the busty figure before me, and even though Carl had no complaints of my weight, I still wanted to get in shape, or at least clean up my eating habits. Cherish and Carl deserved the best of me, and I need to make sure I'm around to give them that.

Chapter Two

"Ok, Zayda," Dr. May said as she removed the purple plastic gloves from her hands and discarded them in the medical trash bin. "I'm all done. You can sit up now."

Finally! I'd been getting vaginal exams since a preteen and still get a bit weirded out spreading it wide open for another woman. You're just laying there, pussy exposed.

"Dr. May, I don't know how you do it," I said shaking my head.

"Do what, honey?" She beamed.

"Look at coochies for a living."

Dr. May burst into laughter, throwing her head back from my blunt statement. "Well, that isn't *all* I do." She held out her hand and assisted me to an upright position. As I pulled myself up on the exam table, I clenched the paper cover-up to conceal my goodies.

"I get to monitor beautiful healthy babies like the one you just had," she reminded me. "How is she doing, anyway?"

"She's good. I dropped her off at my mother's house," I told her. "I finally get a break."

"Humph, I'm surprised your mother isn't staying over your house with you. You know how she can get. She's going to spoil that baby rotten."

Natalie May, who happens to also be my mother's GYN, was a middle-aged, African American woman…and a fly one at that. Her hair was never untamed, and even on her worst day, she'd come strutting into the office with her high heels clicking against the tiled floor and laced in designer threads. She was the only black female doctor in the care center, and the best of them all. She had been my doctor for as long as I can remember. The first time my mother took me to see her was when she found out that I was no longer a virgin. If it weren't for Dr. May, I might have still been getting my ass whooped. It was Dr. May who actually talked to the both of us about losing my virginity.

The check-up turned into a therapy session because my mom broke down. She opened up about everything. We ended up staying at the appointment for an additional thirty minutes. Being a mother of a pre-teen herself, Dr. May understood; but she also helped my mom see how important it was to react from the heart and not from emotions. Hell, now that I am a mother, I'd be damned if Cherish tells me at 13-years-old that she is having sex. I'd flipped the same way, but back then, I agreed with anything Dr. May said as long as it kept my ass out of my mother's line of fire.

"Zayda," she interrupted my thoughts. "Have you given any thought to what we last spoke about? The contraceptive?"

"I have."

"And..."

Taking a deep breath with my lips slightly twisted to the side, I shook my head no. "I'm not going to use birth control. Carl and I want a second baby, so there is no need."

With a concerned looked on her face, Dr. May pulled the wheeled-stool from under the desk and took a seat.

"Zayda, you know this pregnancy—"

"Was a high risk. Yes, I know."

"I'm not sure you fully understand the risk and complications."

"I am very aware, Dr. May," I said. "My cervix is damaged. But you were also the one who told me as long as I take it easy, me and the baby would be fine. And we are."

"Yes, Zayda, but a second baby, right now...could be life threatening. Just because your body carried this baby full term doesn't mean it will happen again. You need to put your health as a priority. If you're not here, then who is going to take care of your child?"

Hopping off the table, I retrieved my clothes from the chair sitting against the wall. I guess Dr. May could tell by my actions that I wasn't going to further engage in the conversation. She stood to her feet and grabbed the files from the desk.

"Ok, Zayda," she spoke, calmly. "You know how to reach me if you change your mind about birth control."

Smugly, I smiled. "Yes, I do. Thank you, Dr. May." I dismissed.

Nodding her head, she eased out of the room and closed the door.

My attitude wasn't towards her. Honestly, this was a touchy subject for me. Certain choices I made put me in this situation. During my freshman year of college I had gotten an abortion that, at the time, my mother knew nothing about. Yes, I was going to be a mother way before I'd planned. I wasn't ready. I did the only thing I could...I got rid of it. Doing so did more damage to me than I knew. I suffered from cervical injuries. The damn doctor nipped my shit and left me with a weak cervix. It was nothing but the grace of God that allowed Cherish to go full term. I prayed every day while carrying her that she would make it. The thought of never being able to have another child was devastating, especially since Carl wanted a few more. I have to be able to give that to him. It was my job as his wife.

Quickly, I dressed back into the casual attire I sported; a pair of stone-washed denim capris, a yellow graphic tee with the word DIVA in white letters printed across my chest, and a lightweight white quarter length blazer. My toes weren't well manicured, but they weren't hideous either. I was able to get away with rocking a yellow pair of Steven Maddens open-toe flats.

Now my hair was another story. My appointment wasn't until tomorrow, so I had to manage it on my own and the best way I knew how. You'd think after living with such long and thick hair I'd learn how to handle it...hell no. That was one battle I refused to face. Using a small amount of gel and water, I brushed the thick patch back into a tight bun and called it a day.

On my way out, I stopped at the front desk to schedule my next appointment. A woman holding on to a pink double stroller with a visually protruding belly stood in front of me signing her name on the clipboard.

The two young girls in the stroller were very close in age, and yet she was due to have another. Her innocent features gave away her young age range as well. Between eighteen and twenty, I'd guess.

My eyes traveled down to her left hand, and I noticed she wasn't wearing a ring. Hopefully, the father of her children was pulling his weight. Knowing how men, especially young men, can maintain a habit of neglecting their responsibilities, I wouldn't be surprised if she was taking care of her family all on her own.

A sympathizing feeling had overtaken my body. I could have been her. Having the abortion was, in a way, a blessing in disguise. Selfish, yes. But I would've done more damage as a mother at that age then I could handle. College wouldn't have been in the picture, and I would have never met Carl. I came to the conclusion a long time ago that things were supposed to happen this way. But I will make it up to my first seed by having many children now, and promise to love them no matter what.

It took almost thirty-five minutes to get across town to Carl's office, but finally, I made it. Carl and I locked eyes through the office glass door the moment I entered his workplace. He held up one finger halting me in my tracks. The two men standing near him, dressed in all black, evidently did not work at the firm.

Carl focused his attention back on them, and I could see the vexed look smacked on his face. They didn't notice. But me, I'm his wife. Something was going down, and it wasn't good. His firmly tilted brow never flinched. His jaw was locked tighter than a bolt. If he was a few shades lighter, he might have turned red. It was the most serious I'd ever seen him at work. Even dealing with his clients never burdened him with such discomfort.

I waited at the front desk engaging in small talk with the receptionist, Marcy. She was a few years older than me, but she was cool...down to earth. Marcy worked there long before Carl had. She knew all the scoop and didn't mind sharing. In fact, Marcy was the one who kept a close eye on the men for their wives. She'd let me know whenever Carl had a bit too much to drink at an out-of-town business trip, or if his new clients sat or stood to pee. Luckily for me, I never got any bad news about my husband. This time, she had no information about what was going down.

"FBI," was all she had for me.

"Are you serious?" Her enlightenment came as a shock. Why on earth would the Federal Bureau of Investigation be there?

"As a heart attack." Marcy assured.

"What do they want with Carl?" I kept my voice lowered and eyes trained on him through the crystal clear glass door of the conference office.

Marcy shrugged, "Your guess is as good as mines. They came up in here about thirty minutes ago and asked for him, Spencer, and Marcel."

"Marcy!"

Both she and I looked over to Sean Cartman, the CEO of the law firm, standing in the threshold of the hallway. Mr. Cartman was an extremely attractive older man. I would love to have a sip of whatever youth juice he'd been drinking, because that fifty-plus year old man could easily pass for late thirties. He probably had bitches going crazy over him back in the day...plus he was educated. His wife, Margaret, hit the jackpot. The only thing that seemed to age on him was his salt and pepper colored hair. He was caramel complexion, and stood about 6'1. From the way he walked with his shoulders broad, it wasn't hard to tell that underneath his suave attire he had the body of a god.

With both hands on his waist holding back the opened flaps of his black Kenneth Cole suit jacket, Mr. Cartman's legs were planted wide on the floor. Normally, he would have acknowledged my presence, but today it was as if I was transparent. From his heaving chest, flared nostrils, and his protruding eyes as he glared at Marcy, I could tell by his unwelcoming demeanor that he was pissed. He tried to remain calm, but I'm willing to bet that his head would have popped off of his shoulders if it weren't attached to his neck.

"Come to my office." He ordered. "I need to speak with you." Mr. Cartman turned and headed back down the hallway to his private office area.

Marcy slowly stood to her feet. "I'll be right there."

"Shit." I whispered. "You in trouble, too?"

Shaking her head, Marcy walked around the receptionist desk in her blue and black knee length dress. "I'll be right back." She mumbled.

I watched as she disappeared down the hall and into Mr. Cartman's office. Carl and his colleagues were just finishing up their own little gathering with the FBI agents. One of the black-suited men opened the glass door.

"We'll be in touch," he said before he walked out of the room and down the hall as well. Carl emerged from the room loosening the tie from his neck.

"What going on?" I asked him as he approached me.

The look in his eyes was terrifying. It was a look I wasn't familiar with on him. It was the look of uncertainty. Nothing in our lives has ever affected us to the point where he couldn't handle it. Carl always had the answers, but seeing the question marks welling up in his eyes sent quivers up my calves.

"I'll tell you when we get home," He replied.

"You're coming home now?"

He nodded his head yes. "Let me get my things, and I'll be ready to go."

"Carl…"

"I can't go into details now, Zayda…not in here. Just go back to the car and wait for me." He kissed me on my forehead and left me standing there, clueless.

Like a good wife, I did what I was told and sat in the car. I couldn't help but to wonder what could've happened. Was he in trouble? Was the entire firm involved in something illegal? Five minutes turned to ten and ten to twenty that quickly. Carl still hadn't come to the car. I retrieved my cell phone from the bag to dial his number. Not wanting to cause too much of a scene with Mr. Cartman already on edge, I refused to go back inside.

Just as it began to ring, Carl was coming out of the front door. Mr. Cartman was right on his heels. They stopped just outside the door, and Carl turned to face him. Even though my window was completely rolled down, I couldn't hear what was transpiring over the noisy city traffic. By Carl's fidget movements, I could tell that he wasn't happy with whatever his boss was telling him.

Carl's eyes shifted from the door to Cartman as he inhaled a well-needed breath of fresh air. With the agents hounding him, he felt like he was going to suffocate. Their surprise visit didn't give them any time to make sure all closet doors were closed and sealed shut. Cartman & Associate were now under full investigation of the FBI. Although he kept a steady flow of clientele that paid him well, Cartman accrued the bulk of his wealth through money laundering. He was the cleanup man for one of the most infamous kingpins in Philadelphia. Cartman was smart. For years he'd been inserting dirty money into a legitimate German financial institution and then making various financial transactions to change its form to make it difficult to follow. Through bank-to-bank transfers, wire transfers between different accounts in different names in different countries, and making deposits and withdrawals to continually vary the amount of money in the accounts, Cartman's operation was top notch. He'd also purchased items of high-value, mostly boats, houses, cars, diamonds, you name it; anything to change the form of the money. This is the most complex step in his laundering scheme, and he had to make the original dirty money as hard to trace as possible. It was the perfect white-collar crime, and he was good at it. The best. For him to come under scrutiny now only meant one thing. There was indeed a rat in the ring, and he was certainly going to catch the bitch by its tail.

The Feds were seizing everything. From computers to hard files, they were ready to bust open Cartman's entire operation.

"What did you tell them?" Cartman asked as his eyes scanned around them making sure no one was eavesdropping. All of the agents were still inside, and not too many pedestrian walked the sidewalk of the building.

"I didn't tell them anything." Carl said, confidentially. "But someone in this office is. They knew too much. Even if we've been under their eye, all of our paperwork checks out. They can't trace us back to anything.

"Oh?" Cartman questioned in a low tone. "Not even the home you recently purchased in Germany?"

Carl's eyes shot open.

"You didn't think I would find out about that?" Cartman hissed through clenched teeth. He took a step in closing the small space between them. His low tone spoke volumes. "A three hundred and sixty thousand dollar purchase in your god damn name."

"But it's overseas. The feds don't have jurisdiction—"

"Mutha fucka, if you believe that they can't trace an amateur move like that then you have no business being at this firm in the first place." Cartman silenced him. "Eleven years and not once did I ever pop up on their radar. Just know that I will do anything to keep it that way. And if you have to burn in the process, then so be it." Thick veins emerged from his neck that could be seen from a mile away.

Carl knew Cartman meant business. He wasn't a killer, but he certainly had a plan to save his own ass. Carl knew firsthand how, Cartman played. Most likely, Cartman had the backup paperwork already made up to pin all of this on Carl. He'd seen it happen before. As a matter of fact, he assisted Cartman in the setup about a year ago on their ex-colleague, Nixon. After Nixon was caught with his hand in Cartman's cookie jar, Carl had the duty of leaking Nixon's income history to the IRS. Of course, he'd altered them first. Nixon got booked for tax evasion.

Carl's heart thumped rapidly inside his chest as the bottom of his stomach knotted up. "That house won't prove anything. I've got the trail to prove my assets."

"You better be right," Cartman warned before going back inside the office building.

Carl looked at me before storming over to the car. I remained calm as he yanked open the passenger side door and flopped in the seat.

"Let's go." He said, keeping his eyes forward.

"Where is your car?"

"In the parking garage," he answered, yet his mind still in the firm. "I'll get Neil to run me by here later to get it."

Nodding my head, I turned the key and started my ignition. I wanted to ask him what happened again, but I knew now was not the time. The last thing both he and I needed was to get into an argument over his misplaced anger. Knowing my boundaries, I decided to drop the matter until he was ready to talk about it.

Chapter Three

The aroma in my house was entrancing. I did what I could in the small amount of time that I had to get ready for Carl's meeting. Smothered turkey wings, jasmine rice, and fresh grilled asparagus were on the menu. Normally, I would settle for just ordering a few pizzas and a tray of Buffalo wings from the pizza shop around the corner, but since Carl's day was a bit rocky, I decided to make his favorite southern meal. I wasn't, at all, a stranger in the kitchen. When we first married, I cooked a full course meal just about every night. That was until the pregnancy started to take a toll on my body. It'd been a while since I used my appliances, but I moved around the kitchen as if I was a professional chef.

After rinsing off the last pot in the sink, I cut the water off and turned around to hang it on the hook over the center island.

"Shit," I grabbed hold of my chest. "Carl, you scared the hell out of me. Why are you sneaking up on me like that?"

"I wasn't sneaking," he nonchalantly responded from the kitchen's entry.

"Well, whatever you want to call it; I didn't hear you come downstairs. How was your shower?"

He walked over to the center island, pulled out the barstool and took a seat. As if something heavy still boggled his mind, he rested his elbows on the black marble counter top and continued to stare at me.

"Do you want to eat now, or wait for the guys?" I said trying to ease into a conversation.

"I don't have much of an appetite." He shook his head.

"Well, hopefully that will change in a few—"

"Zayda, there is something I need to tell you." He cut me off.

"Okay…"

"I just hope when I say it you'll still love me the same way…just as much as you do now."

When Carl peeled his eyes away from mines, my heart fluttered. *What is so bad that he can't even look me in the eye?* I automatically pictured him with another woman, again. To be quite honest, even though the text message earlier today was a misunderstanding, I couldn't rid myself of that feeling. The, what if's. Carl had been perfect. Flawless. Which made me realize that the perfect person didn't exist. Did he not look at other women? Fantasize about them? Carl didn't even watch a single porno. He was too clean, which only meant it was to cover up his dirt.

"Just say it," I leaned up against the island directly in front of him. "Whatever it is let it drop.

Don't try to cushion the blow... *that* will only piss me off more."

He paused for a second as if he was gathering the correct words to say. Licking his lips, he cleared his throat of the dryness. "I haven't been completely honest with you."

"Really?" His statement only heightened my intuition. "We're lying to each other now?"

Carl hesitated.

"Just say it, Carl. I'm a grown woman. I can handle it."

"It's about my position at Cartman's."

Ready to reach across the counter and slap him, I halted when I realized it wasn't about what I'd thought.

"Oh...your job." I cocked my head back, shocked.

"Yea...What did you think it was about?"

"Nothing." I lied. "I just wasn't expecting you to tell me about work. You were silent the entire ride home. What? You're a drug dealer, or something?"

"Really, Zay?"

"Well...I come to your job for our lunch date and the FBI has you sized-up in a room. Now, you're telling me that you're not really a Business Attorney."

"I never said that."

"Then what *are* you saying?"

His perturbed stare was anything but soothing. The bulges in my gut tightened by the second. The way he was beating around the bush, I was liable to have a nervous breakdown any minute. I am not good with *give it to her easy*. Just rip the damn bandage off!

"Dammit, Carl, just say it."

"I need for you to just listen and not ask any questions. I really don't want to involve you in all of this, because the less you know, the better. But this is something you need to know. And you are the only person I trust."

I watched his jittery fingers tap hastily on the countertop as he appeared to be organizing his thoughts on how he would break the news.

"The feds are investigating us for money laundering," he finally confessed.

"Money laundering?" I exclaimed. "Are you fucking serious? Tell me you are not that stupid."

"Lower your voice, Zay."

Anger flooded my body. I couldn't believe what I was hearing. The man I married is a fucking criminal.

"How long has this been going on?"

"Zay, that's not important."

"No, I think it is. Carl, we have a child together. *A life.* And your selfish ass put it all on the line. The feds, Carl? The fucking FBI." I began to pace the kitchen floor. "What? So you've been helping some drug dealers clean their money. Does Cartman know?"

He didn't respond, but his silence told me all I needed to know.

"He's fucking in on it too." I concluded, shaking my head in utter disbelief. "Whose money are you cleaning?"

He looked at me as if I asked him something unusual. "I don't ask those types of questions for reasons like this. If I don't know, then I am protected under plausible deniability."

"And you're a plausible jackass to believe that." I chastised. "Money laundering is a federal offense. If you go down, what the hell is gonna happen to me and Cherish?"

"That's why I'm telling you this now. If the ball drops, we have to be prepared for them to take it all. The money, this house, the cars... You'll be fine. It's me they are coming after. I have a safety account in a Swiss bank—"

Ding Dong!

The doorbell tolled just in time. I felt myself about to backhand the hell out of my idiotic ass husband. How can someone be so smart and so dumb at the same time?

"We're *going* to finish this conversation later," I let be known before leaving out of the kitchen and opening the front door.

"I said, MY SOROR!" My sorority chant was the way Jennifer, Neil's wife, and I greeted each other...especially if it's been awhile since we've last hung out.

"Yea!" I chanted back.

"My sweet, sweet soror!"

"Yea."

"Tell me, *what* is a Delta?"

We embraced one another with an extended, long-overdue hug.

"One of these days we are going to finish that damn chant." Jennifer said passing me the bottle of Zinfandel she carried.

"Enough of the reunion," Neil came trudging up to the front door. "Y'all Deltas always got to make an entrance."

"Oh hush," Jennifer playfully slapped his arm. "You and Carl aren't any better."

"Where *is* my boy at?" Neil reached in and gave me a hug.

"You know I'm never too far away," Carl approached us, and gave a hand dap to his best friend.

Shutting the front door, I discreetly shot Carl a menacing look reminding him not to forget what I told him.

"It smells delicious in here, Zay," Neil rubbed his stomach in a circular motion as his eyes roamed towards the kitchen.

"She put it down, bruh. I hope you're hungry," Carl added. There was no trace of the fallout we'd just encountered. That was us. Smiles covered any dispute we had inside these walls.

Jennifer and I headed to the kitchen.

"Just let the other brothers know we are in the basement when they get here," Carl yelled back before descending the basement steps.

"Will do, honey," I offered a half smile.

"So, what he got you up in here cooking?" Jennifer asked as she removed the lid to a simmering pot on the stove.

Placing the bottle of wine in the stainless steel refrigerator, I retrieved the small tray of fruit I threw together a few hours earlier.

"Too much," I said placing the tray down on the counter beside the stove. "He's lucky I did something for his ass...especially after telling me about this last minute."

"Hell, Neil better be grateful I even cook for him at all." Jennifer grabbed a handful of grapes and bit into one.

"Why you say that?"

"Cuz he doesn't deserve it," she shook her head. "Not after me finding an opened pack of condoms in his car. And I know we don't use them."

"Bitch, lies." My eyes widened in shock. She didn't waste any time spilling her tea. That was the difference between us. Jenn didn't care. If she was pissed, especially at Neil, the world was going to hear about it.

"I wish I was lying." She huffed.

"What did he say?"

"His two-faced ass talking about, it must have been there from the last time they car pooled to DC for a Kappa's event. My name must be Boo Boo because he thinks I'm fool enough to believe it."

"You think he's cheating?" I asked with my eyebrows raised.

"Or cheated."

"Well, girl how the hell can you be so cool about it?"

"Because until I have solid proof, there is no need for me to be raging around like some mad woman... at least not until I find out what this private investigator has to say."

"A what?" I had to chuckle at what she slyly blurted out. "You hired somebody to spy on that man?"

"Hell... yes!" The chin length bob-cut she rocked swayed back and forth as her head dipped with each word. She leaned up against the counter and folded her arms across her chest.

"Girl, you are crazy."

"No, what's crazy is his ass thinks I let it go. It's been a week, and I haven't bought up the situation since the day it happened. But...when I have to—"

"*If*...you have to."

Jennifer paused from her snacking and looked at me dead on. "*When* I have to...I will have the evidence to kindly show him."

Men. It's always some shit with them. Why can't us woman have a moments peace of mind. If it's not one thing, it's another. I mean, don't get me wrong, both Carl and Neil are providers. Much like myself, Jennifer reeled in a husband who takes care of all the finances. The only reason she works is because she is the owner of Stylish Foot Boutique. After college, she turned one of Neil's investment properties into her own shop to keep her busy during the day.

Jennifer was beautiful; blessed with high cheekbones, and big brown eyes lined with thick natural eyelashes. Her facial features were the talk of the campus back in college. The thirty dollar an hour fitness trainer kept her body in shape...well worth every penny. Jennifer prided herself on retaining the same figure she had when she and Neil met. And not to mention, the bitch was stylish. From head to toe, Jennifer could have walked the runway at any given time. She was a trophy wife, to say the least.

It's hard to believe that a man could be stupid enough to eat at McDonalds when, clearly, he has a good cooked feast awaiting him at home. That is one thing about a man I will never understand. Even after reading *Think Like a Man* by Steve Harvey, I was even more confused.

"Let's just say...this is my insurance policy." She nodded towards me and popped another grape in her mouth.

"I don't know about this, T. I mean, maybe you are taking things a little too far. What if he is cheating, or cheated. After you bring it to the light, then what? Are you ready to just walk away—just end it like that?"

Jennifer took in a deep breath. "Honestly, Zay, I don't know. I guess, I'm hoping...praying to God, actually, that I am wrong—that Neil was telling me the truth. I love him, Zay. He worships the ground that I walk on. I never thought we'd ever come to this. I can't see myself leaving him, but I also can't see me ignoring his infidelity."

The hurt she felt surfaced to her face. I could tell by the way she gazed into space that this was an ongoing battle between her mind and her heart. Jennifer was usually in control. She was on top of everything in her life, and inside, this was killing her. The only thing I could do was be there. She was my girl, and I was going to lend my support no matter what her decision is.

After hearing her drama, I figured now we both needed this night. She had no clue that I was battling my own war with clairvoyance. And now that Carl dropped an even bigger bomb on me made me regret this day ever happening. If I could turn back the hands of time, lord knows I would. But life doesn't work that way. All I can do now is suit up and wait. Besides, my war had just begun, and depending on whether Carl was going to continue to feed me a story to justify his mistakes, or not, was the determination of how big this war will get.

Chapter Four

The night, for both Jennifer and I, had taken a turn. After a few hours, and multiple glasses of wine, we found ourselves lounging in my living room laughing and joking at old stories of the time we were pledging. Brandy and Krystal, two of Carl's frat brother's wives who were also members of their black Greek organizations, had joined us. Even though we didn't all attend the same university, or join the same sisterhood, our stories were all similar.

Brandy, the oldest of us all, had been married to her husband, Ronald, for ten years. Somehow, we got on the topic of men… which wasn't unusual considering that just about every woman had their own horror story about one.

"The key to a successful marriage…is wine," Brandy held up her glass and took another sip. The group excavated into laughter.

"Now *that* I can drink to," Jennifer contested.

"You'll drink to anything," I hooted.

"You damn right," T's voice had taken on a slight slur from her alcohol consumption.

"I'm serious," Brandy said. "This was the best thing introduced to woman since the tampon. Wine has helped me keep my lips zipped when need be, and turned me into a porn star when it was time to put it down in the bedroom. Shit, even when I didn't feel like doing a damn thing. This is a multipurpose drink. It makes your husband think you're just being an obedient wife while all along you are three steps ahead of him."

I've known Brandy for a few years, and I've learned when to take her advice seriously and when she was just talking out of her ass.

"Well, right now, this wine got you delusional," I stood up from the chocolate colored sectional holding my empty wine glass in one hand. Reaching for the empty bottle on the glass coffee table, I held it up, "And it looks like we could use more of this *multipurpose drink*," I mocked.

On the way to the kitchen, I poked my head in the basement doorway. I could hear much debating at the bottom of the stairs... sounding more like a Friday night bar meet up rather than a chapter meeting. Whatever they were discussing didn't sound too serious. The men were probably doing the same thing we were...a bunch of loose conversation.

I closed the door and went into the kitchen. Sitting the empty wine bottle on the island, I noticed my cell phone lighting up. I had forgotten that I left it in the kitchen. Retrieving it from the counter, I swiped my thumb across the screen as I made my way over to the fridge to grab another bottle of wine—our third, by the way.

A missed call from a number I hadn't recognized blared on my screen. At least the caller had enough sense to leave a voice message.

"Where is that bottle?" I heard Brandy yell from the living room.

"Calm your drunk ass down," I joked back. Tapping the screen, I raised the phone to my ear and listened to the message.

Hi, Zayda, it's Dr. May. Listen, I was hoping that I got you because I didn't want to leave this on your voicemail. You need to come in to the office as soon as possible.

The chatter in the living room increased causing me to pin my free ear close to hear the rest of the message.

The labs from you're PAP exam came back. You've tested positive for Chlamydia. You need to come in for treatment. I'll be...

After hearing the word Chlamydia, everything Dr. May had said following it didn't register. My heart must have stopped beating. If not, the air in my lungs had surely sucked completely out of me. *Chlamydia?* That was the last thing I'd expected to hear. This had to be some kind of mistake. If I have an STD then the only person who could have given it to me was Carl. So she is telling me that my husband *has* been, not only unfaithful, but neglected to protect himself while doing so. No. this can't be right.

Just as the room began to spin, in walked Jennifer fanning herself. "Girl, what is taking you so long?" She headed straight for the freezer and pulled out an ice tray. Even though I could hear her, and see her movements through my peripheral, I was stuck in my own thoughts.

"We ran out of wine, or something?" She turned to look at me. "Zayda?"

"Huh?" Finally ripping my stare away from nothing in particular, I shot my eyes at her.

"You okay?" Jennifer asked with her forehead creased up. "You look like you just saw a ghost."

"Huh? Oh… no," I exhaled trying to sound as normal as possible. "I think the wine is getting to me." I guess my pretentious smile was enough to convince her.

"Let me find out you can't hang with the big girls anymore." She chuckled and retrieved the new bottle from the counter. "You need me to get you some water?"

"No, I'm fine. I'll be there in a sec."

"Alright. Don't go passing out on us." Jennifer left the kitchen and rejoined the others.

"Chlamydia?" I whispered again, in sheer disgust. Slipping out the second doorway that led to the dining room, I was able to make it to the guest bathroom without them noticing. Once inside, I locked door and quickly pulled down my Capris and panties, and took a seat on the toilet.

The first thing I thought to do was check the lining of my underwear for any discharge. Not seeing any, I bent over to take a whiff. There was no funny odor, or unusual scent that would've alarmed me. Double checking, I wrapped the toilet paper around my fingers, wiped my vagina, and pulled the tissue back to look at it. Still…nothing.

Dr. May's message had me buggin' out. What the fuck was I supposed to do? I wanted to call her ass right now, regardless of how late it was, and have her retest me.

I am married. A happily married woman. This shit is not supposed to be happening to me. My husband…the man who made me the queen of his castle, the keeper of his heart, and the key holder to mine, wouldn't do something so low down and dirty...would he? The more I thought about the last time Carl and I made love, I grew angrier. I trusted him with my body. If it was this easy for me to catch this, what else is his ass bringing to our bedroom?

"Fucking liar!" I screamed. "The feds....now this? It's like I don't even know who the hell he is anymore."

I closed my eyes as tears began to fill them. This can't be happening to me. Not again. I was safe with him. He can't be just another nigga who let me down in my life. Carl is the only man I've ever loved after what Valdis did to me. I swore I wasn't going to let another man unlock my heart again.

Ten Years Earlier...
Overbrook High Senior Year

I couldn't help but let out a soft moan when he slowly swiped his tongue across my hard nipples. His firm grip on my breast made my brown melons appear much larger than what they actually were. He took one of my nipples into his warm, wet mouth. I quivered. I've waited so long... too long for this moment. He sucked on me in the same slow motion, and I could hear low snippets of his baritone grunts. He was into it just as much as I was. My heart raced, and I could feel his lips placing a trail of kisses down my belly. Normally, I would've stopped him from witnessing the worst part of my body. The fat trap is what I call it. But this time, I didn't give a damn. It's been over a year since I last had some dick, and my pussy was craving like a coke fiend on her worst day. Masturbating was the only thing that held me over, but there was nothing like the real thing. My fingers didn't compare. I wanted it. I needed it, badly.

He kissed passed my belly button and down to the top of my vagina. *Is he... Oh shit, I think he is.* He used his fingers to spread the lips of my flower. At that point, I knew he wasn't going to stop. He was going for gold.

"Relax, ma." He whispered. "Just enjoy what I'm about to do to you."

I guess he could sense the way my body tensed up. I never in my life had a man go down on me. I didn't know what to expect or what his reaction would be. I hope it taste like it supposed to. I was nervous, but I did exactly what he instructed me to do. I rested my head back on the bed and closed my eyes.

"Zayda!"

Startled, I quickly shot my eyes open.

"You fell asleep, again." My girl, Jessica, said as she stood in front of me with her hand planted on her hip.

Her green polo pull over uniform shirt with the Weller's Senior Citizens Home logo reminded me where I was.

"You got the nerve to be sleeping at the front desk? Your ass would be fired right now if it weren't for me."

"My ass would be able to sleep peacefully around here if it weren't for you, too." I snickered, adjusting myself in the black swivel chair. "What time is it?"

"Almost time to go." She grabbed a chart from behind the desk where I sat. "First shift will be in soon. I'm going to finish up my rounds. Try to stay awake this time." She playfully hit me on my shoulder before leaving the front area.

My mind just played a horrible trick on me. That dream felt real. So real that I could feel the moisture built up between my legs. I was completely turned on, but at the wrong damn time. Thank God I hadn't unconsciously slipped my hand down there. Jess would have never let me live that shit down.

Get it together, Zay. My self pep-talk did me no good. All I could think about was the man in my dream. I didn't know his name, or him for that matter, and for the life of me I couldn't even remember what he looked like. He wasn't a resemblance of anyone I knew; just a figure created for one purpose. I know…I'm such a pathetic loser.

Shaking the thoughts from my mind, I got up and went to check on my clients.

Finally, it was 6 A.M. Time to roll out of this place. I don't normally snag the overnight shifts but fuck it, it was Friday night and I didn't have anywhere else to be. I convinced Jess to accept a shift, too. That way I wouldn't be bored all night. Besides, graduation is right around the corner, and I needed all the overtime I can get. My mom told me that if I wanted a car before I leave for college in the fall, then I was going to have to pay for it myself. But I bet her ass will be the first person to ask to borrow it when I get it.

Thirty-five hundred dollars. That's all that stood in the way of me burning my monthly bus pass and cruising around in a cherry red 2005 Nissan Altima. It wasn't brand new, of course, but it was going to be mines.

I finished my final progress notes in the overnight Log Book, closed it shut, and placed it back on the chart rack before heading down the hall to the staff lounge. The next shift had already started to come in. I bypassed them without a single word. I hadn't made friends with any of my other co-workers, and I didn't care to. Jess was all the friend I needed in this place. I was there for one thing and one thing only. I was on a money mission—period.

Jess was standing over by the water fountain talking on her cell phone when I entered the room. A few other workers were there securing away their belongings in their personal lockers. I retrieved my bag from my small locker, pulled out my work ID and swiped out. My regular Saturday shift started at 2 P.M., so I had no time to waste getting home. I needed a good nut and some rest. I walked back to the front and sat on the couch in the waiting area until Jess was ready.

As usual, I checked my cell phone for missed calls and text messages. This place had strict rules about having a cell phone on the floor while caring for the residents, so I had to keep it in my bag the entire shift. It isn't like my shit is blowing up, anyway. The same three people always call my phone. Since Jess was here, that left only two other people, my mom and our other friend, Aja. Just as I expected, I had two missed calls from her. I already knew what she wanted. She had been talking about this senior pool party for weeks. She had to make an appearance at every kick-back, BBQ, school dance, you name it. That was her…the party girl. We met in 9th grade. She had just moved to West Philadelphia from Washington, DC. We were paired together to do a freshman project on social stereotypes… go figure. I never intended on her and I actually becoming friends. Aja was one of the pretty girls. The ones you would think was as shallow as a creek, or dumb as a door knob. She was light skin with long silky black, wavy hair. Her wide grey eyes, exotic tone, and defined cheekbones had everyone assuming she was biracial. Back then, she'd always wear her hair pulled back into a tight bun with full bangs cut just above her eyelids. She rocked big hooped earrings and never left her home without beating her face with her Mac collection. Her type only hung with their own…at least that's what I thought.

Turns out, she was far from what I had made her out to be. Aja was cool—down to earth. She was the true definition of *real recognize real*, and never bit her tongue for anyone.

She was the first person that had ever stood up for me in school. Being around her gave me a little confidence; enough to make my high school experience better than junior high. I mean, I was still practically a nobody, but the teasing and jokes stopped. Well… to my face, at least.

Jess, on the other hand, was a childhood friend. She had moved back to her home country, Ghana Africa, just after fifth grade. Needless to say we lost touch for a while, a long while. Just before high school started, this bitch shows up at my front door. I embraced her, thrilled to have her back; especially after Tony's shiesty ass turned on me.

Personality wise, she hadn't changed a bit. She was still the same shy and quiet Jessica. But honey, Jess grew up in more ways than one. Her body had finally caught up to her once over-sized head, and she had the physique of a super model. Her figure was one that women killed plenty of hours in the gym trying to attain. It was given to her naturally. She had a smooth chocolate brown skin tone, with high cheek bones, and an award winning smile that showed off her pearly white teeth. Yeah, she made bitches mad.

And then you have me. Over the past couple of years, I've came into my own image. I wouldn't say I'm pleased with my size 18 body, but I am a little more accepting of it. I've learned how to dress it up. Being plus sized is not easy. I spend every Sunday in the hair salon to keep my shit done. Any extra money that I had after helping my mom and my cell phone bill, I spent it on clothes and shoes. I had to keep up with the Jones'. Being the fat girl out of the group, there wasn't a chill day for me. I couldn't just rock a cap, tee-shirt and some sweats without looking messy. It was bad enough that I was big, but I refused to be big and a hot mess. So, I worked twice as hard than what my girls had to. There was no excuse for me not to look good at all times.

I found it to be true when people say that looking good makes you feel good. I had the attitude to match my big girl swag. By senior year, everyone noticed my confidence. We were now at the top of the high school food chain, and I was the popular *big girl*. But no matter how popular I was, I was still lonely. Aja and Jess both dated guys from our school; but me, I never had a boyfriend. To a teenage dude, I guess I was acceptable enough to be cool with but I wasn't datable. Once in a blue moon when I did meet a guy it was from the internet or a popular phone network called The Party Line. The AOL chats and phone connections would last a few months, but when I would actually meet them face-to-face, it shortened to a few days. Either they weren't as appealing in person to me, or they were only looking for one thing…an easy fuck. I gave up on meeting guys all together.

"Zay," Jess called as she flopped down beside me. "Ryan's here, you need a ride home?"

"Hell no. Girl, you and Ryan are like a walking porno." I laughed. "I'll pass on the front row seat of you and your boyfriend swapping spit."

"Oh, is that hate?" She said.

"Bitch, please."

We both laughed.

"Girl, I can't help it." She admitted. "Why does he have to be fine? I can't keep my hands off of him."

I rolled my eyes to her sarcasm. "You and Mr. Fine go ahead. I'll be cool."

"You sure?" She asked with one eyebrow raised.

"Positive." I grabbed my bag and stood to my feet. "I'll call you later."

"Alright." Jess responded as she stood up as well. We began to walk out of the exit door. "Well, we can all ride to the pool party together."

I shook my head. "I'm not going. I have to work later today."

"Zay, this is the last party of our senior year. Why would you miss it?"

"I couldn't get off." I lied. Truth was, I wouldn't be caught dead in a bathing suit around any of our classmates.

"So call out." Jess pleaded.

"Let's see," I held out both of my hands, "Partying…Making money… Partying… Making mo—"

"Fine," Jess sucked her teeth. "Be a loser all of your life."

The tooting of a car horn diverted our attention. Ryan sat in his idling car waving for Jess to come over.

Jess held up her pointer finger and gestured for him to wait a second. She turned back to me. "Well, I'll call you later to see if you change your mind."

"Alight, girl."

We hugged before parting our separate ways.

Chapter Five

The shrieking of my cell phone alarm had awakened me out of my sleep. I reached over and grabbed it off of my nightstand. It was just a little after 12 P.M., and it was time for me to get ready for my next shift. That little cat-nap didn't do a thing for me. I was tired as shit. I didn't bother to even take off my work uniform when I came home.

After turning off the alarm, I could hear the muffled sound of R. Kelly's *Step in the name of Love* creeping through my bedroom walls. I slid out of my bed, walked out of my room and down the stairs of our two-story row home. My mom, Jourdon, was in her own little world swaying her curvy hips to the melody. Quietly, I stood at the bottom of the steps. Her back was toward me, and she had no clue she was being watched. Her dark, shoulder length hair shined as it swung along with her head movements. I could tell mom was in a great mood; but, from what or *who* was the question. She was even wearing a new outfit. It had to be new because I hadn't seen it before. She wore a white linen halter top that revealed the majority of her chocolate backside, and a pair of white linen capris. Her fresh pedicure toes peaked out the top of her white opened-toe wedged heel shoes. She clapped and stepped to the beat repeatedly. Finally, she slowly turned to me and paused. The two of us broke into laughter.

"Someone's feeling good, huh?" I asked with my arms folded across my chest.

"I'm looking good, and feeling good." She replied as she continued her dancing. "It's a good day to be *good*, baby."

"Going somewhere?"

"Just out to lunch." She said as she grabbed the remote from the coffee table and turned her music off.

"It must be a pretty jazzy lunch date because you're looking fly, mom."

"It's nothing to get all excited about...yet." She said grinning. She turned to walk into the kitchen.

"Oh no, mother dear," I said as I followed behind her. "You are not getting off that easy. I need more details. Who is he?" Pulling out the bar chair from the kitchen table, I sat on down and rested my elbows atop it. "So, shoot."

"Zayda, it's nothing— really." She leaned up against the counter. "Just a guy I met a few weeks ago."

"That you neglected to tell me about."

"Why are you so interested?"

"Mom, I haven't seen or heard you talk about a man in years. The last man I remember that made you glow the way you are now was my dad, and—" I paused when I noticed the smile fading from her face. I purposely steered clear of bringing up my dad around her. She never talked about him, so I assumed it was a touchy subject for her no matter how tough her exterior was. I didn't mean to just blurt him out in the middle of her living in the moment.

"And what?" She asked, breaking our brief silence. Her eyes were focused on me but I could tell she was thinking— about my dad, perhaps.

"And...it's a good day to be *good*. You seem happy, and that is all that matters." I said trying to quickly heal whatever wound I had just punctured. I picked up her white and silver clutch from off the countertop and handed it to her.

She took the clutch and kissed me on my forehead. "Thank you, baby. Call my cell if you need me." She grabbed her car keys. "But try not to need me until after 4."

I laughed. "Have fun."

*****

Work was nothing amazing; same old boring and quiet routine. Easy money, I'd say. The most exciting thing that ever happened there was on the days when we had fire drills, and we had to clear all of the residence out safely. The senior citizen home was a one-level building, which made it easier, but it was always timed. In order to pass we had to get the fifty-four bed facility emptied in less than six and a half minutes. Other than that, the shifts ran smoothly.

By the end of my shift, I was starving. I hadn't eaten anything beside the Oreo cookies, corn chips and Pepsi I bought from the vending machine. I walked a block and a half down to the local shopping center. It was after 10 PM and all of the retail stores were closed. Bertucci's Italian Restaurant, however, was opened and by the multitude of cars parked in the lot I knew it was packed inside.

I had no intentions on dining in. I've had the taste for their chicken parmesan all week. I placed and paid for my *to-go* order, and waited for it in the vestibule where it was a lot less crowded. A man sat on the green bench by the wall, and a woman stood by the door with a young boy. I took a seat on the opposite end of the green bench and pulled out my cell phone to occupy my time during the wait.

"Ticket 247, your order is ready." A soft woman's voice announced over the intercom. That must have been the woman's order. After the announcement, she grabbed hold of the little boy and left out of the waiting area.

I sent a text message to Jess and Aja. Neither one responded. They must still be at the pool party. A part of me wished I would've gone. I know they are having blast; but the mandatory swimsuit rule turned me off. This summer I'm going to hit the gym hard. With Jess going to West Chester University, and Aja deciding to go to Community College, I'll be on my own at Cheyney University. It'll be like starting all over again. I have to get this weight off of me. If I could get down to a size 10 or 12, I'll be cool.

"Is tonight a holiday that I didn't know about?" I heard the man near me ask. I looked up from my phone. He stared at me.

Confused, I raised one of my eyebrows. "Excuse me?"

"I mean, I've been waiting over forty minutes for my food," he said. "I've never had this long of a wait here. If the food wasn't so good I might have been left."

"Yea, it is pretty busy tonight." I responded before focusing my attention back to my cell phone.

"Have you ever tried the Shrimp Rossini?" He continued.

"Nah, I usually get the pizza or the chicken parm."

"Really?" He asked.

I nodded my head.

"That's not a good way to live. You've got to try new things, you know, live on the edge a little."

"Well, I'll be sure to add that meal to my bucket list."

He laughed. He extended his hand to me. "I'm Valdis."

I caught a whiff of his cologne. *Damn!*

"Zayda." I said shaking his hand.

"Nice to meet you, Zayda." He smiled. At that moment, I noticed how attractive he was. His complexion was a well-blended shade of a creamed coffee, and his teeth were ideal. They were the straightest and whitest teeth I'd ever seen. His hair was cut low, but dark enough for his waves to be visible. The suit he wore made him appear as a business man. He must have had his shit together because he didn't look a day over thirty. In Philadelphia, men his age don't normally have such a professional swag with them. Most of them strived to be the next Jay-Z or Frank Lucas. Valdis was sexy. Mature. I don't know what made him talk to me because he was definitely out of my league.

"Are you going to let go of my hand, Zayda?" He asked in a low tone.

"Oh my god." I said. I hadn't realized I was still shaking his hand. "I'm sorry."

He smiled again. Things had gotten weird for me, fast. I was fine until this gorgeous stranger spoke to me. Now, I didn't know how to act. *Calm down Zayda. He's only making conversation. Don't get ahead of yourself.* I tried to play it cool, but inside I was a nervous wreck.

I looked down at my work uniform. *Yea, he's just being nice,* I thought. *I looked a hot mess. He couldn't possibly be interested in me.*

"Ticket 248, your order is ready." The woman on the intercom announced.

"Ahh," Valdis said as he stood to his feet. "Shrimp Rossini."

"Enjoy life on the edge." I told him.

"I always do." He winked. "If you're not in a rush, how about you join me?"

His invitation caught me off guard. I didn't know what to say. I have never been on a proper first date, let alone a pop-up one. I wasn't prepared for this, and I damn sure wasn't going to stuff my face in front of him.

"Come on," he encouraged. "I doubt they have an available table in here but we can sit at one of the picnic tables outside."

My silence must have given away my hesitant feelings.

He reached for my hand. "This is the first step to living on the edge."

"Umm, sure," I finally spoke up. "Why not?"

Just as we walked up to retrieve his food, the woman announced that my order was ready as well. We sat outside and finished our conversation. The weather was just right; not too hot and not too cool. He tried to get me to try his meal, but I refused. I hadn't even opened my own meal, even though I was hungry as shit. Hell, I could have eaten both his and mines.

I looked at the time on my phone when I noticed people starting to clear out of the restaurant. It was almost 1 AM. Time passed us by so quickly. Surprisingly, we had a lot in common. He was a 28-year-old college graduate with no kids. He graduated from the same university that I planned on attending in the fall. I was honest with him about our ten year age difference, but he didn't seem to mind. He was born in Haiti, but moved to the states when he was 8-years-old. Now, he worked as a tax accountant for a foreign business.

I was enjoying myself, but I knew this was all too good to be true. I didn't expect for this to go any further than tonight.

"Well, Valdis, thank you for the company." I said. "But it's getting kind of late; I should start heading home while the buses are still running."

"Do you need a ride home?" He offered.

"Ok, you're a nice guy and all, but I don't let strangers know where I live."

He chuckled. "Yet, you stay out late with a complete stranger. Makes perfect sense." He sarcastically stated.

"I was living on the edge!" I laughed.

"So why stop now when you can go all out, and let me drop you off." He said. "Besides, I'm a gentleman. I wouldn't dare have you traveling alone this late at night."

I really didn't feel like catching the bus. Who knows how long I would have to wait before one arrived, and then still had to take the ride home. At this time of night, it would take at least an hour to get home by public transportation.

"Ok," I replied. "But you can drop me off at the 7-11 near my house, deal."

"You drive a hard bargain," he smiled. "But, ok. It's a deal."

The ride was quick, about fifteen minutes. He pulled alongside of the curb at the 7-11 and put the gear into park. Just as I reached for the door handle, he got out of the car and came around to the passenger side. He opened the door for me. I have never had that type of treatment. He *was* a gentleman.

"I had a good time with you tonight, Zayda."

"So did I. Thank you." I had been sneaking peeks at him all night, but this time when our eyes met it was different. It was like my body was melting. The look he gave me had me creamin' in my panties. I could feel a pulsating beat between my legs. He had no clue as to what he was doing to me at that moment all from one look. Yea… it *has* been too long.

He reached into his suit jacket, pulled out a card and held it out for me. "My cell number is at the bottom."

Slowly, I took it from him. "When would be a good time to call?"

"Whenever I cross your mind."

Shit, you don't want to tell me that! I thought. *My ass would be calling you all damn day.* I put the card in my pocket. "Ok."

"Have a good night." He said before walking back around to the driver's side.

I watched him pull off before I made my way down the street to my house. It was completely dark when I entered. I didn't need any light to find my way upstairs. I stuck my head into mom's room. Just as I suspected, she was stretched out across her bed asleep. I closed her door and retired to my own room.

Valdis. Just saying his name made me blush. I pulled out the card with his number and stared at it. I hated being the one to call a guy first. The first person to call always had to be the one to lead the conversation. I didn't give him my number, so I knew I had to call him eventually if I'd ever wanted to talk to him again. Always thinking on my feet, I pulled out my phone and sent him a text message.

Hey, it's Zayda. I got home safely. This is my cell number, lock it in. Good night.

Genius! That way he will have my number. He can call me when he's ready. When my phone buzzed a few minutes later, it was his reply.

Ok. Sweet dreams, beautiful. -V

I took off my uniform and slid into a t-shirt before lying in my bed. For once, I was going to bed with a smile on my face. Thank you, Valdis.

Chapter Six

Was it real? Was he real? I thought as I lay on my back and stared at my bedroom ceiling. Valdis was in my mental heavy. It all felt like a dream; never in my life would someone that fine actually be interested in me. I looked at the text message he sent me last night for the 5th time already. I debated if I should send him a good morning text. I didn't want to seem too eager, but since I was up and his scent seems to still fill nostrils, why not?

Good Morning Valdis! Hope you had a good rest.

Just before hitting the send button, I noticed the time on the top of my screen and I paused. It was 7:30 in the morning. I must be out of my damn mind. He would think I'm crazy. It was early; too early to be texting somebody I barely knew. What if he wasn't a morning person? I'm probably the only one who wakes up this early on a Sunday. No matter what time I went to bed, I never slept past 8 AM; as if my body had its own alarm clock. Shaking my head, I quickly deleted the message. Guess I'm going to have to wait it out until he calls me.

Since I was up, I figured I'd knock out my Sunday cleaning. My room was a mess. Shoes showered the floor and clothes covered the love seat in the corner. A few used cups still sat on my dresser from a few days ago. During the week, shit just seemed to pile up in my room. I wasn't always the neatest person, but I made sure to do a thorough cleaning at least every Sunday.

After turning on my Monica CD, I went downstairs to get the broom. As I approached closer to the bottom of the steps I could hear my mom laughing. She sat at the dining room table with the cordless phone attached to her ear.

"Um hmm, here's my child now." I heard her say as I walked by her and into the kitchen. I could tell by her instant change of tone that she wasn't happy about something. *What the fuck did I do now? And why the hell is she even up this early?*

"Let me call you back." She said. "If I need bail money, I'll be sure to call you."

I grabbed the broom and a bottle of water out of the refrigerator.

"Zayda!" She bellowed. Before I could even answer her she was standing right in front of me.

"Damn, mom," I accidently let slip out of my mouth. "What's wrong?"

"First off, watch your god damn mouth." She scolded as she pointed her finger in my face just barely missing the tip of my nose. "I'm not one of your little girlfriends, Zayda."

"Sorry..."

"And what did I tell you? Hmm?" She put her hand on her hip. "If you're not working, or if your name is not Jourdon Nicole Jones, you don't not come strutting you ass in this house anytime you feel like it.

Here I am thinking you're at work, but when I called there this morning they said you didn't work the overnight. So where were you?"

"Mom, I'm eighteen. I—"

"I don't give two shits if you're old enough to vote," she interrupted. "Because that's the only thing *eighteen* means to me. This is my house, and you *will* respect it. Do I make myself clear?"

I nodded my head. My mom was cool, but she had no problem letting me know who the queen B was around here. When she got in her angry mood, I never went back and forth with her. It was pointless. Even the times when I'm right and she wrong, she's still right. I just agree and keep it moving.

"And whoever *he* is that got you thinking you're grown I hope he's worth it." She said before turning to walk away.

"Who said anything about a *he*?" I questioned. The cordless phone rang from the dining room table.

"Zayda, please. Ain't no pussy got you coming home in the middle of the night. You just better had made him use a condom?" She said before answering the phone.

Shit, I wish. That was my chance to go back upstairs before the questioning started. I never told my mom about any guys I talked to. For one, meeting guys over the internet was not a popular choice. She would kill me if she knew I did that. And two, they never stuck around long enough. I didn't want to have to always explain what happen to *so and so*. It was easier for me to just keep it to myself.

The lavender scent from the lit candles around my room filled the air. It took me about two hours to clean the entire upstairs including my mom's room and her private bathroom. Hopefully, this will help my mom start to forget about me coming home late. I even threw in a load of laundry, took a pack of chicken breast out of the freezer for dinner, and all before noon. I love Sundays. It was the only day I could really chill out. Lifetime Movie Network and ice-cream occupied just about every Sunday.

I checked my phone hoping that Valdis had called. No missed calls and no messages. I know he had to be up by now; no one sleeps this damn long. I tossed my phone on my bed. *He has my number.* I thought. *If he wants to talk, he'll call.* I dismissed the thought of texting him, grabbed my towel, and headed to the bathroom to shower. Half an hour later, I was down stairs sitting in my favorite chair, relaxing in a t-shirt and a pair of dark blue sweatpants. My mom had stepped out for a store run. I clicked on the television with the remote just as my cell phone buzzed.

Aja's name flashed on the screen. I sent the call to my voicemail. It wasn't anything personal; I just didn't feel like hearing about everything I missed at the party. That's when I noticed another missed call. I tapped the screen to see who it was. My eyes widen in excitement when I saw Valdis's name. He must have called me when I was in the shower.

I put the television on mute and dialed his number back. *Damn.* His voicemail came on after two rings. I didn't bother to leave a message. I was just happy that he called. I checked the volume on my ringer and made sure that it was set at the loudest ring. I didn't want to miss his next attempt. I'd been waiting to talk to him…to hear his voice again. My phone chirped, and it was a text message from him.

Hey babe! I'm in the gym. Can't talk right now, but let me know if you are free to hang out later. I have a business dinner at 8 but I'll be free after that. –V

A smile grew on my face as I read the message. "Babe? He called me babe."

Yes—Yes—and Yes! That is what I really wanted to say back to him, but I know my mom was still on her pedestal about last night. Because she is a little pissed off, I knew she would find some fault in me going out and on a school night at that. But there was no way I was going to pass this up. I had to be strategic about it. I didn't answer him right away. I needed to first make a solid plan to get out of this house without my mom all up in my business.

I put my phone on the coffee table and got up to start dinner. I was going to pamper her. She loved shit like that; a clean house and dinner on the table with a glass of pink Moscato. I'll slide in that Aja and Jess is coming over after dinner. Knowing how she is, I can almost bet that she is not going to want us all up in her house today. So, when she says no, I'll tell her we'll go to Jess's house instead. She should be cool with that. Lying to my mom was as easy as ABC. Lies flowed from my mouth as if it were the truth sometimes. I did it so much that sometimes I convinced myself that I *was* telling truth. We all did; me, Aja, and Jess. If our parents knew about half the shit we got ourselves into we'd all be in boarding schools. The shit we did wasn't all that awful, but they would probably think so. And like Will Smith said, parents just don't understand. So, we lie.

As I started to season the chicken breast in the pan, I heard my mom come in the front door.

"Man that heat ain't no joke," she said as she put the bags down on the dining room table. "It's so hot outside my eyelashes started sweating."

"How many pieces of chicken do you want for dinner?" I asked her.

"Oh, none for me," she said. "I'm going out to eat tonight."

"Another date with my new stepdad?" I joked.

"Ha, with the way he's been acting you just might be right." She replied as she unpacked the grocery bag.

This was perfect. Since she would be out having a good time, she would be less focused on me. I just had to make sure I got home before she did.

"So, things must be getting pretty serious." I continued as I put the pan of chicken in the oven. "When am I going to meet him?"

"Soon." She answered. "I need to make sure this is real before I start bringing him around."

"Oh mom, Aja and Jess are coming over later, is that cool?" I purposely mentioned to get my plan rolling. She wasn't the only one who had a hot date tonight.

"Are you asking me or telling me?"

"Uh, both… I guess. I kind of already told them it was OK." I said.

"Zayda, no." She shook her head. "I need to come home to a nice, peaceful, and quiet sanctuary. You and your little girlfriends can find somewhere else to *chill.*" She said before heading upstairs.

Yes! I thought. *So far so good.* I grabbed my phone from the table and headed up to my room. I was going to call Aja and Jess so they can cover for me; but first I had to figure out what I was going to wear. There were more than enough clothes in my closet to choose from.

The problem was I felt like nothing was good enough. I mean, when he first saw me I had on my work uniform. This time I had to turn it up, but now it felt like the shit I had wasn't all that appeasing compared to what he wore. He seemed like the suited and booted type. I had to step it up if I wanted to impress him.

There wasn't enough time for me to go shopping, and I damn sure couldn't fit anything in my mom's size eight wardrobe. I had to make do with what I had.

"Zay," my mom popped her head in my bedroom. "Change of plans. I got called in to work tonight. Three of the other nurses called out and they are really short. Looks I'll be working a double. Make me a plate, will you?"

"Ok," I nodded.

"Thanks baby." She said. "Wake me up at 5 so I won't be late." She left out my room and closed the door behind her.

Things couldn't have worked out any better. I was going to have a good time with Valdis and didn't have to worry about rushing back home.

Oh shit! I forgot to text Valdis back. I quickly grabbed my phone and sent him a text.

Yes, tonight is good. What time?

A few minutes passed. I expected him to text me back, but he didn't. Instead, he called me. I answered the moment I saw his name flashing on the screen.

"Hey beautiful." He greeted when I answered. "How's your day going?"

"It's going good." I replied. "No complaints over here. How was your workout?"

"Hard, just the way I like it." He laughed. "Maybe one day you could come and sweat it out with me."

"Nah, I probably couldn't keep up with you in the gym."

"I'll go at your pace. It won't be that bad."

The thought of him topless with sweat making his skin glisten started to turn me on. He probably has some nice cut arms and the chest to match. He didn't seem that buff when I met him, but I bet he's working with something.

"You still there?" he asked interrupting my fascination.

"Uh, yea," I replied. "I'm here."

"So about tonight, my business dinner got canceled. If you want to meet earlier we can; about 7, maybe."

"7 is cool." I agreed.

"Great. So, I'll pick you up at the seven-eleven?"

"Yea that's fine." I smiled. "I see you in a little while."

After trying on nearly half of my closet, I finally settled on a knee-length, dark blue denim dress with silver buttons that trailed down the front. I topped off my outfit with a pair of silver and dark blue flat sandals, and accessories to match. I waited in my room until my mom left. As soon as she was gone, I headed right to the seven-eleven to meet Valdis. I was early, but I didn't mind waiting. He pulled up at 7 o'clock on the dot. As I expected, he got out of the car to greet me.

Damn, he's finer than what I remembered.

"Were you waiting long?" He asked as he walked around the car to me.

Smiling, I shook my head no. "Not at all."

"Good," he leaned in and kissed me on the cheek. He greeted me as if we had been dating for a while. He just seemed so comfortable in doing so. It wasn't normal for me, but hell, I didn't mind getting used to that shit.

"Come on," he said as he opened the passenger door. "I've got a surprise for you."

Small talk and lame jokes kept us occupied during the thirty minute drive. We arrived at a popular park near the Art Museum. Famous for the beautiful view of the city skyline and romantic first dates, it was rumor that plenty of babies were conceived there. Without saying a word, Valdis got out of the driver's seat and shut the door. A few seconds later I could feel the vibrations of him rumbling in his trunk. I didn't know what to expect. When he suggested going out, I assumed we would hit the movie theater or pizza joint like everyone else does. We were at a park; grass, mosquitoes, dirt, trees, and a few pedestrians staggering around.

The trunk slammed shut and up walked Valdis carrying a basket and a blanket. He nodded his head for me to come. I stepped out of the car and followed his lead. We walked to an area where there weren't too many people around.

"Should I be scared?" I asked. "You're not one of those crazy ass psycho killers, are you?"

"I have a clean record," he laughed. "I promise." He unfolded the blanket and spread it out over the grass. He sat down and began to unload plastic containers from the basket. "Are you going to sit?"

I looked away for a split second before easing down onto the blanket.

"You've never been on a picnic before?"

"Actually I haven't. This is one of those types of dates you only see in the movies."

"Ha, well we need to get you out more often." He smiled. "I love eating out, but I love cooking even more. I figured what better way to impress a woman than to cook for her. Anybody can spend a few dollars."

"No man has ever cooked for me." I admitted. "I am impressed, but is it any good?" I joked.

"Girl I got skills in the kitchen." He took the lid off one of the containers and grabbed one of the plastic forks. "Here, taste this."

He scoped a piece of what looked like grilled chicken and held it out to my mouth. The aroma of the meal hit my nostril as he got closers. It smelled delicious. I slightly opened my mouth to invite it in.

"No, wait." He pulled back. "Close your eyes."

I frowned up my face and gave him the side eye.

"Just trust me," he explained. "It will make this experience even grander."

This nigga spoke as if we were about to go sky diving or some shit. But I didn't refuse. Skeptically, I did as he requested. I closed my eyes and took in my mouth what he had created.

"Oh my god!" I exclaimed. My taste buds were on fire. This has got to be the best chicken that I have ever eaten. It was moist with just the right amount of seasoning. The sauce he coated it with was like no other. It was sweet but zesty; spicy but not enough to make it uncomfortable to eat. I finished chewing my food and swallowed it. Just as I opened my eyes, Valdis leaned in and placed one of the softest and gentlest kisses on my lips.

Caught off guard, I pushed him away. An awkward silence briefly lingered between us. I wasn't used to this…this romantic shit. By the look on his face I could tell he knew that I was a bit apprehensive. Taking a deep breath, I fixed my lips to say something, anything, but nothing came out.

"Listen, I'm sorry if I offended you," he started. "I just couldn't help myself. You are so beautiful, Zayda. I've wanted to do that the first time I saw you."

That tingling feeling you get when your nerves start spinning out of control…yea that was exactly how I felt at that moment.

"You don't have to apologize." I assured him. Even though it was sudden, I liked it…and I wanted more.

"I do." He said. "I should have asked. It's not like me to—"

I moved in so quickly if felt as if a magnet had pulled my lips to his. I kissed him and it felt good…so damn good. I shocked myself on how aggressive I was being. I never in my life took a leap like that, but once I finally did, a huge adrenaline rush inundated my body. I couldn't fight this feeling, nor did I want to.

He took me into his arms and pulled me on top of him. Our lips never parted as strong hands began to caress my body. My dress was slightly raised as I straddle his lap. I could feel the lively thump of his manhood tapping against my peach. His kisses lead down to my neck as he started to unbutton the top of my dress. Breathing heavily, I stopped him when I realized we were in a public park.

"We can't do this here." I shook my head. "Someone might see us."

"No one is coming back here," he whispered. "I wouldn't do it if I didn't know for sure that we had privacy." He looked me in my eyes. "Just trust me."

Something about the way he persuaded me never made me want to refuse. Sex in a park was way out of my character, but being around him made the daring side of me want splurge on the excitement. I slowly nodded my head and mouthed the word OK.

He grabbed my hand and kissed the back of it without taking his eyes off of me. "Lay down." He instructed.

I climbed off his lap, and on to the blanket. He swiftly turned over and on to his knees while at the same time laying me onto my back. The way his eyes lit up when he scanned me from head to toe was like an artist admiring his masterpiece he just created; studying every chisel, every curve, its perfect imperfection, appreciating its true beauty.

God! I think I'm in love.

Valdis lowered to me connecting his lips to my neck once more. The second our skin touched my body jolted. His tongue teased my collarbone as he pinned both my hands above my head. My breathing got heavier, deeper. I through my head back as his oral massage intensified.

I quivered. What was he doing to me? If was as if he was making love to my soul. His hands began to explore the depths of breast using his teeth to slightly lower the cup of my bra. A soft moan escaped my month when he exposed my hardened nipple.

"Oh, God!" I whimpered. I couldn't help but slowly squirm from the way my pussy yearned for him. I needed to feel him inside me. And I was ready and willing to beg for it.

"Fuck me." I pleaded.

Before I knew it, my entire dress was unbuttoned. Valdis continued to kiss on me. I wanted to cover my exposed body. I hated to see my own nakedness in the light, so I could imagine what he must have thought.

Surprisingly, he didn't stop. He trailed pecks down my large frame and slid off my panties. Firmly lifting up one of my legs, he pinned it back and took my vagina into his mouth. He went at it like a vulture. His tongue swerved in different directions as my pussy got wetter. I've always dreamed about having my pussy licked, but this shit was better than I ever imagined. For the first time, I was experiencing what the women on the X-rated movies were feeling. No wonder they were so dramatic. It was the best feeling in the world.

My toes curled up as my body grew weaker. I tried to hold in any noise by biting my bottom lip, but it was no use. I let out a loud moan and I'm sure someone could hear me from afar. I didn't give a fuck. I was in heaven and no one except Valdis could bring me back to earth.

Moments later, my body began trembling uncontrollably. I let out another loud squeal as he bought me to my climax. My juices exploded and he never bothered stopping. In fact, he made my love come down twice more before even coming up for air.

He crawled up and lay down next to me. I waited to see what was going to happen next. I assumed we would go all the way. I just knew he wanted me to return the favor...I mean, what man wouldn't? I've only done it a few times. I was nowhere near a pro, but I was going to give it my best shot.

We lay there quietly for a moment taking in the cool fresh air. It was perfect for me, especially after the little sweat my body worked up.

"Are you ready to eat now?" He looked over at me and smiled. I guess his mission was just to please me. He didn't even try anything else.

I shot him a smile back. "I don't think I'm hungry anymore, but that *was* the best chicken I ever had."

"Is that because it came with a little something extra?"

If my skin tone was lighter, my face would be red from blushing. "Yea…that too."

He leaned over and kissed my forehead. "Well, we can't leave until you try everything."

I sat up and fixed my dress; needless to say that I enjoyed the rest of our date. We talked, he fed me, and we talked so more. I got home a little after 10 pm. He was everything I imagined and more. It was like a scene straight from a movie. Guy meets girl and makes her fall in love. No, I wasn't in love with him yet, but was slowly catching feelings. There is no doubt in my mind that he would soon have my heart; especially if he kept this up.

Chapter Seven

As Mr. Leuter, the senior class advisor, went over the commencement practice schedule, all I could think about was my night with Valdis. The way he handled me was in a way that I never imagined in my wildest fantasy. He was gentle, but rough; passive, yet aggressive. He knew what to do and just when to do it. He wasn't shy, and he explored my body like he was on a worldly adventure. I thought for sure that my flabby frame would turn him off, but it didn't. He worked me as if my body fat didn't matter. For the first time, I felt comfortable naked in my own skin. He wasn't like these little boys trying to bust a nut. He was a man who knew the anatomy of a woman's body, and he had making me cum down to a science. I could still feel his tongue circling my pussy.

The ringing of the school's bell disrupted my thoughts. It was 11:45A.M. Second period was finally over. I grabbed my Chanel shoulder bag and headed out of the classroom to meet up with Aja and Jess at our usual lunchroom spot. I was the first of us to arrive as upper and lower classmen began to fill the large cafeteria. For most, lunch period was the highlight of the day. It was *the* social hour; a break from learning and nagging ass teachers. Most importantly, it meant that the school day was half way over.

The lunch line was always long at the start of lunch period. We had an hour to kill, so I always waited until the line died down before grabbing my meal. I sat down at the brown lunch table closest to the vending machines.

"The champs are here!" I heard a male voice yell out. I looked over to the entrance and a few members of the boys' varsity basketball team had come into the lunchroom.

"Do they always have to make a grand entrance?" Jess said as she and Aja walked up behind me, both sitting down at the table.

"Shit, if I had their skills on the court I'd be bragging too." Aja said, "Especially after that blowout championship game. They're undefeated!"

"Since when did you become such a basketball fan?" I asked.

"Since she started talking to Jamal." Jess answered.

"He is not the reason why." Aja explained. "I've always supported our team. I went to every game before me and Jamal started dating, Ok. But now, his fine ass just makes the game worth looking at."

We all laughed.

I momentarily looked away and spotted Tony and Tiffany standing by the entrance door. I watched as the two engaged in their own conversation. He reached up and touched her face. She smiled and caressed his hand in return. He followed up was a kiss to her lips. They seemed happy. They've been together the entire time; from freshman year til now. They even got accepted to the same college, and will be attending Hampton University in the fall. Tony's hoop skills landed him a full ride. Things seemed to turn out well for him. Despite how corny he was for what he did to me, I was happy for him.

The two of them kissed once more before Tiffany disappeared down the hallway. Tony walked into the lunchroom and passed the table where I sat. Briefly, we locked eyes. He looked away and continued walking to join his teammates in the café.

Sometimes I wondered how it would have been if he and I were still friends. We never spoke after the day he dissed me, but I can tell by the look on his face when those eye-catching, awkward moments would happen that he thought about it as well. I knew that he knew he was wrong for how he treated me. Truthfully, I didn't need his apology. It wouldn't really change things. We would still be on two separate levels. The unspoken truth that we shared was all that I needed.

"Zayda," Aja said hitting me on the shoulder. "Are you listening?"

"What?" I asked not hearing one word she said.

"We're going downtown to the Gallery to shop for graduation outfits today. You down?"

"Sorry," I shook my head. "I've got plans."

"Plans?" Jess interrupted. "What plans do you have that we don't know about?"

"I don't tell y'all bitches everything I do." I smiled.

"Yes… you do," Aja said, "Now spill."

They both stared at me waiting for an answer as if they were obligated to know.

"Well?" Jess said.

"Okay, Okay," I gave in. Truth is I really wanted to tell someone anyway. I couldn't hold it in any longer. A smile grew on my face as I mumbled the words, "I've got a date tonight."

"A date?" They sung in unison.

"Damn, is it that shocking?" I laughed.

"A date with whom?" Aja asked. "You never told us about a new nigga. You've been holding out."

"Because it's not much to tell." I lied. I didn't mind telling them about my new friend, but I wasn't about to say that he gave me oral sex already. "We met on Saturday, and I'm just now seeing y'all so how would I be able to tell you?"

"You have got to give us the rundown, Zay." Jess said as she twisted the cap off her water bottle. "What's his name? Is he fine? Where is he from?"

"Aww shit!" Aja said winding her body as if she were dancing to music. "Zay got her a Mr. Boo Thang!"

"When are we going to meet him?" Jess asked.

"Slow down," I put my hand up. "We just met. I don't need y'all scaring him off already. He's a little bit older than us so I don't need y'all acting a fool around him. He'll be my little secret until I know for sure what this is going to be."

"Well Mr. Boo Thang must have something on you because you haven't stopped smiling since we started talking about him." Aja noticed.

She was right. I couldn't stop smiling. I couldn't get him off my mind, and his head game…this man had me going through it and I haven't even known him a week yet. I was anxious to meet up with him later today. My mom was working the overnight shift again, so needless to say, Valdis was definitely on my agenda for tonight.

Later that night.

Naked and alone, I lay on Valdis's bed staring at the ceiling in shock at what I just let happen. I don't know what came over me. Why I would let a nigga go up in me without any protection was beyond me. I've made a lot of stupid decisions in my life but this was by far the worst. Gripping the black top sheet, I pulled it up to cover my body. The worst thoughts traveled through my head at the speed of lightening. *You don't even know this man. He could be out here burning bitches and you just let him stick his dick all up in you.* Silently, I scolded myself as tears rushed to my eyes. The fact that he was so cool with not using a condom had me worried. In the heat of the moment, I wasn't thinking with a clear mind. I just went with the flow. But now, I was regretting my decision. He could have an STD or worse, AIDS. *How could you be so stupid, Zayda?*

Valdis walked into the room carrying two glasses of orange juice. His cell phone rested between his ear and his shoulder as he took a seat on the edge of the bed. I sat up on the bed making sure I kept my body concealed with the sheets. He passed me one of the drinks. I wasn't really thirsty so I only took a small sip before sitting it down on the night stand. I remained quiet while he finished his phone conversation.

"Alright, thank you." He said before tossing his phone on the bed. He looked back at me and smiled. "You good?"

"Yea," I answered, doubtfully.

"They just called me into work," he continued. "Somebody fucked up one of the accounts and now the client is talking about removing all of his accounts with the firm. I have to go in and try to clean this shit up." He shook his head. "So, I'm not good."

As I stared down at the sheets, my thoughts dominate my hearing. I heard his voice, but didn't quite make out what he said.

"Hey?" He tapped my leg. "Are you sure you're OK? You look worried."

"I've never done that before." I blurted out.

"Done what?"

"I've never had sex without a condom," I confessed. "Especially with someone who I just met. I'm just hoping that there isn't something I should be worried about."

"I'm clean...disease-free if that's what you're implying." He said with his eyebrow raised.

The slight change in his tone caught me off guard.

"I'm not saying you aren't. I'm just—"

"Just what?" He said. "Zayda, I'm not sure what type of men you're used to dealing with, but I would never do that to you. I don't play around when it comes to my health, or anybody that I care about."

Were my ears deceiving me? Did this nigga just say he cared about me? He's only known me for two days, how could he care about me? I looked at him with the, *yea right,* look.

"Yes Zayda, I care about you." He confessed as if he could read my mind. His tone changed to a more soothing one. "What can I say?" He shrugged. "Call me a hopeless romantic, but I believe in love at first sight. I don't expect you to feel the same way but I'm willing to wait as long as it takes until you do. I'm not going anywhere, Zayda. And I hope there's nothing *I* should be worried about."

"Of course not." I responded, slightly offended. But I guess he felt that same way when I questioned his status a few minutes ago.

"No one has ever expressed their feelings to me." I confessed. "Honestly, this is all new for me. I'm just not sure how to take it."

"And I'm not rushing you. Take all the time that you need. I'm not going anywhere."

Did I believe him? I don't know, but I wanted to. He was open enough with me to put it all out on the front line so the least I could do was meet him there. Besides, it's kind of pointless to ask him that shit after we fucked. He had just as much on the line as I did, but he trusted me. So, I was going to trust him. So far, he hadn't given me any reason not to. I'm a big girl, I can handle this. But first chance I get, I will be getting tested.

Dropping the issue, I scooted towards him. I put my hand on his chin and slowly guided his face to mines. I kissed him, gently and passionately. Shivers shot down my body as he took me into his arms, and made love to me all over again.

Chapter Eight

Things between Valdis and I had been nothing less than amazing. Most of my off days were spent with him, and on the days we didn't see each other he made it up to me by showering me with gifts. And the sex…Oh My God! A permanent grin embellished my face. Everything was right. Even when shit went wrong, especially at work, I didn't let it phase me…I had a man; a real one.

I still had yet to introduce him to my mom or my girls, but with college only two weeks away I thought it might be time. He'd been away on a business trip for the past week and a half, but as soon as he gets back I'll tell him I'm ready. Knowing him, he is going to be thrilled to meet my family. We've talked about it before, but I didn't think it was the right time. Now that I'm going to be on my own, it's best for my mom to meet the person who will be keeping me company. Cheyney University was only an hour away, and Valdis already expressed that he had no problem coming there to see me.

I missed him; especially in the mornings. I was so used to getting a text or call from him every day, that this week and a half felt like torture. He was out of the country. With the time difference, it made it difficult for us to talk. But damn, he could have sent me a text or something.

Truth be told, we needed this little break. I haven't spent time with Aja or Jess in a while. As much as I love being with Valdis, I was missing my girls. So when they called me to go shopping I was all for it.

It was Saturday and we had been at the Springfield Mall all morning. I picked up a few new outfits for when I go to those campus fraternity parties. Aja and Jess did their usual by trying on damn near everything in the stores. It was pushing 2pm and I was ready to head home.

"Are y'all bitches done yet?" I huffed. "They're going to think we in here stealing or something."

"Please, a bitch ain't got to steal a god damn thing." Aja said loud enough for the store workers to hear. "How do you like this skirt?" She held up a black pencil skirt with thin pink pencil stripes.

"Um, I like the lime green one better." I told her. She assessed her outfit in the mirror. "Yea… me too. The black don't pop enough. A bitch got to stand out." She laughed and twisted her body to get a look at her ass in the mirror.

God, I would kill for a body like hers. She looked good in anything she put on. I mean this girl could wrap a tablecloth around her body and make it work. It was easy for her to shop, but me, I had to find clothes that fit my body; nothing too clingy and no bright colors.

"Ta-da!" Jess announced as she stepped out of the dressing room wearing a fitted, floral mini dress with thin straps. She walked in front of me as if she was on the runway and gave a twirl for her big finish.

"Do that, honey?" Aja said. "If you don't get that dress, I will."

"Girl please, you know you can't rock this dress like I can." Jess joked.

"One of y'all needs to hurry up and buy something because I'm ready to go." I interrupted.

"Where the hell do you have to be?" Aja asked. "I thought this was our girls' day out. Don't be rushing now, Zay."

"Listen, I'm getting tired, and I'm starting to feel a little sick. I just need to get home and lay my ass down."

"What the fuck, are you pregnant or something?" Aja asked. "Let me find out Mr. Boo Thang done knocked you up." She laughed.

"Girl, bye." I shot at her. "I am not about to be anybody's mama."

"Shit, I remember the time when my period was late and I thought I was pregnant." Jess shared, "I was scared as shit. I swear my life flashed before my eyes. Like a week later, she finally came on. Girl, I've never been so happy to leak blood."

"I bet you learned your lesson with ya little fast ass." Aja laughed. "You can always count on good old Bloody Mary to tell you if you're really pregnant."

"Exactly," I agreed. "That's how I know I'm not pregnant. Just a little sick, so we need to go. Please and thank you."

"Alright, alright," Aja moaned as she walked back to her dressing room. Jess followed suit and headed to the one she had just came out of.

Aja was crazy. Pregnant? Me? Yea, right. Valdis and I used condoms. Well, sometimes we did. Okay, most of the time we didn't, but he made sure not to nut inside of me. He wouldn't fuck up like that. Kids would be a burden to his life as well as mines. I know for a fact that he made sure to pull out every time. And like she said, getting a period was the official pregnancy test, and I always mark down when she comes and goes.

I pulled out my cell phone and thumbed my way to the calendar app. It automatically opened to the current month, August. I hadn't logged my period for the month which is odd for me. I know I had it because I remember getting it. It normally comes around the 4th of each month.

I thought hard about where I was when it came on. Valdis had left on the 5th and we had sex the night before. *Oh Shit! I didn't get it this month; that was last month.* I thought.

It was already the 12th of August which means I was eight days late on my period. I started to panic a little…no, a lot. My heartbeat sped up as the thought of me being pregnant danced around in my head. "Calm down, Zay." I told myself. "You don't know for sure, so just calm down."

I took deep, slow breaths attempting to stagnant my nerves, which didn't work. I needed to know—now.

"Um, I'll be right back y'all." I shouted out.

"You're rushing us to go so your ass better not be long." I heard Aja say behind the curtain. I ignored her and headed out of the store.

There was a small convenient store on the level below the clothing store we were at. I rushed to the escalator and headed down to the next level. When I entered the store, a short Indian man wearing a red smock greeted me. "Can I help you?" He asked.

I looked around making sure no one was in close proximity of me before I asked, "What aisle are the pregnancy tests in?"

"They are in aisle 5," he responded.

I found exactly what I was looking for. There were so many different brands; different prices…shit, I didn't even know which one was the best. Some had digital readings, plus or minus, one line or two lines—I just need one that worked. I grabbed the one I remembered seeing a television commercial for, First Response, and took it up to the front. There were no other customers at the front of the store, so I was able to get in and out. I made my way to the public restroom by the food court. A woman and her daughter stood at the sink counter washing their hands when I entered.

I went into the first empty stall and locked the door behind me. I wasn't even sure how to use one of these because I never had to. After quickly lining the toilet seat, I pulled down my jeans and panties and sat down on the seat. I opened the box and pulled out the test along with the directions.

Are you kidding me? I thought as I skimmed over the instructions. They really put little pictures of a woman with her pussy exposed peeing on a stick. Do they really think girls are that stupid? Shit, I guess they had to dumb it down for the girls stupid enough to get pregnant so young. Like me, of course. I shook my head in disbelief that I could possibly be in that category.

I took off the plastic cap and dangled the stick between my legs where my pee would flow. A few seconds later, I felt the urge and handled my business.

When I was finished, I cleaned myself up, fixed my clothes and leaned up against the wall of the bathroom stall. The directions said it would take up to two minutes, but it seemed like forever waiting for the results to pop up. I started to think about what I would do if it came out positive. My life would be over. After hearing my mom's mouth for a few weeks, I guess she would finally come around. But I know her ass ain't babysitting shit. I know she loves me and would do anything for me, but a baby, man she would purposely make me do it on my own to teach me a lesson. I would probably be stuck working at the old folk's home because I would really need the money. And college would definitely be out of the question for now. I mean, how could I? With a baby and all, I'd be lucky to find the time to go to a junior college.

God please just let this be all one big misunderstanding. I thought.

Well, God straight ignored my fresh ass today because the stick had a light pink plus sign which meant pregnant. I stood there staring at it for almost ten minutes hoping that the results would change.

"Fuck my life. What am I going to do with a baby?" I mumbled. More importantly, what was Valdis going to say? Coming home to news like that was going to be crazy. I don't think I've got the nerve to tell him face to face. I felt like this was all my fault. I should've gotten on the pill. I should've made him use a rubber. I'm not like those hood rats running around town, careless. I know better. But I guess none of that shit matters now. I pulled out my cell and called Valdis. I didn't know what I was going to say but I needed to talk to someone before I went crazy in this bathroom. His voicemail came on after a few rings.

"Hey babe, I hope everything is going well on your trip. I really need to talk to you. It can't wait. Call me any time. Even if it's late, I'll wait up."

Not wanting to leave the details on the message, I had no choice but to wait for his return call. I stuffed my phone in my pocket, put the test back in the box and slipped it into my bag before washing my hands and leaving out of the restroom.

Aja and Jess were standing outside of the store when I returned.

"Where the hell have you been, Miss *I'm ready to go?*" Aja asked when I approached. "You were gone for like a half an hour. You good?"

I took a deep breath. "Yea, I'm good." I responded with a straight face. I didn't need them knowing just yet. "We can go now."

Just about the entire bus ride home I sent Valdis text message after text message telling him that I need to talk to him. I knew he was getting them so why the fuck hasn't he responded to any of them? This shit was driving me crazy. Now that I had time to think, it was really fucked up that he hadn't reached out to me at all. They do have phones in China— shit, they are the mu'fuckas who makes the phones! His ass could have Skype me or something...anything! Did he even miss me? He was going to hear my mouth when he got back next week.

"Zay?" Jess called interjecting my inner rant. "Are you sure you OK? You haven't said a word since we left the mall."

"I said I'm good...really."

"OK....but if you want to talk we're here," she said.

"Well, we are going to your house with you to make sure you're good." Aja chimed in.

"What?" I laughed. "Y'all don't have to go out of the way. There is nothing wrong with—."

Aja cut me off. "You said you didn't feel well earlier so we are coming to take care of you— end of discussion."

Aja was such the demanding type sometimes. I didn't put up a fight. At least if they were there my mom wouldn't be all up in my face. I just had to prepare myself for the million times they were going to ask me if I was ok.

Chapter Nine

"Surprise!"

I nearly fell backwards out of the door when everyone shouted. Yes, I was surprised.

"Congratulations, college girl," my mom said over the clapping and cheering. She embraced me in her arms and hugged me tightly. She had managed to plan a trunk party without me noticing. I guess being the first one in my family to go to college was a huge deal. She went all out too. The living room featured blue and white balloons and streamers, Cheyney University's official colors. A banner hung from wall to wall with my picture airbrushed on one side, the words *CU Later College Girl* across the top, and the University's crest on the other end. Gifts were stacked up on one side of the living room, and a full buffet style layout was prepared in the dining room. My mom invited a host of family and friends including my nana, my mom's baby sister and her two children, my uncles, cousins and some of my mom's friends from work. Aja and Jess were in on it as well. They purposely kept me out all day for the set up.

As crazy as I felt on the inside, I made sure to keep a smile on my face. Out of all the times my mom could have planned this event, she did it just when my life took a turn for the worst. My feelings were all over the place. I was nervous, pissed, sick, hurt, and disappointed all at once. Valdis still hadn't returned any of my texts, and I just wanted to go in my room and sleep. My mom would know something was up if I left my own party, so I had to push through it. The last thing I needed right now was to hear her mouth. This pregnancy was going to stay on the hush until I figured out what I wanted to do my damn self.

I wasn't there for longer than thirty minutes before my mom pulled out old photo albums of my childhood. She talked on and on, to whoever would listen, about how proud she was of her baby girl. Her words were so piercing, and she didn't even know it. Every time she spoke highly of me, it felt like a dagger jabbing at my heart. It was as if God was punishing me. If she knew that her baby was having a baby she'd be so disappointed in me right now. I never envisioned that this would happen, at least not this early on. How could I have been so stupid? I wasn't like those girls at school who walked around with their pregnant bellies. A baby was going to put a hold on a lot of things. Was I ready to become a mom? No. I had no clue how to raise a kid.

I heard the doorbell chime in the midst of my thoughts.

"I'll get it." My mom said. She put the photo album on the dining room table and headed to the front door.

"Girl this seafood salad is the bomb." Aja said as she took a seat on the bar stool next to me. She continued to stuff her face with the pile of food on her plate. "You've got to taste this shit."

She held her plate out to me.

"Bitch, I don't want that shit." I joked. "The way you're eating it you probably got spit all up in it."

"I wasn't really sharing with you anyway." She laughed. She sat her plate down on the counter top and wiped her mouth with her napkin. "So, are you ready for college? It's not like high school. You're going to be on your own up there."

"I guess." I replied, nonchalantly. I reached over to her plate and took a piece of the BBQ chicken.

"You don't sound too excited," she said. "A few weeks ago you couldn't stop smiling. Shit, earlier today you seemed happy. Now you look like someone stole your best friend. And since me and Jess are both here, that can't be the reason either. So what's up?"

"It's nothing." I took a bite of the chicken and never looked her way.

"Bitch, I know you like the back of my hand." She snatched the chicken out of my hand and put it back on the plate. "You were never a good liar. Is it your Mr. Boo Thang?"

"Aja it's nothing, really?" I huffed. "Can you please just drop it?"

"Something is going on and I'm not shutting up until you tell me."

One thing about Aja, nothing got passed her. Her observant ways was going to land her a job as a detective of some shit. As much as I wanted her to drop the issue, I knew she wasn't going to until I told her. Besides, I needed to tell someone before I went crazy. Aja was my girl and I knew I could trust her with my secret.

"Ok," I started. "Aja I'm—"

"Who is that fine piece of a god with your mom?" Aja interrupted. "You didn't tell me mama was getting her groove back."

I looked up to see what she was talking about. My bad day had suddenly gotten worse. I felt like my entire stomach dropped out of my body. I couldn't believe what my own eyes were witnessing.

"Zay, come here." My mom called me from the living room. "I want you to meet someone. This is Valdis…my fiancé'…"

Knock! Knock!

"Zay, you in there?" Brandy called from the other side of the bathroom door ripping me away from my daydream. "Girl, I've got to pee. This wine is running right through me. You better hurry up or you're gonna be cursing me out for pissing on your floor."

"I'm almost done," I assured her. Getting up from the toilet seat, I pulled up my pants, fixed my attire, and did a quick hand wash at the sink before opening the door.

"Damn, girl you were in there for almost an hour. Any longer, I was sending the SWAT team." Brandy said as she shuffled her way into the bathroom. Before I could even close the door, this hussy had her shit down and on the toilet. That was Brandy.

The remainder of the night was a blur. I couldn't get this shit out of my head. Not suspecting a thing, the ladies continued their drunken conversation. I was ready for everyone to get the hell out of my house. Luckily for me, the guy's meeting didn't last too much longer after Dr. May's devastating news.

After we said our goodbyes, Carl escorted our guests to the door. I stood over by the mantel, quietly, as the sight of my husband chilled the blood running through my veins. It rose from my feet to my head in 0.10 seconds like an avalanche of ice from the world's most massive mountains. The moment he closed the door, the black glass elephant figurine on the mantel went flying towards his head. Fortunately for him…I missed.

"What the fuck!" Carl shouted when it hit the door and shattered. He quickly turned and looked at me. By the time we locked eyes, I had another one coming at his ass. You would have thought I was a pitcher for the Phillies the way I was beaming them at him.

"Zayda, what the hell is your problem?" He dodged yet another hit.

"Chlamydia! That's my fucking problem," since there were no more elephants, I grabbed the next thing closest to me. The large, Bahama Bay Breezes scented candle could barely fit in one hand, but that didn't stop me from using it. This time, I didn't miss.

"What?" He winced from the candle hitting him in his side. "What the hell are you talking about?"

"You know good and well what the fuck I'm talking about. You dirty bastard."

"Baby, calm down, and tell me what's going on."

"I want you out!" My jaw's grit was so tightly clenched, my tooth almost cracked. "Get out of my fucking house! You lying, cheating, asshole!"

"Zayda, enough," Carl's voice echoed throughout the living room. "What the hell happened? Huh? Did one of those women tell you something? Put an idea in your head? Why the heck would you think I'm cheating on you?"

"Yes." I screamed. "Someone told me something, alright. My damn doctor that's who. The nerve of you to bring some dirty shit like that to me. Who the fuck do you think you are?"

I don't know if I was more hurt, or disgusted. But whatever feeling bubbled inside me had turned on my flow of tears. They just kept streaming down my face. I couldn't even look at him...no longer be in his presence.

Brushing passed the sofa; I stormed over to the staircase to go up to my room.

"Baby, wait." Carl said as he hurriedly met me at the foot of the stairs blocking my path. "We need to talk about this."

"Get out of my way, Carl. Leave me alone. You have nothing else to say to me."

"So you're just going to believe whatever the hell that doctor is telling you?"

"Tests don't lie!"

"Yea, but they tend to get wrong readings. It's not true, Zayda. I would never do anything like that. You know me." He reached up and gently grabbed me by the arms. Instantly, my body quivered from his touch...not in the least bit soothing way.

"Listen, I don't have anything," he continued. "I'm clean. I can go to my doctor's first thing Monday morning. You can even come with me. I didn't do this to you."

Yanking away from his grip, I pushed passed him and continued up the stairs.

"S...T...D." I yelled with my back toward him. "Do you know what that stands for?"

Carl's heavy footsteps trotted up behind me.

"Sexually-transmitted disease," forcefully turning around I met him face-to-face at the top of the steps. My finger violently waved in the closest proximity possibly to his cheek, "Which means I got this shit from sex. Sex with your trifling ass. Sex with *my unfaithful* husband."

"Zay—"

"And since we know the source of this *STD* between the two of us, do you know who *you* had sex with to get it?"

"I told you I didn't cheat on you. I didn't have sex with anyone."

"Well, until you're ready to be honest with me you can go and *not* have sex with your wife in the guest room."

Without another word to his ass, I turned on my feet, stormed off into my bedroom, and slammed the door shut. Outraged was an understatement. I wanted to kill him. My adrenaline wouldn't let me calm down, so I paced the carpet back and forth trying to make some sense out of all of this. And you know what... I couldn't. His ass is lying. He's been lying.

First the job, and now this? And as far as I'm concerned, fuck this marriage, fuck this life, and fuck him!

Chapter Ten

Getting out of my bed the next morning was forced. Literally, I had to muster up every bit of what little energy I had to start my day. Cherish needed to be picked up from my mom's, and I needed to get out of this damn house. I didn't really want to see Carl. He didn't even bother to check on me after I dismissed him last night. Maybe it was for the better. I cursed his name most of the night, anyway. When I wasn't doing that, I cried. I cried hard. The swollen pockets underneath my eyes were the proof of my sorrowful night.

"I'm leaving him." That was the conclusion I came up with after my crying session. I can't be with him if I can't trust him. And what he did to me was below betrayal. It was the unthinkable. The type of shit that will get a bitch locked up real quick. Cheating is one thing. Maybe if I would have found condoms like Jennifer, I'd be able to look passed him cheating. Maybe I would be more willing to work things out. But this shit isn't that simple. Say I do forgive him, and a couple of months down the line he steps out on me again. Next time, things could be far worse. What if he contracts AIDS instead of something a pill or shot can cure. How am I supposed to explain that to my daughter? If he isn't going to be the man I need and protect this family—*protect me*… then I am going to make sure she and I are both out of harm's way.

Before heading downstairs, I showered and dressed. The black Nike yoga pants and black t-shirt fit my mood perfectly. I wasn't trying to impress anyone. It was one of those *Give me 50 feet* kind of days. The moment I stepped foot in the living room, I spotted my cheating ass husband in the kitchen. Surprisingly, he was already dressed in a pair of loose ball shorts, t-shirt, and sneakers.

Going to talk to your bitch about the disease she gave you? I thought to myself. I really wanted to say it, but I wasn't going to give him the satisfaction of seeing me hurt. In fact, I told myself from this point on I would not cry. Too many times, even before Carl, I found myself whimpering over a man that didn't deserve my love. Well you know what? Now, I love myself too much. So, I won't.

"Good morning," Carl said as I made my way over to the refrigerator. I opened it and grabbed a bottle of water and a peach from the drawer. Without looking his way, I could feel his eyes gazing at me.

"You hungry?" He continued without so much of an acknowledgement from me. "I made us some breakfast. It's your favorite. Tilapia, grits and cheese eggs."

The nerve of him to think that everything was okay after his wrong-doings surfaced last night. The nigga must've really bumped his head if he thinks that we're just going to pick up like nothing happened.

Kindly, I rolled my eyes and headed straight to the front door.

"Are you really going to act this goddamned childish?" He followed behind me. "Zayda, we are married. Do you know what that means? It means whatever comes about, good or bad, we talk about it. We...communicate; not parade around here like some little ass girl who can't control her fucking emotions."

Halting dead in my tracks, I snapped my head back around to face him. "Excuse me? You're the reason why I have this damn attitude. Maybe if you would keep your dick in your pants where it belongs, I wouldn't have to act like this."

"How many times do I have to tell you I didn't do anything?"

"Stop lying, okay. Even after everything is laid out on the table you're still lying. That shit didn't magically appear. It didn't just fall out of the sky and land in my pussy."

"Well, how the hell else do you think it could have gotten there, Zayda?" His eyebrows rose with suspicion as if *I* was the culprit.

"What exactly are you trying to say, Carl?"

"That maybe you know a little bit more than what you put on."

"Are you saying this is my fault? *I'm* the one who did this?"

"Well it damn sure isn't mine," he took a few steps back. "You know I've been doing a lot of thinking myself last night. I know for a fact that I haven't had sex with any other woman since you and I first started dating. So don't stand here and act all innocent like I'm the only one capable of fucking somebody else."

"No. No. You're not going to do this to me, okay. You know I haven't been fucking around."

"Yet you still have an STD. Zayda, I've been to the doctors. You were just there with me last week. I didn't have anything then, and we haven't even had sex since. Unless my mouth is infected, cuz that's the only part of me that was between your legs, there is no way you got that shit from me."

I couldn't believe this. This pussy was too much of a coward to admit what he did. Now he wants to turn the blame on me? The last thing I wanted to do was argue, but Carl was completely out of line with his accusation.

"Carl, you know damn well—"

"I don't know shit." He gritted through his teeth. "I only trust and believe the things you tell me are true. But you're accusing me of something I know I didn't do, so you need to figure out how *you* got Chlamydia and keep it real with yourself. I thought you knew me better than that. Do you honestly believe in your heart that I would give you something so disgusting? Zay, if I was cheating, and I'm not saying that I am, I know well enough at least to protect myself…and to protect you. You and Cherish are the best things that ever happened to me. If you don't see that, where does our love really stand? You don't even have *that* much trust in me."

Swiping the keys from the coffee table, Carl took one last look at me and left out of the house. A few seconds later, I heard the car's engine start up from the driveway. And there I was, standing in the middle of my living room, speechless. *Did that really just happen?* Not one sympathetic bone in his body. I had never known him to keep something going for so long. If he was ever wrong about anything, no matter what, he had no problem coming forth; just as he did about the FBI situation at his job. But now, I don't know what to believe. If he *is* guilty, he was not letting it show. Plus, Carl was right. He and I hadn't had sex in the past week. Something was definitely up. The look on my husband's face was that of a hurt man. What if I was wrong? What if that damn test was a mistake?

"Ugh," I dropped my arms to my side and closed my eyes. It never fails. Here come the tears.

Dr. May wouldn't be in her office until Monday morning, which means I had two whole days before I can see her. I needed to be retested, and I'm praying that these results come back clean.

My cell phone vibrated in my pocket. Honestly, I was hoping it was my husband. Something inside of me was telling me that he was being somewhat truthful about this. The little tugging at my stomach just wouldn't go away, and we needed to talk. Digging in my pocket, I retrieved my iPhone. I was wrong, it wasn't Carl. Jennifer's name blared on my screen.

I wasn't in any mood to talk to anyone, so I sent the call to voicemail. Before I could put my phone away, she was calling, again.

"Hey, T, let me call you back later, I—"

"Zayda, oh my God! I need your help." she cried. Her voice was hysterical. Her frantic wailing was so loud I could hardly understand what she was saying to me.

"T, what's wrong? What happened?" I worried.

"Zay, you have to come to me. Help me, please."

What the hell could have happen? Maybe she finally confronted Neil, and told him about the private investigator she hired.

115

"Ok, I'm on my way," I told her. "I will be there shortly."

"Zayda, please hurry," Jennifer cried. "He's dead. I think I just killed my husband."

Chapter Eleven

When I arrived at Jennifer's house, she met me at the door. Violently swinging it open to let me in, she turned and walked back into the house.

"It's his fault. He made me do this to him." I heard her mumble.

I closed the door behind me and followed her into the dining room.

"Oh shit!" My jaw dropped when I saw Neil's body lying face down on the hardwood floor in a pool of blood. Using my hand, I cuffed my palm over my mouth. I couldn't believe what I was seeing. Instantly, I became frightened. Not of Jennifer, but of what was going to happen next.

Neil's white tank top was saturated in his crimson blood. A butcher knife with a black handle stuck straight up from the center of his backside.

Jennifer slowly moved about the dining room. I looked at her, and then back down at Neil's body in complete shock.

"What did you do, Jennifer?" I asked in a low tone, but loud enough for her to hear me.

She didn't respond. She just looked at me and continued her slow pace. Jennifer didn't even look the same. Distraught was written all over her face.

When I saw Neil's body slightly heaving, I bent down to check his pulse.

"Jenn, he's not dead. You have to call the ambulance." I informed her.

"No." she shook her head. "No, I—I can't do that."

"You have to. If you don't then he *will* die. What would even make you do such a thing?"

"He had her in my house," she cried. "He had that bitch in my house and lied to my face. He had her in my goddamn bed. This is my house. I live here. How could you be so damn disrespectful?" She shouted as she looked down at Neil. "And I hope you can hear me, you slimy son-of-a-bitch."

"What are you talking about, Jennifer? How do you know that?" I stood back to my feet and walked towards her.

"Zayda, last night when we got home… I saw it." She started. "I was drunk, but I know what I saw."

I grabbed her by the arm to stop her stride, "You saw what?"

"The texts… the pictures… everything. He didn't even have the sense to delete this shit from his phone."

"You actually saw the woman in his phone?"

"No." she shook her head. "I saw the pictures he took of the house. He had it all decked out and shit; rose petals around the tub and on the bed, and candles every fucking where. I never came home to that shit, so I know it wasn't for me."

Jennifer picked her pacing back up. "It had to have been that week I was in Texas for that conference. I wasn't even here, so who the fuck did he make this house up for?"

Taking in a deep breath, I continued to stand quietly and listened.

"And when I questioned him about it, he started that stuttering shit. Saying that I'm tripping, I need to trust him, and I had no right going through his phone." She halted again and looked at me, "I'm his wife! I have every goddamn reason to go in his fucking phone."

Jennifer finally took a seat at her dining room table. The tips of her finger tapped rapidly against the wood. "So, this morning when we woke up, I nagged him about it. I nagged... and nagged... until he finally admitted it. He told me he did have an affair. Twice. But I should be grateful because I'm the one who got the house and the cars. He had the nerve to say that women would commit murder to live my life. That is when I snapped. The knife was the closest thing to me, and I blacked out. All I remember is me standing in back of him and his body dropping to the floor."

"Honey, I know you're upset." Reaching over to her, I put my hand on top of hers. A few spots of Neil's blood had dried to her skin. "But you're smart enough to know that you cannot just do nothing. You can't let him die. We have to call an ambulance and get Neil to a hospital now."

The way her pupils zeroed in on me, I could tell that Jennifer had lost it. She glared at me as if I was crazy. I know she loves her husband. There wasn't a day that went by that Jenn didn't make it known. Neil was her real knight in shining armor. The ones you would only hear about in the fairy tales. They were the definition of uncontaminated, factual love. Jennifer's marriage was my hope for all black marriages. They had it going on. They were living proof that successful black unions still existed...until now. This news had struck both her and me to the heart.

"Sweetie, I promise I'll be right there with you. I won't let you do this alone, but I cannot have you go to jail for murder. Neil needs help."

A brief moment of silence lingered before Jennifer looked at me and broke down into an even harder cry. She covered her face as the tears crept down the back of her hands. I waited for her to answer. Honestly, I was going to call the police whether I had her approval or not. But finally, through her tears, sobs and heavy breaths, she slowly nodded her head yes.

I was afraid to tell the police what happened over the phone. When the police operator asked, I just kept it simple.

"Someone has been stabbed," I informed, and gave her the address. After making the call, I rushed back to Jennifer's side and held her until the authorities arrived.

When the first responders showed up, it was evident what had happened. They had no choice but to put Jennifer in handcuffs, and haul her away in the back of the cop car. The paramedics put Neil on a gurney and into the ambulance. Sirens shrieked as they rushed him to the hospital. Before they left, I found out what hospital they were taking him to. I was going to go there, but first, I had to make sure my girl was good. I followed behind the police car down to the precinct. This shit was way over my head...out of my league. There was only one person who I knew that could help the situation, or even knew what the next move should be. Jennifer needed a lawyer and my husband, Carl, was the only one I trusted to handle this...even though he was just a business attorney.

The phone call went to his voicemail each time I tried. On the fourth call, I just left him a message letting him know to meet me at the police station. Keeping it brief, and not wanting to alarm him, I figured I'd fill him in when he got there.

An hour passed, and Carl never called me back. But when I saw him walking through the front doors of the police station, I sighed in relief. "He did get my message." I could tell by the look on his face that he was worried. He didn't see me sitting on the chair on the side of the room. He headed straight to the front desk.

"Carl." I called out.

Our eyes locked when he turned my way. Worry turned to liberation when he saw me on this side of the bars. He must have thought I was the one in trouble.

"What happened?" He asked as he approached, "Are you alright?"

"Yes. I'm fine, but Jennifer… they arrested her."

"Arrested her for what? Is Neil here?"

"No. Neil was taken to the hospital, baby, something happened at their house. Jennifer stabbed him." I whispered the last part.

"What?" His voice carried throughout the precinct grabbing the attention of a few bystanders.

I watched his anger rise, quickly. This wasn't the reaction I was expecting.

"Neil's not dead, but he's hurt… badly. He is down at Temple University Hospital."

"What the fuck did she stab him for?"

"Keep your voice down." I warned. "I'm not going to get into all of that right now, but she needs your help."

"No," he said as he vigorously shook his head. "She doesn't need my help. That crazy bitch needs a goddamn psychiatrist."

"Lower— your— voice. We are in public." The threatening look I sent him with the second warning eventually got through.

Carl took a deep breath. "Why did you call me down here?"

"I told you, Jenn needs your help."

"You want me to help your friend, who just tried to kill my friend?"

"The *both* of them are our friends."

"My loyalty is to Neil, not Jennifer." He said momentarily closing his eyes. "If she stabbed him, then she is exactly where she's supposed to be right now."

"It was a mistake, Carl. You know Jennifer would never do anything like that." I defended.

"But she did!" He bellowed. His words silenced me, and everyone else, it seemed. Carl quickly scanned the room and back at me. "Excuse me, but I have to get down to the hospital." He said before turning away.

I grabbed his arm from behind, "You can't just leave her in here; she needs an attorney."

"And I'm pretty sure she has enough money to afford one that can help her." He said over his shoulder. "You are right about one thing; she is going to need a damn good lawyer to get away with this if I've got anything to do with it."

Again, I watched his backside as he walked out of the door.

"Fine," I said to myself almost in tears. "You be there for your friend, and I'll be here for mines."

Chapter Twelve

It had been over nine hours, and I still had yet to see Jennifer. The detective who oversaw her case kept telling me it would be soon. Well, soon turned into never. It was already after midnight, and I was tired. My bed was calling my name, and I hadn't seen Carl since he left me earlier in the day. Thank God my mother was willing to keep Cherish one more night. I hadn't told her what happened between me and Carl, yet, or Jennifer for that matter. My mother never minded keeping her grandbaby. In fact, she was ecstatic when I asked her if she could keep her an additional night.

To my surprise, Carl was still awake when I got home. He was sitting on the living room couch with a lit cigar in one hand and a drink in the other. He knew how I felt about him smoking in the house. I guess any consideration he had for my feelings went out the window due to today's events.

Closing the door, I secured the locks and punched in the code on the alarm system.

"How's Neil doing?" I asked softly.

Carl turned his head, slightly, and looked over his shoulder at me through the corner of his eye.

"Stable." He responded and leaned forward tapping out the cigar in the glass ashtray on the table in front of him.

"Did he wake up?"

"No."

This is going to be like pulling teeth. The one word answers he was giving me was a clear indication of the attitude he was still holding on to.

"Well, what did the doctor say?" I walked around the couch and took a seat on the opposite end.

"Jennifer just better be lucky that Neil is not dead." He assured. "The doctor said that he's going to be just fine. She stabbed him eight times and not one puncture hit any major arteries."

Grabbing my chest, I sighed in relief. "Oh, thank God. Jennifer is going to be glad to hear that."

"Why are you so worried about what she's going to be glad to hear? She is the cause of all of this shit."

Here he goes, again. Picking yet another fight with me for the same exact thing he was doing; being concerned about a friend. I had a long enough night already. That was my cue to go to bed.

"Carl, it's late, and I am tired. Please do not start this… not right now. "

For now, I was waving my white flag. Whatever he was feeling could be dealt with in the morning. I was just thankful that my girl wasn't going down for any murder charges. I got up from my seat and headed for the steps.

"But I really wish you would reconsider helping her." I said as I started up. "Maybe when Neil wakes up you can talk to him… come up with a story to clear this thing up."

"Zayda, I can't do that. And I won't. I'm not going to ask Neil to lie for her crazy ass."

His comment made me pause midway up the stairs, "But, you do it all the time at work."

"Well right now, I can't. I have too much to deal with at the firm. Cartman got me completely boxed out at the firm. I don't know a single thing that is going on or what his next move is gonna be. I could be facing some serious charges, and if the shit hits the fan, it's our asses only that I'm worried about."

"That was the bed *you* made. Don't bitch out now."

Standing from his seat, he turned towards the steps where I stood. "And Jennifer made this one."

"That's different, and you know it. Jennifer snapped because her husband was cheating. But you… you made the decision with a clear conscious mind to help a criminal hide his money."

"So you're saying she was right for what she did?"

"All I'm saying is that it could have happened to anybody." I put my hand on my hip. "Hell, it could've been us."

"Then you are just as crazy as your friend, I guess." He shrugged.

"You really don't see anything wrong with what Neil did?" I questioned, "I'm not saying that Jennifer was right. You know I don't condone that shit, but he hurt her—far worse than what she may have done to him."

"Neil didn't deserve to be stabbed half to death. I don't care what he may have done to her. If Jennifer's life was that goddamn bad, she should've just left. Because if it were me, I..." he paused and shook his head.

"If it were you, what?" I made my way back down the steps and met him at the bottom. "What? Go ahead and finish. If it were you, then what?"

"Never mind. Forget it. Like you said... it is late, and it's been a long day. So drop it."

"No, I want to know. If it were me sitting in that cell right now, you would let me rot, wouldn't you? Even if you know what you did got me there."

"That's neither here or there," he implied. "It's not us, so don't worry about it. We've got bigger problems if I don't find out what Cartman's got up his sleeve."

"Oh, so it's we now? Should *we* be getting an attorney?"

"I've got my frat brother, Ronald, all over it. He's the best lawyer in the city. Ron's already informed me that this case has no weight. They are trying to build one."

"So that means now Brandy knows everything that's going on?" I huffed, throwing my hand up in the air. I took a few steps back, shaking my head.

"I would assume so. She *is* his wife."

"Great. Now everyone knows my fucking husband is a criminal." I turned to walk back up the stairs.

Carl grabbed my arm stopping me in my tracks.

I looked down at his hand and back up to him. "Let me go, Carl."

"Zayda, look. I know you're pissed. But can we just cut this shit until after this investigation blows over. I can't—I won't have my house falling apart with everything else."

Snatching my arm away, I stared at him, spitefully. No matter how hard I tried, I couldn't sympathize with him. I didn't feel sorry one bit for what he was going through. "Well it's too late for that now, isn't it?" I hissed.

"Just let me worry about taking care of Cartman, and you continue to make sure home is straight." Carl barked. "That *is* what you do best, right?" His mockery was rude and unnecessary.

Asshole! I thought as he brushed passed me and went up the stairs. And what the hell did he mean by that?

"I'm scheduled to go in on Monday for more questioning with the agents, just so you know." He informed before retiring to the guest bedroom.

Why was he, all of a sudden, treating me like I am his enemy? None of this was my fault. Not the feds, not this STD, and definitely not what happen with Jennifer and Neil.

This wasn't my husband. He was cold and careless as if he didn't love me anymore. I just wished things could go back to the way they used to be...before our lives took on this downward spiral. You know that saying, when it rains, it pours? Well, right now, I was in the middle of Hurricane Katrina, and I was sinking by the day.

Chapter Thirteen

Finally Monday had arrived, and I was up bright and early. My plan was to be the first walk-in at Dr. May's office. Both Cherish and Carl was sound asleep when I left the house. Carl had also planned to visit his doctor, and decided to take Cherish along with him. Besides, I was going to see Jennifer after my visit. Yesterday was just too hectic of a day for me to get down to the precinct. I didn't actually do anything, or go anywhere, but I needed a break; a break from the world, a break from the chaos… just a mental break.

Knowing Jennifer, she was probably going crazy in the holding cell. Hopefully, I'd be able to see her today, and find out what the next step is for her. She didn't kill her husband, but attempted murder is just as serious.

It took me no time, at all, getting to downtown Philadelphia where Dr. May's office is located. Besides the young female receptionist, I was the only one in there. Thank God I didn't have to wait. My nerves were all over the place, and I needed my questions answered. My marriage depended on it.

Just as I was signing in, Dr. May appeared from the back.

"Zayda, honey, I'm glad you came down," she greeted with a smile. She approached me and leaned up against the desk. Reaching over, she grabbed the file from the young woman who had already begun checking me in.

"I'll print out the information when I get to the back, don't bother." she told the girl.

Dr. May looked back at me. Her smile faded into a look of worry. "Are you okay, sweetie?"

You called me down here because I may have a sexually transmitted disease, and you're asking me if I'm okay. I thought as I nodded my head, yes, and forced an, "I'm okay," out of my mouth.

"Okay, well come down to my office so we can talk."

Dr. May held open her office door for me. I took a seat on the chair in front of her desk. Since she moved her practice here a few years ago, this was the second time I'd actually been in her office. Our visits always took place in the exam room. My intentions were to be retested, and I knew it wasn't going to happen in her office.

She came in, closed the door behind her, and took a seat behind her desk.

For some reason, I couldn't look her in the eye. She knew me too well, and I guess you can say I was embarrassed. Now she, too, knows that my husband had been unfaithful.

"I know what you're about to say," I blurted out just as she fixed her lips to speak.

"Oh?" she sat back in the leather chair.

"Listen, you already know my husband and I do not use condoms. So you can't say that I should've been protecting myself. That wouldn't be a fair statement. Dr. May, he is my husband."

"Zayda, I—"

"Wait. Let me finish." I said, "My husband was the one who did this. I trusted him, and I shouldn't be looked at any differently than the average, faithful wife."

Dr. May just sat quietly with her hands folded on her lap, and stared at me. A few moments of silence went by and she still hadn't spoken.

"Well?" I asked, "Aren't you going to say anything?"

"What is there for me to say?"

"I don't know." I shrugged. "Something. Anything."

"Zayda, what goes on in your bedroom is none of my business. But it's still important, married or not, to always have yourself checked... both you and your husband. I'm just glad we caught it in time."

"Are these tests ever wrong?" I'm sure she could hear the desperation in my voice. I needed her to say yes.

Opening the desk's drawer, Dr. May retrieved a green folder and placed it in front of her.

"Chlamydia is one of the most common sexually transmitted diseases in the U.S." she said opening the flap of the folder. She pulled out a few sheets of paper and laid them on her desk.

"There are a few different tests to diagnose Chlamydia. What I did was a cervical swab of your urethra. The specimen was tested in our labs and came back positive. Just to be sure, I also sent in your urine sample to check for the presence of the bacteria."

She slid the paper in front of me.

"I don't know what I am looking at." I admitted as my eyes scanned the paper.

"That is the laboratory's report. It says that the bacterium is active."

Standing from her chair, Dr. May walked over to a tall cabinet. She reached up to the top shelf and pulled out a sealed syringe, and a small clear-liquid filled jar with a white label.

"I'm going to give you a shot to cure the disease. This, along with an oral antibiotic, will clear the Chlamydia."

Tears began to surface as I faced my reality. I had actually psyched myself up to believe that the test was wrong.

"Can you roll up your sleeve for me?" she asked as she slid on a pair of latex gloves.

Placing the paper on the desk, I did as she asked.

"Now Zayda, it is very important that you finish the oral medication." She warned, "Don't miss a day or you run the risk of not killing all the bacteria completely."

"How long do I have to take it?"

"Seven days." Pinching the fat on my upper arm, she gave me the shot and put a bandage over the punctured area.

"I want you to come back in a month to be retested." Dr. May remained professional as she treated me. I thought there would be more to it, but there wasn't. She really had no words or no comments about how I contracted it. I was in and out of her office in about fifteen minutes, tops. I scheduled my four-week follow-up with the receptionist and headed to my next destination.

The police station wasn't nearly as packed as it was on Saturday. And luckily for me, the same ignorant detective who handled Jennifer's booking wasn't there either…thank God. Detective Ardmore was the one on duty today. He was a lot nicer. I didn't have to wait to see Jennifer at all. Detective Ardmore escorted me down to a room where I waited for her. Like in the movies, I thought that I'd be sitting behind thick glass talking to her on the phone connected to the other side. To my surprise, it wasn't at all the way I pictured; just a large spacious room with no windows. In the middle of the floor sat a table and two chairs. A big mirror practically covered one of the walls. It had to be a two-way mirror so the detectives could watch what transpired in the room. I wouldn't be shocked if someone stood on the other side watching me at this very moment. It didn't matter, though. I knew how to deal with these types of situations.

When the door reopened, in walked Jennifer wearing the same thing she had on when they arrested her. *Damn, they could at least given her a clean white T-shirt so she wouldn't have to wear Neil's blood.* I thought. That was probably a constant reminder of what she had done to him… a punishment in itself.

"Zayda!" She approached and embraced me with a hug. Relief coated her voice. I could only imagine what she had been dealing with since she's been in here. Yes, it was only a holding cell, but hell, they probably treated them just as bad as the real prisons.

"How are you holding up?" I asked her eagerly and concerned.

She continued to hold me as if she didn't want to let me go. "Girl, it's crazy in here. The toilet is in the middle of the floor. When I have to pee, it's in front of everybody…wide open." She began to explain as she took a seat on one chair, and I sat back down in mine.

"I haven't taken a shit all weekend." She continued, "And the smell. Oh my god! It stinks so bad, I am scared to breath in the air. Not to mention there are eight other ladies sharing the cell with me…or so I think they're ladies." She shook her head. "I have to get out here. How is Neil? Have you seen him?"

Her rambling only confirmed to me how nervous she was.

"He's alive." I enlightened her.

Jennifer sighed, hard, and grabbed her cheeks. "Really? Oh thank God. Have you seen him? What did he say? Does he even remember what happened?"

"Jennifer, no I haven't seen him. I mean, Carl has been down to the hospital, but me and him haven't really been on good terms lately. I just figured I'd lay low and let him handle the visits."

"What's going on with the two of you?" Her eyebrow rose.

"I don't want to get into all of that right now. I just came to make sure you were okay, and we need to figure out what to do next."

"Is Carl here?"

Regretfully, I shook my head no.

With her nostrils slightly flared, she sighed. "I knew it. Of course he wouldn't come. I just damn near killed his friend. Why would he help me?"

My eyes immediately shot towards the two-way mirror and then back at her, "Jennifer, don't talk that way while we are in here," I whispered.

"We just need to get you a lawyer, or do you have one already? I can get him down here today."

"Yes, of course, but…"

"But what?"

"It's Neil's uncle, Jeffrey. We always used him. I never thought I had to get my own attorney. It's always just been me and him."

"Well listen, I will make a few calls and get someone here as soon as possible—someone with no affiliation to Neil or Carl."

She nodded her head in agreement.

"Zayda." She looked at me dead on. "I need you to go see him. Please. I need you to go see my husband, and you have to tell him how sorry I am. I didn't mean to do it… I love him, Zay."

"Jennifer, I don't think that's a good idea. Not right now."

"Please, Zay." Her forehead creased with lines, "I don't know when the next time I'll have a chance to talk to him. I need him to know this. I love him. Even if he doesn't say it back. He should hear it."

Jennifer wasn't going to let up until she had an answer. I couldn't lie to my friend, especially while she's in here. But I wasn't going to make false promises, and give her false hopes, either.

"I'll think about it," I told her. That was good enough to calm her nerves. With a simple head nod, Jennifer broke down into tears. I felt bad for her. My problem seemed so small compared to hers. She could be facing a long sentence. No big beautiful house… no business… Nothing. I can see how her situation weighed heavily on her.

I got up and walked around the table to where Jennifer sat. Comforting her, I let her tears soak up my shirt. Not too long after, Detective Ardmore came back into the room and interrupted our moment.

"Times up." he announced from the door.

Jennifer lifted her head and glared up at me with despairing eyes, "Please Zay," she stood to her feet, "Give Neil my message."

Chapter Fourteen

"Hey mom," I spoke into the speakerphone as I fastened my seatbelt, "Are you home?"

"Where else am I going to be when I got this beautiful little baby? *Yes I do, yes I do.*" She responded in a playful babyish talk.

"Whose baby?" I frowned.

"Zayda, whose baby do you think I got? I am not a daycare. My house is only set up for one baby. And that's my Cherish-poo."

Shocked, my brows furrowed. "What is she doing there?"

"I don't know. Carl called me about twenty minutes ago and asked if he could bring her over. He said that he had somewhere important be."

"Mom, you've had her for the past couple of days. You should've told him no. You need a break."

"Now you know I am not going to say no to my grandbaby." She laughed. I could hear Cherish jabbering along in the background.

"Yeah, whatever." I rolled my eyes. "I'm on my way over. I need to talk to you."

"Is everything okay, sweetie?"

"If by okay means that Jennifer is sitting in a jail cell, and I have Chlamydia… then yes, everything is just perfect."

"Zay, what are you talking about?"

"I'll explain everything when I get there." I said before tapping the end button. Turning the key, I started my engine and headed out of the police station's parking lot.

What the hell did Carl have to do that was so important he couldn't take his own daughter? I thought as I merged onto the expressway. I knew he didn't have to be at the firm for questioning until later on in the afternoon. He specifically said he was taking Cherish to his doctor's appointment with him. There's only one other thing that I could think of. Even after all of this, he still hasn't learned his lesson. He's probably with his side bitch. If she's still able to snap her fingers and he jumps after she burned him, then Carl must really have feelings for her. And I shouldn't have to compete with anyone for his heart. She can have him for all I care.

By the time I got to my mom's house, Cherish was sound asleep.

"Are you hungry baby?" My mom asked, "I just made some homemade beef stew, and it is the bomb."

"No thanks. I'm good." I flopped down on her couch. "Where is Zaire?"

"Thea took him to the movies."

"Thea?" I asked. "Those two are friends now?" My 10-year-old brother, Zaire, had a vendetta against my mother's lover. From the day she came out of the closet, Zaire wasn't having it. "I wonder what changed his mind." I spoke.

"Hey, I'm not complaining." My mom laughed. "They had left before Carl bought the baby over, otherwise your brother would've changed his mind about going. That boy loves his niece." She took a seat on the opposite end of the couch, and stretched her feet out on the empty cushion between us.

"So what's this about Jennifer being locked up and you got an infection?"

Deeply exhaling, I shook my head not sure of where to begin. "It's been a hell-of-a-long weekend. Jenn stabbed her husband—eight times."

"Oh my lord!" she gasped. "Are you serious?"

"Yes…Neil is okay, though. He's in the hospital, but Jennifer isn't. She'd been in jail since Friday. She found out that he was having an affair."

"Wow."

"It's crazy, right?"

"Yes, but that's no reason to destroy your life." My mom stated, "A man is going to be a man, and when a man has that much control over you, that you try to literally kill him, it's not healthy."

"Mom, that's the last thing you think about when you're pissed off."

"Well I hope you aren't thinking it," she dropped her head to one side.

"Of course not."

Twisting her lips to one side, she picked up the cup of tea she had been drinking. "So then what are you thinking about your situation?"

"Honestly, I don't know. I went this morning to get treatment for the Chlamydia. And, of course, Carl is denying that he ever had an affair."

"And you know for sure he did?"

"Yes," taken aback, I replied with a bit of offense in my tone. "I haven't done anything if that's what you're implying."

"Hey... I don't know," she shrugged. "I'm just asking, baby. You are human, too. People make mistakes all the time."

Snapping my head sideways, I looked at her through the corner of my eye, "And that makes it ok for a person to cheat?"

"It's never okay to be unfaithful, Zayda. But you can't control a person's actions either. The only thing you can do is trust that your spouse will make the right decision when they are faced with the dilemma."

"Yea, but that is easier said than done. What if they don't make the right decision?"

"Then *you* have to make a decision; probably the hardest one you will make in your life. Walking away is never easy... if that's what you decide to do."

"I don't know what to do at this point. I just wish that he would admit what he did." Staring at the wall in front of me, the night I got Dr. May's message replayed again in my head. "It's still a fresh wound that'd been picked. And the fact that I got it taken care of, doesn't excuse me getting it in the first place."

"It's not supposed to, baby. But you have to ask yourself, is he worth fighting for? Is your marriage worth working it out? And honestly, what will it change for him to confess?"

Her questions stumped me. A confession from Carl most likely wouldn't change a thing, but to hear him say it *would* make me feel better, right? And as far as me fighting for our union, that was up in the air too. My mom didn't know the half of it. I'm sure if she knew, she herself would help me pack my things to leave him.

"If he can admit it to me, then that tells me he wants to gain my trust back." I concluded. "If he can't, then I can't be with him. I need to be with someone that I can trust...a man who has my best interest at heart."

"Zayda." She shook her head and dismissed my somewhat of an explanation. "That only means *you* want him to gain your trust back. No matter what he says or does, the fact of the matter is... it happened. If you are going to forgive him— and trust him again, then it has to be because you want to. Not because you backed him into a corner to tell you something you *think* you want to hear. You will have a life full of disappointments if you operate that way."

My mother never held back in her delivery. She either told you like it is, or stayed out of it completely. I kept quiet as she continued her lecture.

"When it comes to your marriage, remember why you got married in the first place. Continue to lead by example—be his wife. Men and women say things all the time just because we think our spouses want to hear it. Yet, the actions that follow behind it go against everything we said. Words can mean a bunch of nothing, so a confession is merely dead weight. Actions speak louder than words, even your actions. Value your vows. Through thick and thin, remember?"

"But mom, he gave me an STD. I don't think I can ever see passed that."

"Okay. But let me ask you this, would it be any different if he would've gotten the girl pregnant, instead of contracting the disease."

"No," I quickly answered. "I mean, maybe. A baby isn't a disease. It would take some time, but I can't honestly say that I wouldn't divorce him; especially if it was a one-time thing."

"So what's the difference? The act is still the same...its unprotected sex. If you are willing to work it out if it were a baby, then I think you are looking at this all wrong. Not once did you say he was a bad guy, or he mistreats you. This just may have been a one-time deal. Unfortunately it happened, but thank God, it's something that you can get rid of, and hopefully he learns from all of this."

She swung her legs around and planted them on the floor, "Now, I have gotten to know Carl quite well."

Not well enough. I thought.

"I'm not saying what he did was right, but he made a mistake. Men make mistakes all the time, but a real man will fix it. And baby girl, from what I see, you do have a good man; better than the ones that I had back in my day." She chuckled, "Hell, why do you think I like women, now. Thea has been nothing but good to me. And yes we have our days, and there was a time that she was unfaithful, but we worked through it. The bigger picture is that we love each other, and *our* relationship is worth it.

Chapter Fifteen

On my way home, my mind was going non-stop; so much that I don't even know how the hell I was able to make it to my house. I wasn't at all focused on the road.

Talking to my mother was very much needed. She always helped me to see things from another perspective. It can be hard for me to see passed my own feelings sometimes. I don't fully agree with what she said, but it made me think. I'm still mad— pissed at my husband actually, but one thing I did realize since everything happened was we had yet to essentially talk to one another. Hell, I can admit that I wasn't trying to hear anything he had to say, and he probably felt the same way about me. So tonight, I want to do just that—talk. I was going to listen to him, and I wanted him to hear me out, uninterrupted. This is my first challenge of taking the lead in this marriage. Truth be told, I love my husband, and I am praying that he fixes this. Even if it takes time, just fix it. If Carl is willing to work on us, then I'm willing to do whatever it takes to save my marriage.

My mom didn't want me to wake the baby, so she told me to come by tomorrow to pick her up. I guess she knew that I wanted to talk to Carl, as well, but when I reached home his car wasn't in the driveway.

I looked at the time on my dashboard, and it was just after 4 PM. By now, Carl should just be finishing up with his interview at Cartman's. That was another thing we needed to talk about. He never gave a clear explanation of what was going on at his job. Even if we can see beyond our martial problems and federal mishaps, Carl has to be willing to leave Cartman's, and bury whatever they got going on.

As I backed my car in to the driveway, I noticed an unfamiliar black sedan pulling over alongside the curb in front of my house. Momentarily, the driver looked up at my house before getting out of his vehicle.

"Who the fuck?" I watched the black-suited African American male climb out of his car and close the door. He and I locked eyes just when I was getting out of my own vehicle.

"Excuse me," he shouted. "Are you Mrs. Kinsley?"

Looking at him strangely, I asked, "Can I help you?"

"Mrs. Kinsley, my name is Agent Bennett." He waved his badge out for my view as he neared me. "I'm looking for your husband, Carl Kinsley?"

Just then, I recognized his face. He was one of the agents at the firm the day I went to meet Carl for our lunch date. But why was he here? *Shit!*

"Listen, if you're here for information to build a stronger case against my husband, you can escort yourself off my property."

Agent Bennett slyly chuckled as he stuffed his badge into the inside pocket of his black suit blazer. "Your husband was supposed to meet me at Cartman's law firm, but he never showed up. It's imperative that I speak with him. Do you know where I can find him?"

The news hit me with much surprise, but I didn't show. "So you come here? Is my husband under arrest or something?"

"No, but—"

"Then no," I interjected. "I don't where he is." *Hell, his guess was as good as mines, anyhow.*

"Mrs. Kinsley, do you mind answering a few questions?"

"Me? Why?"

"I figured since you're his wife maybe you know something about what is going on at the firm."

"I don't work there. What's goes on at Cartman's is not my business." I coldly told him and headed to the front door.

"I noticed you were talking to Ms. Marcy Wiley the first day that we came down to the firm," he continued as if I hadn't dismissed him. "Are you and she good friends?"

Annoyed, I took a deep breath. "Agent Bennet, now is not a good time. I'd be happy to answer your questions to the best of my knowledge. I'll schedule it with my attorney." Again, I turned away, opened my front door and quickly entered the alarm code on the keypad. Agent Bennett had made his way up to my front door step.

"What about Carl and Marcy? They're pretty close, right? I mean, they do work together, and they just happen to take frequent out of town trips; majority of them being *non*-business matters."

"Out-of-town trips?" Cocking my head slightly to one side, I scowled my face at him. He was dropping bomb after bomb. It was time to end this. "If my husband's been anywhere with her, trust me... it was all business. And I'm fully aware each time."

"Mrs. Kinsley, we do have evidence of them checking in to various hotels outside of Philadelphia; a few times in Miami, Las Vegas, and Chicago. We have surveillance of just the two of them, and when we checked the dates against the company's records, there were no business trips scheduled during the times they were spotted. Do you know of any reason why your husband and Ms. Wiley would visit these places?"

And there it goes again. It never fails; that pesky knot forming in my gut. Carl neglected to mention Marcy going on any of these trips with him. As a matter of fact, his ass outright lied to me, AGAIN!

Now it was all starting to make sense. That was the reason he had an excuse of never having time for another woman. His side booty worked with him. I trusted him at work because Marcy always told me everything…except for the fact that she was the one fucking my husband. *That little stink bitch.*

If it hadn't been for Agent Bennett standing here, I would've screamed. I would have screeched so loudly that it would've woken the dead. Agent Bennett stood in silence staring at me. He probably could see the rage twitching at my jaw bone. Yet still, he wasn't going to get a thing out of me.

"Thank you," I forced a half smile. The tingling in my toes began working its way up to my legs and in to my thighs. I was literally going numb standing in front of him. My mouth dried up, and my ears began to pop as if I were on an airplane.

"You will have to speak to my husband." I said. "Any questions you may have about Carl, I suggest you save them for him."

"I see," He nodded. "Thank you for your time, if you—"

"I won't." Before he could finish his sentence, I shut the door in his face. Snatching off my jacket, I tossed it on the couch and walked over to the window. Agent Bennett was just walking back to his car. He got in and pulled off.

"Son of a bitch," I said as my body nervously shook from the can of worms Agent Bennett had no idea he just re-opened.

"All of this time… the many conversations this bitch had with me, smiling in my goddamn face and shit, and her little dirty ass has been screwing my husband."

If it weren't for the investigation going on, I would've went right down there and paid Ms. Marcy's ass a visit. Most likely, she wasn't there, anyway. But her ass better believe the next time I see her… I'm fucking her up on sight.

Chapter Sixteen

As the dark blue night cascaded over the sky, Carl still hadn't stepped foot in the door. It was almost 10 PM., but guess what? I was going to sit right here on this couch and wait for his ass. In the past few hours, I had already packed all of his shit; his pants, shirts, shoes, jewelry, vitamins…you name it. Everything was neatly packed in the black Calvin Klein luggage set I had gotten him for his birthday a few months ago. Who would have thought it would come in handy to kick his ass out of the house. What couldn't fit in the suitcases, I stuffed in three of his gym bags, and stacked them all in the living room by the door.

Me? I was dressed as if I was about to beat a bitch's ass in the street. My sneakers were laced up. The grey oversized T-shirt and black tights allowed me to move comfortably and freely. My hair was pulled back into a ponytail with a gray scarf wrapped around my head.

Fighting Carl was never my aim. I knew for damn sure he wasn't going to lay a finger on me—or crazy enough to try. But that wouldn't stop me from pouncing all over his cheating ass.

Looking down at the empty wine bottle in front of me, I realized that I went through the whole damn bottle by myself. Needless to say, I was a little fucked up. But he was still going to hear my mouth.

As more time passed, thoughts of Carl and Marcy invaded my mind like a swarm of killer bees. How could I have been so dumb? Marcy was too nice to me, too quickly. Ain't no woman that damn pleasant to another woman unless she was out to gain something from her. Women. Either they wanted to be your, or jealous enough to hate your fucking guts. I don't know what game that bitch think she is playing in, but she'd about to lose.

Damn, he could have at least fucked with a bitch I don't know. The audacity of him to bring me to his job knowing what the two of them had going on. She probably loved that shit, too; I was so blind to the messiness right under my nose.

Purposely sitting in silence, I listened to hear his car when he pulled into the driveway. When he finally came, it was almost 11:30PM. I heard his car alarm chirp after the door slammed shut. Waiting for him to enter the house seemed as though time had slowed down. From the time he locked his car to the time he got to the front door felt like forever.

My eyes remained focused on the black television screen mounted on the wall above the mantel. The doorknob jiggled, and seconds later, I felt the cool night's breeze hit against the back of my neck when the draft from the opened door rushed in. It felt good considering the amount of heat my body drew from the alcoholic intake.

"What is all of this?" He asked from behind me. I still hadn't turned around to look at him. "Are you going somewhere?"

"No." I leaned up and sat my half-empty glass of wine on the coffee table next to the empty bottle. "But you are."

Just as I stood up, he closed the door. I walked around the couch and stood directly in front of him. It wasn't until we were face-to-face that I noticed his reddened eyes and distraught look. Carl looked as if he'd been crying. I wasn't at all expecting that.

"Zay, listen, can we please just talk?" His voice was low and sorrowful, and it sparked an ounce of worry in my heart. Everything that I planned to say to him left my mind that quick.

He pulled out a piece of paper and held it front of me.

"What is that?" I asked never ripping my eyes from his.

"These are the results from my appointment today." He told me.

Because of my slightly blurred vision, I had to squint trying to read what was on the paper.

"It says that I'm clean, Zayda. I don't have a sexually transmitted disease. Which means you didn't get Chlamydia from me."

"What!" My breath shortened and my knees buckled. I would've fallen to the floor if Carl hadn't caught me. I couldn't stop my eyes from filling with tears as he lowered me to the floor. Someone must have hit my volume button, because my drunken screeches increased.

"Where could I have gotten it from? None of this is making any sense. I haven't done anything with anybody else."

"Zayda, I don't even want to know." He said in a calm yet disappointed tone.

"But I didn't do anything," I repeated through each sob. "I would never do that. I gave birth to your child."

Carl used his thumbs to wipe the tears gliding down my cheeks.

"Agent Bennett said you've been going out of town with Marcy. Why were you at hotels with her if you weren't cheating on me? How come you hid that from me?"

"Marcy? Zay, I'm not sleeping with Marcy. I don't give a damn about any other female. I keep telling you you're the only one I want...the only woman in this world for me."

"But Agent Bennett already said—"

"When did you see Agent Bennett?"

"Today." I said as my bawling began to simmer. "You didn't show up to the office so he came here looking for you. Where were you at all day?"

"I missed the meeting today because I was at the hospital with Neil." He began to explain. "When my results came back negative, I needed to vent. Neil is the only one I could talk to about this. Honestly, he helped me get my head straight because my first intention was to just leave you. But then..." He hesitated.

I looked up at him, "But then what?"

Carl sat completely on his bottom and looked me in the eyes. His hands gently massaged mines as he took a deep breath.

"I probably should have told you this a long time ago. Maybe this was karma coming back to kick me in the balls."

I didn't respond. The only thing I could do was prepare myself for more hurtful news; door after door of surprises, and not the good kind. I was becoming numb to it all. We were just so happy a few days ago. Now, it felt like my life was falling apart and I didn't have the glue to keep it together. With more bad news, how am I ever going to begin to patch the wounds?

"When we first got married... I did have an affair." He confessed.

"What?" I tried to snatch my hands away, but he only gripped them tighter.

"It was only one time," he continued. "And ever since then the guilt ate at me. It was the worst mistake I've ever made in my life. I felt bad coming home to you afterwards. I was reminded how much you would have been hurt every time you smiled at me, or told me you loved me. I promised myself that I would never sleep with another woman again....and I haven't. I just know if you would have found out what I did back then, I would want you to give me a second chance to prove to you that I can do better; which is why I said I need to give you a second chance. Baby, I love you. And I just want us to move forward from here. We are going to get through this."

I sighed...hard. Everything he was saying sounded so convincing, so sincere...so pure; much like the man that I married six years ago. But I couldn't just sit there and let him place the blame on me for something that I did not do.

"Carl."

"Yes, baby."

"This isn't right. I *know* I haven't been unfaithful, and I refuse to let us continue on with you thinking that I have betrayed you. If I'm wrong, then I would tell you. I would never let it get this out of control. My name and reputation will not be dragged through the mud. No matter what you say…if I let you believe that, then you will always have in the back of your mind that I am capable of being that type of woman. I am a *good* wife. I have been nothing but a supportive, loving, and understanding woman to you. I stayed true to my vows because I meant them. I love you more than life itself, but I would rather see you walk away before I let that lie live on. My heart would never settle for that."

Carl's eyes rolled down to his lap, and the silence grew thicker between us. We sat on the floor in each other's presence without a single word spoken, but his muteness shouted loud and clear… he knew I meant every word I said.

After about five minutes of sedentary, Carl pulled me in to his arms. He lay me down on the plush carpet and positioned his body behind my cradled posture. His arm fit perfectly in the dent of my side as he pulled me closer to him.

"Let me just hold you tonight." Squeezing me just a little tighter, he kissed the nape of my neck.

His lips sent shudders throughout my entire body. I wanted to refuse, but being in his arms gave me the secure feeling I'd been accustom to. It felt too content, too safe for me to leave from it. More tears streamed down my face as I silently soaked in my own contemplations. His hand massaged from my shoulders down to the midst of my thighs.

"I love you." he whispered in my ear. "And I'm not going anywhere."

The next thing I knew, we were fast asleep on the living room floor where we stayed the entire night.

Chapter Seventeen

ONE WEEK LATER

"Bail is set for two hundred thousand dollars." The judge announced. Everyone in the courtroom stood still until the judge banged his gavel against the wooden base. Jennifer turned around and looked at me. I was sitting on the first row. Her smile was bigger than the Kool Aid man himself. I know she was relieved to make bail.

"You'll be out in a couple of hours." I heard her lawyer say to her. Jennifer quickly nodded her head. The bailiff came and escorted her to the back.

Arson Clemens. He was Jennifer's attorney. Brandy had given me his contact information. I told her we didn't want anyone affiliated with Neil or Carl... or her husband, Ronald, for that matter. She assured me that he wasn't. When I asked her how she knew him, she gave me *the look*. You know... the look only a man could make a woman have when he's laying the pipe down right. I just shook my head.

Damn, is anybody faithful these days?

Mr. Clemens was very attractive. He was an older man; about late 40's or early 50's. He was the complete opposite of Brandy's chocolate-complex husband. I didn't even know she was into high yellow men. He sort of favored the NBA basketball player, Tyson Chandler. Nonetheless, Brandy says he's good at what he do, so we used him.

As Mr. Clemens turned to leave, I met up with him at the center aisle and we walked out of the room together.

"So, what now?" I asked him. "I doubt she has that much money sitting around. Neil held all of the accounts."

"The bail is two hundred grand, but we only have to pay a percentage right now so she can get out." He educated me.

"How long is that going to take?"

"The Bail Bonds is right across the street. I'm going to do that right now. After processing, she should be out within an hour or so."

"Okay, good." I sighed in relief. Jennifer had spent over a week in that place. I was glad to know she'd get to sleep in her own bed tonight. Despite what she did, Jenn is not a bad person. She doesn't deserve to rot in a jail. "I'll just wait around with you, then. No need in me going home and have to come back down here to pick her up."

"Okay. There's a little diner on the corner where we can wait." Mr. Clemens held open the door to the outside. "I'll meet you there once I finish handling her paperwork."

"Okay." I agreed. This will give me some time to call Carl, and check on the baby, anyway.

The sun was blazing when I stepped outside the doors of the courthouse building, downtown Philadelphia. It was 11 AM, and already hot as hell. As I made my way to the corner diner, I retrieved my cell phone from my oversized shoulder bag. Carl answered on the first ring.

"Hey," I said with not much enthusiasm in my voice. "What's going on? How's Cherish?"

"She's good." Carl responded in almost the same tone. "We're just about to eat lunch. How did things go?"

"She made bail. I'm waiting around now until the lawyer handles everything… then she'll be out soon."

"Hmmm," was all he offered about Jennifer's situation. I knew he still felt some type of way. His boy was in the hospital, and had to undergo a major surgery because of what she did. But from what I hear, Neil was doing a lot better. This past week did wonders for his recovery. But Carl's feelings toward Jennifer hadn't changed.

"So, yeah, Cherish is fine." he quickly changed the subject.

"Okay. I'll be home later this evening. When she gets out, I'm going to take her home and talk to her for little bit."

"Okay, we'll be here."

"Bye." I ended the call and slipped the phone back in my bag.

Even though Carl and I agreed to work things out a week ago, things between us were still a little rocky. I didn't know how to feel around him, honestly. It was always an awkward situation for me, so I tried not to be around him. When he was downstairs, I'd be upstairs. When I cooked dinner, we didn't sit at the table like we normally did; he would take his food and go to the basement to watch a game on the big screen, or I'd take mine and go upstairs to the bedroom. We even slept in different places most nights. Carl would make up some excuse like, *I fell asleep downstairs,* and ask me *why didn't I wake him?*

But I knew he did it on purpose. He was avoiding me around the house just as much as I was trying to avoid him. At this point, we just existed.

When they finally released Jennifer, almost two hours had passed. Mr. Clemens and I both waited for her in the lobby of the courthouse. He made sure they didn't take her back to the holding cell so we wouldn't have to make the trip to another location. The moment she saw me, she came running to me with opened arms.

"Oh my god, Zay. Thank you so much. I don't know what I would've done without you."

"You don't have to thank me, Jennifer, that's what friends are for." I said hugging her back.

Jennifer looked at Mr. Clemens. "Thank you so much, again, Mr. Clemens. You really just saved my life."

"Well, it isn't over." He warned. "We still have to make it through trial. Right now is when things get crucial. You are going to be under a fine toothed comb. That means you have to be careful of what you do. But the good thing is your husband hasn't pressed charges. He hasn't even given his statement yet, from what I hear. So that may be our only hope. He's the only living witness that can testify against you."

"What did he say?" Jennifer's eyes widened. "Have you spoken to him?"

Mr. Clemens shook his head, no. "He has refused all of my visit requests. I've inquired to see if he had an attorney representing him, and to my surprise... he doesn't."

"He still loves me," Jennifer whispered. A smile crept across her face as if she just figured out where a gold mine was. "Neil still loves me! That's why he hasn't given me up. I need to talk to him, Mr. Clemens."

"No, Jennifer. You cannot go down there— at all."

"Well, can you at least try again," she pleaded. "Ask him if I can at least call him or something?"

"I'll see what I can do. But in the meantime, do not go down to the hospital. Do you hear me?"

Jennifer nodded her head, "Okay."

"Well, you ladies enjoy the rest of your day. I have a lot of work to do, and I need to get back to the office."

The moment Mr. Clemens was out of sight, Jennifer turned back to me. "Did you ever go and see Neil?"

I hadn't really had the chance to see or speak to Jennifer since our meeting in the holding cells.

"No, Jennifer, I wasn't able to go down there." We began walking outside to where my car was in the parking garage across the street. "Shit has been out-of-control." I continued. "I never told you about what me and Carl been going through."

Pressing the unlock button on my key pad, we opened the car door and got in. As I pulled out of the lot, I filled her in on everything that had taken place between me and my husband—well everything besides his business at the firm. Our conversation took up most of the thirty minute ride to her house.

"I can't believe Carl would do such a thing?" Jennifer said as we arrived. "What is going on with these men? I can see Neil being the type, but not Carl."

"You know what they say…Birds of a feather…" I joked trying to bring some light to our crazy situations.

"I'm just glad you didn't react the way that I did, or else we would both be sitting in jail."

"Ha! And then it'll be like old times. You *were* the craziest roommate I had in college. Why not take over cell block D, as well." I laughed.

"We would have all of them bitches in their pledging. We'd have that shit on lock."

"Those were the days right." I turned off the ignition and rested back on the seat reminiscing about when it all had been so simple. My younger days were just as crazy as they were now, but in the short time Jennifer and I were together, life was cool. And it was the same time Carl had come into my life. He was my breath of fresh air…

Chapter Eighteen

Ten years ago...

Okay, pause for a second. This has got to be one fucked up ass joke, right? I mean, Ashton Kutcher and his camera crew better pop their asses out real fast and tell me that I'm being punked. Please tell me that Valdis is not standing in front of me, in my house, at *my* going away party being introduced to me as my mom's *man*.

"Zay?" My mom called again when I didn't answer. She touched my shoulder. "Are you ok?"

A blank stare was all that she received from me. I'm guessing the look on my face alarmed her. My eyes switched back to Valdis. I don't even think I blinked. My chest slowly heaved up and down as I took in the thinning air. From the look on his face, I could tell he was just as shocked as I was. Like a deer caught in headlights, his eyes were widened in mystify. *Oh shit* was written all over his guilty ass face.

"Zay," My mom shook me. "What the hell is wrong with you?"

I still didn't give her an acceptable response. I couldn't speak. I couldn't move. All I could do was stand there and be angry. A film strip of me and Valdis sped through my mind like a train passing by. It was almost as if I could see it playing out right in front of me. His words "I'll never hurt you" echoed in my ears. The more I thought about us, the angrier I got. The higher my anger rose, I started to think about every man that ever hurt me; from my dad abandoning me, to Tony's disloyalty, and now Valdis and his cheating ass. Just when I thought I could trust again he goes and pulls this bullshit. And why the fuck does my mother have to be the other woman…or maybe I'm the other woman, and to top it all off, I'm carrying his baby. Yup, the icing on the cake.

Overtaken with rage, my body went numb. My eyes began to fill with tears of hurt. I've had enough; enough of the games, the lies—everything.

Valdis cleared his throat and unhurriedly extended his hand. "Hi," he managed to force out. "Nice to meet—"

Before he could finish his sentence, I leapt on him sending both of us to the ground.

"How could you do this?" I cried. I pounded my fist on him, connecting them to any part of his body. Valdis blocked his face with his arms. "You dirty bastard! I hate you!"

I felt someone grabbing me, and next thing I knew I was being pulled off of him. "Zayda, what the hell is wrong with you?" I heard my mom ask me. She and my male cousin, Marquis, were trying to contain me. I continued to kick and squirm trying to free myself from their grips. I saw red, and I wanted to kill him.

"Zay, calm down." Marquis instructed. "What happened?"

By this time, my outbreak had commanded the attention of everyone in my house. The music had stopped and all eyes were glued on this ghetto soap opera. Everyone looked on, confused. I was like a mad woman being singled out. My party was now ruined, but hell—that was the least of my worries.

Valdis had picked himself up from off the floor. His yellow button-up shirt was ripped from the collar. He just stood there breathing heavy and looking dumbfounded.

"Valdis," my mom called out. Clearly, she was pissed. "What the hell is going on?"

"Jourdon, maybe I should go." Valdis responded.

"Yea," I huffed. "Maybe *you* should. So you won't have to tell my mom that you're fucking her daughter, too."

I could feel the stares coming from everyone as gasped filled the room. I had put all of the business on Front Street. But hell, at this point, I didn't give a fuck.

"Ok," my aunt, Antoinette, stood to her feet. She was the splitting image of my mom, only younger. "Party is moving to the backyard. There is nothing else to see here." She began to clear out the living room. I could only imagine what was going through the minds of all of our family and friends. As if they didn't have enough to gossip about already.

My aunt was the last to leave out the back door, and she closed it shut behind her. My mom, Valdis and I all stood there loitering in a terse silence. A quick glance at my mom opened up another wound inside of me. The hurtful look painted on her face struck a huge nerve. It was a look that I was all too familiar with. A look that only someone she truly cared about could cause. The last time I saw that look was right after my dad left. It was that moment when I realized she was in love with Valdis. It took her nearly a decade to let another man have her heart, and when she finally does, it's to a man who doesn't deserve it. My mom was tough, but like most women, her heart was soft. She loved pure and unconditionally. It was only so much a heart like hers could take, and it illustrated through the most beautiful part of her. I never wanted to see that look, again. Watching her made my blood boil for Valdis even more.

Valdis took a deep breath, "Jourdon, I—"

"Get out," my mom interrupted. She stared straight ahead at the crème colored wall as if she was watching a movie.

"Baby, please just listen to me." Valdis pleaded.

No sooner than the words left his lips I felt them piercing my heart. He was pleading for her. This was all one big rude awakening for me. He had just confirmed that the feelings I had for him were not mutual.

"I didn't know she was your daughter," he continued, "I was just—"

"You were just what?" My mom snapped. She viciously glared at him. "Just going to keep playing these games with me?" She took a step closer to him. "Just going to keep this little charade going?" She took another step closing the small space between them. Valdis didn't speak. In fact, he was almost in tears himself. His eyes were glassy, and I could tell he was fighting hard not to let one fall. "You were getting the best of both worlds, huh?"

"Jourdon, baby it wasn't like that?" Valdis explained. "Do you honestly think that I would have come here if I would have known she was your daughter? Zayda and I were nothing more than friends."

"Get—out, now!" She yelled. Her teeth were clenched together just as tight as a pitbull's jaw-lock.

"Baby, you've got to believe me," Valdis said. He looked over at me. "Zayda, tell her. Tell your mom that there was nothing serious going on between us. We hadn't seen or spoke to each other in a couple of weeks."

Huh? Was he for real? I know I wasn't that damn foolish. I didn't imagine what we shared. It was real—all of it. He gave me this pathetic look like I was the one who had the power to end his life. He was drowning, and he needed me to throw him a life jacket.

The longer I gawked at him the more disgusted I became. I was completely turned off, and utterly shocked at how he would even insist such an accusation. Warm tears trickled down my cheeks. I literally felt my heart break in half. My stomach was absorbed in a knot so tight that it shot pains up my spine. Suddenly, I got the urge to bring up everything that had settled in my stomach. Before anything erupted, I ran up the steps and into the bathroom slamming the door behind me. I fell to my knees when I reached the toilet just in time. With my head lowered directly into the bowl, I up-routed a day's full of food. My curly weave almost swung right in the path of my vomit. I swooped it behind my ear and let out what was left.

Panting, I sat completely on my butt and leaned my back up against the wall. I felt slightly better that the knot in my stomach had gone away, but the effect of what Valdis had done to me left a pain so unbearable. All I could do was cry. Soaking in my own sorrow, I felt so alone. No one knew of the battle I was dealing with. Over the years, I had grown accustomed to holding it all in; the teasing, the loneliness, the heartbreak—everything. I would let so much shit slide, and convince myself that shit didn't really bother me.

You know, I don't think I was born to be happy. Shit, that's what it seemed like. I couldn't catch a fucking break. I don't have the physical assets to make me acceptable. These guys didn't see me for more than just some ass. Hell, my own dad couldn't give two shits about me right now. I've tried so hard to just be happy, but no matter what I do, I always end up lower than where I started. Just as I began to pick myself off the floor, I heard a light tap on the door.

"Zay," my mom's voice muffled through the closed door. I didn't answer.

Tap! Tap! "Zayda," she called again. "Baby, are you ok?"

I stood at the bathroom sink staring at my reflection in the mirror above it. I was a mess. My eyes were puffy, and my lips were dried up. There was no way I was going back down stairs for everyone to see me like this; especially after that embarrassing episode. I just wanted to sleep. At least then I wouldn't have to face my reality. I flushed the toilet, wiped my eyes, and opened the door. My mom was standing directly in front of me. Without saying a word, she pulled me into her arms and held me. That was the best hug I've had in a long time. Almost instantly, my tears started up again.

"Mom," I said just above a whisper. "I loved him." I confessed.

"I know, baby," she consoled me.

"Why did this have to happen?" I asked. I knew she didn't have any answers for me. She probably had many questions herself, but right there, in that moment I was just thankful to be in her arms. I cried on her chest. I let it all out as we stood there and she softly stroked my hair with her hand.

Chapter Nineteen

"Is this the last of it?" My aunt, Antoinette, asked. She picked up my pink Victoria Secret duffel bag and swung it over her shoulder.

"Yup. That's everything." I said as I took one more look around the living room.

She smiled, "Alright college girl." She wrapped her free arm around my neck, "let's hit the road."

We walked out of my mom's empty house and locked the door behind us. My mom was originally supposed to drive me up to campus on move-in day, but ever since that shit happened at my party a week ago the vibe between us felt weird. We never discussed Valdis, or what happened, after that day. We barely spoke two words to one another. I wasn't angry at her, but for some reason I felt it was hard for me to face her. There was still a secret that I was hiding. The baby growing inside of me was eating away at me. I wasn't sure if I should tell her; nor did I have the courage to do it. So for the past week, I purposely avoided her.

I worked as much overtime that they allowed me to, so I was hardly ever home. The times that I was home, I would either sleep or try to make myself look busy. My mom never pressed the issue, but she wasn't anybody's fool. Yesterday, she finally came to me and told me how proud she is of me. She emphasized on how she never had to worry about me running the streets and getting into trouble, and that she raised a good woman. Lastly, she said that she'd hope that I would come to her about anything no matter how bad it may be. I had a feeling that she knew something was up with me which made me feel even worse. I couldn't bear to be with her alone in a car for the ride to school, so I called my aunt and asked her to drive me. My mom said she was OK with it, but I can tell it really hurt her feelings. That was never my intention, but until I figured out what I was going to do about the baby I needed space from her.

My aunt's SUV was packed tighter than a can of sardines. It never occurred to me how much stuff I was taking with me until I saw all of it in her truck. Most of it was gifts I got from my trunk party. My family really looked out. They had got me appliances and just about everything on the list that I would need for my dorm room. There was just enough room for me in the front passenger seat. She hopped into the driver's seat and we were on our way to Cheyney University.

The ride took just a little over an hour. Just as we pulled on to the visitor's parking lot, it finally hit me. I am going to college. I was going to be up here on my own. I had the freedom to do as I pleased, and when I wanted to do it. No one to tell me when, where, why or how, and it was scaring the shit out of me.

"Hey," my aunt touched my shoulder, "You ready for this?"

With tears built up in my eyes, I looked at her and slowly shook my head no.

"Aww, Zay," she pouted her face. "Everything is going to be just fine. You are going to do your thing up here. You've got nothing to worry—"

"I'm pregnant." I blurted out. I quickly turned my head away as tears gushed down my face.

"Pregnant?" She asked in a calm, yet shocked voice. "Are you sure?"

I continued looking away as I nodded my head yes. I heard her let out a heavy sigh.

"Oh god, Zay." She turned the car ignition off. "Valdis?"

I nodded my head again.

"Dammit." She said.

Hearing the disappointment in her voice made me cry harder. "I don't know how I let this happen." I said.

"What did your mom say?"

"She doesn't know." I confessed. "I don't want her to know yet. I let her down, and I'm not ready to face it."

"Oh Zayda," she said leaning over toward me. She touched my face and turned my head so that I would look at her. "You have to tell your mom."

"No, I can't." I laid my head back on the headrest. "Do you know how pissed she would be?"

"Yes," my aunt said, "But I also know that she will be there to help you through this."

"I don't think I'm keeping it, so there is really no point in telling her. She doesn't need this extra stress right now."

"But *you* need her support right now." She told me, "You shouldn't be handling this on your own. Trust me Zay; she is the best person to talk to right now."

So many thoughts clouded my mind. I wasn't sure if telling my aunt about the baby was the right thing to do, but it felt damn good to finally tell someone. It was eating away at me; I just had to get it off my chest.

"Let me tell you something, Zay" she continued. "When I was sixteen, there was this boy name AJ. He was two years older than me. I really wasn't into the boyfriend thing, but somehow he got me to be his girl. Honey, when I say I fell deep in love, you couldn't dig me out with a shovel. He was perfect. I couldn't have asked for a better first love. Now, at the time, I thought we were going to be together forever. That was until I got pregnant. He changed. Almost as if another soul had taken over his body. He denied even being my boyfriend. He wanted nothing to do with the baby, and called me every type of whore there was. I couldn't believe that was happening to me. He went off to college, and I was stuck at home with a baby in the oven."

"Did you tell Nana?" I asked, intrigued with her story.

She shook her head no. "Just like you, I was petrified to tell my mama. But, my big sister, your mom, was there for me. She had just turned twenty-one, and I figured at least I was confiding in a responsible adult."

I looked at her through the side of my eye.

"Shut up, Zay," she laughed, "I was young, and back then it made sense to me."

I chuckled and shook my head.

"Anyway, the point is, she was there." she continued her story. "She helped me through the abortion, and sat with me when I broke the news to my mom."

"What happened when you told nana?"

"She snapped." My aunt laughed. "But afterwards, she sat us down and told us how dangerous it was to not come to her first. Something bad could have happened, I could have gotten sick, or worse, I could have bled to death. I didn't think of the risks when we did it... neither of us did. It scared her more than anything, and I felt horrible. That's when I promised to always go to her when I'm in a bind— good or bad."

"I feel you, Aunty," I nodded my head, "But I'm just not ready to tell her." I looked over at her, "You're not going to say anything, are you?"

She paused. "No," she said after a short silence, "But you have to promise me you will tell her yourself. Even if you decide not to keep it, you need to tell her."

"Ok," I agreed. I leaned over and gave her a hug.

"Now come on," She said. "Let's get you moved   in."

Chapter Twenty

A few hours later, I was all settled in. I stayed in one of the oldest dorms on the campus, Harriet Tubman Hall. The double occupant room featured two twin beds with metal bed frames, two built-in wooden closets on both sides of the entrance door, two built-in dressers on both sides of the room connected to two built-in desks, and two windows that viewed the front of the dorm. The right side of the room mirrored the left, and the white, cinderblock walls were freshly painted.

I hadn't met my roommate yet. Her side of the room was already set up when we arrived, but she wasn't there. She had her shit hooked up like it was her bedroom at home. She had posters on the wall, little knickknacks on top of her dresser, a floor lamp with the colorful lamp heads bent in different directions; she even had everything from her floor rug, to her window drapes color-coordinated. I was taking notes on everything I needed to buy to hook my side up.

"Alright," my aunt said as she stuffed the rest of the trash into the empty refrigerator box, "I need to get going. I've got to pick up the kids at five. Do you need anything else?"

"No, I'm good." I told her. "Come on, I'll walk you out."

We grabbed all of the trash, and dragged it to the trash room right next to the elevators before one came. We headed down to the first floor. A lot of girls were still moving in, so there was a line waiting to get on the elevator when we got off.

"Thank you," I told my aunt as we walked to the parking lot, "for everything,"

"That's what family is for," she responded with a smile, "just don't forget what we talked about."

"I won't." We hugged, and she kissed me on my forehead before getting into her truck and pulling off.

When I returned to the dorm, the elevator line looked as if no one had moved from their spot yet. Students and parents were waiting with dollies full of luggage, and small appliances.

"The stairway is located at the end of the hall if anyone doesn't feel like waiting." A chunky girl at the front desk said. "Those things can be so slow sometimes."

The girl didn't look that much older than me. She was pretty—very pretty, and she was the first plus sized girl I've seen since I got up here. Her shirt and baseball cap caught my attention. They both were red with white Greek symbols. She was in a sorority. I'd always thought sorority girls were skinny and prissy; kind of like the popular kids in high school. She looked at me and smiled. I nodded and headed to the stairs along with a few others waiting for the elevator.

It took some time, but my big ass climbed the stairs all the way up to the fifth floor. It was then I swore to myself that I was never doing that again. I was completely out of breath. To make matters worse, I damn near stopped breathing when I looked down the hall and saw my door wide open. I gathered up what little energy I had left, and ran down the hall. I stopped at my door and saw a small framed girl sitting at the desk. She looked up at me.

"Hello," she greeted.

"H- Hi," I managed to get out in between breaths.

She got up from the desk and came toward me. "You must be my new roomie. I'm Danielle, but everyone calls me Dani."

I let out a sigh of relief. "Girl, I thought someone had broken into my room already." I confessed.

She laughed. "Well if they did, it ain't much that they would get. I ain't got shit up in here." She extended her hand. "Zayda, right?"

"Uh, yea," I said as I shook her hand, "How did you know."

"I'm cool with the RA on this floor. She told me the name of my new roommate." She walked back over to her computer desk and sat down.

"RA?" I questioned. I took a seat on my bed.

"The resident advisor." She explained. "Each floor has one. They are like hall monitors. Our RA is Karma. She's the coolest one out of them all. She doesn't care if you have company after visiting hours or alcohol as long as you're not drawing too much attention."

"Oh, you're not a freshman?" I asked, "I thought this was an all-freshman dorm."

"It's supposed to be," she replied, "But there are still some upperclassmen in this building. I'm a sophomore. I had this same room last year. I lucked up and had this room all to myself. But I guess now..." she shrugged.

"Well, sorry to ruin your plans." I said with a slightly offensive tongue.

"Oh no," she said. "I didn't mean it like that. I wanted a roommate, but I didn't know how she would feel about me having my son here on the weekends." She grabbed a photo from her dresser and brought it to my bed. "This is my boy, Jalen."

"He is adorable," I complimented. The baby wearing a blue and white plaid jumper with white sneakers and a white hat was the spitting image of Dani. His toothless smile revealed a dimple on the left side of his chunky cheeks. Dani had a dimple on the exact same side. He was a tad-bit lighter than Dani's creamed coffee complexion, but he inherited her green eyes. A soft flutter tapped on my insides. Waves of guilt were rushing toward me at full speed. I knew that getting rid of this baby would be the best thing for me right now, but was it right? Did my baby not deserve a life all because I got involved with the wrong man? I felt myself tearing up but quickly shook off the feeling.

"How old is he?" I handed her back the photo.

"He was nine months old here." She gazed at the photo as if she had never seen it before.

"He's one now. My grandmother keeps him during the week so that I could finish school. I have to get him every weekend to give her a break." She walked back to her dresser and sat the photo back in its original position. "So that's why I said I was lucky to get a single room. I wasn't throwing you shade." She smiled. "You got kids?"

My heart skipped a beat. Her question struck a nerve and she had no clue.

"Me? Nah," I responded. I wasn't about to let my business be the talk of the town. Even though she seemed nice, she was still a stranger to me.

"Take it from me; kids can wait until you are done school." She advised. "I love my baby, but if God offered me a do-over, I would take it. It's a lot harder than what most girls think. I mean, yea my grand mom is helping me, but do you know how much shit she hits me with." Dani opened her top drawer. "Shut the door for me?"

I nodded and did what she asked.

"You smoke?" she asked. She pulled a bag of weed and a blunt wrap from the drawer.

"Nope," I said as I took a seat back on the bed. "It's not my thing."

"I bet you by the end of the semester it will be." She joked as she began to roll up her L. "Nah, but seriously being a mom is no joke. But I am one, and I do what I have to do to make sure my son is good."

Ready to switch subjects, I didn't respond. I just nodded my head.

"Perfect!" she held up her tightly rolled up L. "So, shall I give you a tour of the first HBCU?"

"Ok, cool." I agreed.

Dani showed me the entire campus. First, we stopped at the Café to grab a bite to eat. We also met up with her two friends Secret and Imani, who were sophomores as well. Then, we stopped passed the other four dorms, the historic walkway that they called the Quad, and the infamous Greek Row. That's where all the sororities and fraternities held cookouts, or just chilled when the weather permitted it.

I was glad to meet someone my first day here. I would have been bored out my mind if it weren't for Dani. Seeing the campus and all of the students gave me a bit of excitement. Actually, I was looking forward to my time at Cheyney. I had taken a huge step toward the future by furthering my education. I can't mess that up. I won't mess this up. I am not having this baby.

Chapter Twenty One

My first week on campus seemed to drag. I had finally paid a visit to the closest Planned Parenthood Clinic in West Chester, Pa. It was about fifteen minutes from school. Since I still didn't have a car of my own, I got Dani to take me to the appointment. I told her that I needed to get my birth control prescriptions refilled so she wouldn't think anything of it.

They confirmed my pregnancy and due date. Nine weeks. I was almost out of the first trimester. I informed the physician of my decision about not keeping the baby. She gave me the contacts to another clinic that terminates pregnancies. Their office worked hand-and-hand with them, so it would be easy for my files to be transferred.

As soon as we arrived back to campus, I didn't waste any time. I set up an appointment, and tried to not think about it. But between starting class, my nerves, and the sickness from the baby, I couldn't help not to think about it. Plus, I still hadn't spoken to my mom. She called me a few times and left messages. I just sent her a text back when I knew she'd be working letting her that I was OK. Truthfully, I wasn't quite sure if my aunt had kept her word or not. I had a feeling she told my mother something. Sooner or later I would have to let it be known, but I'd rather do it once I got the baby out of me.

Finally, Friday had come. My appointment was scheduled first thing in the morning. That was a good thing; especially since I had no idea how I would feel afterwards. That way, I'd have the entire weekend to relax.

This time, I took a taxi to my appointment. When I arrived, I checked in and took a seat in the waiting room. There were only two other people in the waiting area; a girl who looked to be no older than fourteen, and an older woman who I assumed to be her mother. The look on the older woman's face was cold—emotionless. The young girl would occasionally glance up at the woman with eyes of pity; however, the woman never looked her way.

Dazed, the woman stared straight ahead and never diverted her attention. I could tell she had a lot on her mind. Worry, fear, disappointment… her eyes gave away it all, but by her being there said that her love for her daughter was stronger than any of it.

As emotions began to rush me, I closed my eyes and said a prayer. I was beginning to regret not telling my mom. My aunt was right. I needed her. I needed someone who loved me to tell me that everything was going to be Ok. But as usual, I was on my own.

"Zayda Jones?" A middle-aged black woman called from the front desk.

I got up from my seat and approached her. "Yes."

"Good morning, Ms. Jones." The woman smiled. "I need you to sign the rest of these consents, and your payment today will be three hundred and fifteen dollars."

I glanced at the badge clipped onto the pocket of her light pink scrubs. It read *Karen Marie*. She and I shared the same middle name. After giving her a slow nod, I signed the forms, retrieved my wallet from my shoulder bag, and handed her the money.

"Thank you," she said. After she collected the papers and the money, she stood to her feet. "You can walk through the brown door and follow me."

As I approached the door, my heart began to thump loudly in my ears. The woman buzzed me in and escorted me down the hall. Goosebumps covered my arms as I walked closer to my assigned room. I was scared...scared to the point where I became sick to my stomach. I was even more afraid of what pain I was about to endure.

When we reached the last room, the woman placed a clipboard inside a slot hanging on the door, and entered the room. She rumbled through a cabinet and pull out a pile of hospital gowns and socks.

"You can change into these." She instructed. "These are the largest size we have, but you can put one on frontward and the other backward so that way you'll be fully covered."

I took the gowns from her without saying a word.

"Take everything off including your underwear and bra." She continued, "When you're done, come across the hall so I can get your weight and vitals."

"Okay," I replied.

She left the room and closed the door shut behind her. An uncanny sensation lurked in the room. It wasn't close to what I expected it to be. I pictured more of a hospital setting; monitors, carts of medicine…something. I at least thought there would be more people around. This room was fairly empty. The walls were painted yellow with a red border at the top. They had nothing to grace the walls with. Not even a single poster about abortions. There was one examination table in the middle of the room already prepared with sheets and pillows, an ultrasound machine next to the table, a light that hung from the ceiling, a sink and cabinet in one corner of the room, two black chairs next to the sink, a black leather stool with wheels, and a cart with drawers that required a passcode to open.

As I began to change into the gowns, my mind started thinking the worst things. *How many girls actually got rid of their unborn child in this very room? What if I hemorrhage? Will they be able to stop the bleeding? Has anyone ever died from this?* All questions I should have been asked, but actually being here was creating a small panic. Thank God a knock on the door interrupted my thoughts.

"Come in," I said.

"Are you ready?" Karen popped her head in and asked.

I nodded my head and followed her across the hall. We were only there briefly. She weighed me, and took my temperature and blood pressure.

"Ok, you're all set," she said, "You can have a seat back in the exam room. The doctor will be there shortly."

I just nodded and turned to head back to the room.

"Oh, one more thing," she said, "You do have a ride home today, right? I didn't see anyone come with you, and with the sedation you will be getting, we cannot discharge you unless someone accompanies you home."

I paused. "Um, yea," I lied, "my mom is coming to pick me up."

"Very well," she said.

I went back to the exam room and nervously waited.

One Hour Later...

Bundled in a heated blanket with my feet propped up, I drifted in and out of a light sleep. The flat screen television that hung on the wall was barely loud enough to hold my attention. I had been in the recovery room for about thirty minutes before the pain meds started to wear off, and I felt my stomach cramping. They were much like menstrual cramps but worse. And I was bleeding—a lot. They gave me this huge, thick maxi pad to wear.

The procedure wasn't as bad as I thought it would be. The doctor performed what is called a Vacuum Aspiration. He literally sucked the fetus from my womb. The most I felt was pressure. My body was relaxed from the medicine he gave me. The procedure only lasted about twenty minutes, but with the loud humming of the vacuum machine it felt much longer.

Again, I was the only one in the room, but there were enough recliners to seat six people. A large glass window next to the door allowed me to see the front waiting area. By this time, more people had arrived.

"How are you feeling?" Karen said when she entered the room.

"Shitty." I moaned.

"Yea, it's going to be crappy for the next couple of days." She said, "Maybe even a week."

I deeply exhaled. "Yea, but after that I can move on from all of this."

Karen bit her bottom lip and slowly nodded her head as if she was agreeing with me. "Are you able to stand?" she asked.

"I think so."

"Let's give it a try; get these legs moving." She bent down and closed the recliner. I scooted to the edge and gradually stood to my feet.

"How do you feel now? Any dizziness? Nausea?"

"No," I told her, "My body feels heavy, but for the most part it's just a lot of cramping."

"Ok." she said. "Well, you can use the restroom to change into your clothes." She pointed to a door located at the back of the recovery room. "Did you bring something comfortable to wear?"

"Yes."

"Good." she smiled. "Seems like you're all set. As soon as your mom comes I can discharge you."

"Thank you," I nodded grabbing my bag and headed to change.

Moments later, I was dressed and ready to go. My only problem was getting passed the front desk without being spotted by Karen. I poked my head out of the door, and spotted Karen at the front desk through the window. She was checking in another patient. I watched her for about a minute before she got up from her seat and walked to the back. The moment I saw her leave, I left out of the recovery room. I walked as fast as I could. Each step I took felt like someone was stabbing me in my gut. I could literally feel the leakage dripping from my body between my legs. I continued to walk through the waiting area passed a few people and out the front door. The fresh air felt so good hitting against my body. There was not a single window to the outside in the entire building. I walked down to a diner at the end of the block, called a cab and waited inside until it arrived.

You don't know how glad I was when I reached my dorm room. Thankfully, Dani wasn't there. I needed some peace and quiet. My body yearned for a hot shower and a good rest. It was a little after noon, and the building was practically empty. Classes were still in session; but on a Friday, I had at least expected a few students playing hooky. It was like a ghost town on my floor. At least I could take a shower in peace and didn't have to wait on an empty one. I changed into my robe, grabbed my shower bucket, and headed to the shower room.

I stood under the running water. Just how I like it, the water was hot, and the steam quickly clouded the tiny stall. As water beads hit my body, I had pictured them rinsing away all of my hurt. It was all finally over, but I couldn't seem to get away from the pain. Valdis' face was like a tumor growing on my heart. The more I tried not to think about him, the more I missed him, the more I hated him, and the more I wondered if things would be different if I would have told him about the baby. In my heart, I honestly rather not know. The way he looked at my mom—the passion that lived in his eyes spoke volumes of the love built up in his heart. I was reliving that feeling all over again.

I finished up my shower, slipped something comfortable on, and climbed under my plush comforter. My past continued to take stabs at my heart, and tears gushed down my face while I immersed in a silent cry. I cried until sleep took its place.

"I know right." I heard Dani's voice fade in. I lifted my head from under my blanket and spotted her sitting on the edge of her bed with her cell phone pinned to her ear. "This party is going to be the shit," she continued, "You know we're up in there tonight. Kappa parties do one thing." She laughed. "Alright, just come to my dorm after y'all get dressed; I picked up a few bottles so we can get buzzed before we go." She said before hanging up.

I slowly sat fully upright in the bed.

"Damn girl, it's about time you woke up." Dani said. "I've been in and out this room a few times, and you were all snoring and shit." She joked.

"What time is it?" I moaned.

"Almost eight o'clock," she said as she began to undress. "Are you going to the Kappa party tonight?"

I shook my head. "I'm not in the mood for a party. I have a headache out of this world."

"What?" She stood in front of me wearing nothing but a purple laced panty and bra set with her hand resting on her hip. "What kind of roommate would I be if I let you miss the first party of the year? I've got a few Percocets and some Peach Vodka for that headache. Trust me; you will thank me later."

"I could use some of those Percocets now." I admitted. My cramps had seemed to increase since I left the clinic, and my breasts felt extremely tender and sore. I had hoped that these were all normal symptoms. Since I hadn't waited for any discharge instructions or my pain medicine prescription, I had no other choice.

Dani walked over to her dresser, "Here you go." She tossed me a pill bottle. "You might not want to take those on an empty stomach."

"Yea I know," I told her as I swung my legs over the edge of my bed. I tried my best not to wince from the pain. "I *am* kind of hungry. I meant to set my alarm for dinner. You got any more cups of noodles?"

"Nope," she shook her head. "I ate my last one earlier. We can go food shopping tomorrow, but for now we could order out." She said as she put on her robe and grabbed her shower bucket. "There is a menu for Brother's Pizza hanging on the wall above my computer. Order me a cheese burger with everything." she said as she left the room.

As soon as she closed the door, I opened the pill container and took back three of the pain meds. At that point I didn't care about the food; I just wanted to ease this pain. And it did. The meds started kicking in about fifteen minutes later. I was feeling gooooood. My cramps were faint, and I was relieved. I put a couple more pills in a stash for later, and then placed the bottle back on Dani's dresser before ordering our food.

About forty minutes later, Dani and her friends, Secret and Imani, were all in our dorm room grooving to Lil Wayne's Lollypop. Dani stood at her mirror piling her face with Mac's latest creations. She sported a white, tight spandex tank top that showed off her flat waist and a neon orange high-rise skirt that hugged her hips and stopped just below her ass cheeks. She slipped on a pair of white pumps, and complimented them with an orange and white clutch. Secret and Imani swayed their bodies to the melody in their too small dresses, both with a cup in hand filled with drinks they've thrown together. It was like their ritual; Dani had already told me how they get it poppin' before each party. She even bragged about a time when she pissed herself because she was drunk. As if it was cute. I just smiled, and shook my head. I was in no place to judge a god damn soul.

I sat on my bed scrolling through my Facebook app on my cell phone when I was interrupted by a call.

"Hello," I answered. I plugged my finger into my other ear so I could hear the caller over the loud music. "Ok, I'll be right down." I said and hung up the phone. "The food is here." I said loud enough so Dani could hear me.

She gave me a nod and pulled a twenty out of her clutch. She walked over to me and handed me the money. "You can give him three dollars of mine towards the tip."

I hopped off the bed, slid my feet into my slippers, and retrieved my wallet from my top drawer.

I opened it and paused. *Where the hell is my money?* I thought to myself. I grabbed the shoulder bag that I carried to my appointment earlier that day thinking maybe it fell out into the bag.

The music's volume decreased. "What's wrong?" Dani asked.

"I think I…" I mumbled as I shuffled through my bag. "My money is missing. I'm hoping it didn't drop out of my bag while I was out. I know I put it in my wallet but it's not there."

Fuck! I cursed at myself. *Someone went into my bag while I was at the clinic. That bitch Karen was just a bit too friendly. She saw me when I put the rest of my money into my wallet after paying her. She was the one who handled my things while I was having my procedure. It had to be her. I didn't go anywhere else.*

"I can't believe this shit." I huffed. "A hundred fucking dollars—gone!"

"What!" Secret said. "Girl, I'd be crying right now if I lost a hundred dollars."

"How much did the food come to?" Dani asked.

"Twenty-five and some change." I responded. I dumped out everything that was in my bag and continued searching.

"Here," Dani handed me a ten dollar bill. "Just pay for the food and you can pay me back. They have a serious issue when we cancel orders after they get here.

"Thanks Dani, I'll go to the ATM in a few to get you the cash." I said before leaving out the door.

On the way to the first floor, my missing money was still on mind. *I had never been robbed, and for it to happen in an abortion clinic, shit they're already getting money from their patients why in the hell would that woman go into my bag. I was going back up there tomorrow to speak with her ass. And the way I've been feeling lately, shit, she stole from the wrong bitch.*

The elevator doors opened to the front lobby. I guess parties were the highlight of college life because the way the girls were dressed leaving out was like they were auditioning for an Uncle Luke video. I spotted one girl leaving out with damn near a bikini on. *Why even get dressed?*

The pizza guy was leaning up against the front desk grinning from ear to ear. He was so focused on one of the girl's plumped ass that he hadn't noticed that I walked up on him.

"Delivery for Zayda?" I asked.

He quickly adjusted his posture and his facial expression. "Uh, yea ma," he said, "That will be twenty-five, twenty."

I handed him thirty and told him to keep the change for his tip.

"No party for you tonight?" he asked.

"Excuse me?"

"I noticed you have on PJ's and ordering food." He smiled. "You must not be going to the Kappa party tonight."

"No, I'm not in the partying mood." I admitted.

"But it's a *Kappa* party." He continued.

"I could care less if Jesus was going to be in the VIP. Y'all say their name like it's supposed to ring bells or something."

He laughed. "Well, they are kind of a big deal."

"And what do you know about them? You got time to keep up with college parties?"

"Actually I do," he said as he stuffed the money into his denim jeans. "I'm Carl, I'm a junior here." He held out his hand. "*And* I'm a Kappa."

I shook his hand. "I'm Zayda. A freshman."

"Zeta? Like the sorority?" he raised his eyebrow. "You're mom one of them or something?"

"No, it's Zay-da. With a D." I smiled. "My mom doesn't know anything about a sorority." I laughed and grabbed the food from the front desk. "Well *Kappa* Carl, don't let me hold you from your epic party."

"Oh, you're not. You were my last delivery tonight." He nodded. "But I do hope you change your mind about coming tonight. If you do, just save a dance for me, Ms. Zayda with a D."

"Yea, maybe…" I said as I got back on to the elevator.

The last thing I needed right now was to meet a new guy friend. I was not about to fall for the pearly whites and fresh Caesar haircut. He was only making conversation, no need to get all gung-ho about it. *Save a dance for me*. Boy, please. Was that their way of saying let me grind on your ass in a dark room full of other horny college students? I'll pass. So what if he was cute, and his chocolate skin was as smooth as a baby's bottom; I've learned my lesson.

As soon as the elevator doors opened up to the fifth floor, the bass from the music blasting rattled the brown paper bag I carried in my hands. There were about five different songs playing from different rooms.

Damn, was the party on the fifth floor tonight?

I walked down my hall by passing room after room of girls getting ready for the party with their doors wide open. There must have been a contest on who can wear the least amount of clothing to a party.

I walked into my room and closed the door behind me. "The building director don't say anything about this loud music?" I asked, sitting the food down on the desk.

"Honey, this is Cheyney." Imani said. "You've got a lot to learn." she laughed.

"Ms. Jacobs is hardly ever here to do any directing." Dani said. "But you will have a few haters from other floors calling campus security. When they do, I always get a call from Glen; he's one of the security officers. He likes me, so he looks out from time to time."

I grabbed my food and sat down on my bed. "Y'all want some?" I asked Secret and Imani.

"Hell to the yes!" Imani said. "This liquor got me starving. I need something to coat it before I start throwing up."

She took a seat on my bed next to me. "Did fine ass Carl deliver this?"

"Please, don't pump his black ass up." Dani said.

"You just mad because he turned down the pussy you was throwing his way." Imani laughed.

"I was drunk, Bitch." Dani snarled. "That nigga didn't deserve my goodies anyway."

"No, he didn't *want* your goodies," Secret teased. "I told you he like them good girls."

"I am a good girl." Dani rolled her eyes. "When I want to be." A conniving smirk spread across her face.

All three of them shared a laughed; an obvious inside joke that I knew nothing about.

"Naw, but I'm on to bigger and better now." Dani continued. "But the mutha fucka is fine as hell though. I can't deny that." She opened her food container and took a bite of her burger.

Dani was flawless. How could anyone turn her down? Most young guy's goal is to bag a bad bitch, especially if you have the freedom to do it. I could name a hundred guys who would hop on that if she made a pass at them. Maybe Carl is different. And they were right; he was a nice looking young man. He was slightly taller than me, and he was husky. Not fat husky; he was all solid. He reminded me of an NFL player. And for the first time since I got here, for a moment, he took my mind away from my chaotic life.

"We need to be heading out," I heard Secret saying from the door. "It's almost ten and I know it's about to start jumpin."

"Yea," Dani said. "We can roll out now. I got to tap the ATM for more cash to get in the party anyway." She said grabbing her clutch. "Zay, you're sure you don't want to come?"

"We'll wait for you to get ready if you do." Imani said. She was still stuffing her face with my food.

Even though the pain meds had me feeling a lot better, I knew I should not have been going to a party. But hey, now that I've thought about it one dance with Carl wouldn't hurt, right?

"Um, you know what?" I responded. "I'll go for a little while. I need to get out of this damn room."

"Yay!" Dani smiled. "We are going to have so much fun."

A quick shower, bump in my hair, and two Percocets later we were headed to the dining hall where all the campus parties were held. Compared to Dani and the girls, I was completely overdressed. There was no way I was going to wear anything but jeans with this heavy flow of blood my body was releasing. I must say, I looked cute in my off the shoulder, sheer, loose neck, black top, with a black halter underneath, black tights, and a pair of black and gold Gucci flats.

Some of the big girls that I've seen walking to the party could really take some tips from me. They had no shame in their game with what they wore. Anything that could hang out, did. My mom always said just because it comes in your size doesn't mean you should wear it. They were the true meaning of that statement.

We stopped at the security building next to the dining hall to get money out of the ATM. I withdrew one hundred and fifty dollars. I gave Dani back the money for the food and stuffed the rest in my gold mini hand clutch. Dani and I were going to ride to Jersey to pick up her son in the morning, and go food-shopping for the room, so I just figured to get out all I might need. This time, my clutch was not leaving my sight. I damn sure can't afford to lose any more money.

Just as Dani had been saying, the party was jammed packed when we entered. We didn't have to wait in the long line or go through the metal detectors thanks to Dani's security friend, Glen. We weren't the only ones. I spotted a few guys doing the same thing, and passing off money to security. Go figure.

The music poured loudly from the speakers, while the infamous DJ Flow worked the turntables. We walked through the dark musty building, finding our way around groups of grinders, twerkers, and perverts trying to get their dicks hard from a dance. Lights from the DJ booth barely lit the room.

We found a spot on the wall near the gigantic windows, which didn't open. It wouldn't have hurt if a breeze or two blew through there. My nose had to adjust to the sweaty aroma.

"Yo, Yo!" a gang of guys chanted out from one end of the room. They began to move in unison in a straight line.

"What are they doing?" I leaned into Dani and asked loud enough so she could hear me.

"Party walking," she informed me. "All of the Greeks do it. You're going to see that shit all throughout the party."

I nodded my head and continued watching the Kappa's do their thing. Secret and Imani were already on the dance floor bending over for some guys.

"Zayda," Dani called, "I'll be right back. I see a friend of mine."

I mouthed the word OK. She sashayed through the crowd and her petite frame disappeared in the sea of people.

Left all alone, I stood there and bobbed my head to the music. The Kappa line was making their way around to the side where I stood.

"Move. Move. Move." The guy leading the line kept shouting. The crowd spread apart as if Moses himself was parting the red sea. They had an obvious respect from the students here. I was honestly fascinated by their party walking.

"I see you made it here." A male voice said into my ear. I turned to look at him.

"Hey Carl." I said trying to play it cool. Even in the dim lighting he was fine.

"Aww, that's so sweet," he said. He put his hand up to his heart, "You remembered my name. I feel special."

"Yo dog, come on." A guy from the party walk line shouted. Carl put one finger up as to tell him *in a minute*.

"I'm bout to hop on this line, but when I come back I want my dance you owe me." He smiled.

I just laughed not sure of how to respond. He quickly got behind the last person in the line and fell right in with the moves.

Moments later, a commotion broke out near the DJ booth. I spotted a few security guards squeezing their way through the crowd to find out what was going on. Quickly, I scanned the room for Dani. I finally saw her standing next to this tall guy on the other side of the room. They, too, were staring at the uproar.

As I began to make my way to her, gun shots rang throughout the room. The fun atmosphere quickly turned to screams and panic. Like a stampede, people headed toward the doors trying to get to safety. I was scared out of my mind. Living in Philly, I heard gunshots all the time, but being this close to it was no joke. My heartbeat sped up as I too ran for safety.

I was nearing the door when I slipped and fell to the ground. No one seemed to give a shit. They just stepped on me like I was a doormat. Unable to get up right away, I covered my head with my arms.

When the room was just about empty, I sat up in a panic. The lights had finally flicked on. I saw a guy lying on the ground. His white shirt had red stains splattered all over it. He was being attended to by one of the few security guards.

"Call the ambulance," he shouted, "he's not breathing.

A few feet from them sat a girl holding her shoulder. She appeared to be in great pain. She rocked back and forth, as she screamed for help.

I instantly recognized her from my dorm. She stayed in the room next to me, but we had never spoken. I picked myself from off the ground and headed for the door.

The girl screamed again. Her scream shot through my body. It was as if I could feel her pain. I looked back at her. She was scared and alone; two things that I knew all too well. I couldn't leave her there. I knew if it was me, I would want someone to stay with me, so I ran to the side of a total stranger.

Chapter Twenty Two

I ended up riding in the ambulance to the hospital with the girl who had been shot. The ride to the hospital was only about ten minutes. The main thing I wanted to do was keep her mind off of the pain. I kept asking her questions about where she was from and what she was majoring in. The most I got from her was her name, Jennifer. I assumed that was a nick-name given to her reflecting her dark skin tone.

Jennifer was pretty, but I could tell she had edginess to her. She wore her hair pulled back into a weave ponytail with the hair extending down her back. She was from Baltimore, Maryland and had the heavy accent to show it.

As I sat in the Emergency Room lobby of Riddle Hospital waiting for a report from the doctors, the Percocets that I had taken earlier slowly started to wear off. A slight tightness developed in my abdomen. For now, the pain was manageable, but I needed to get to my room soon before it got any worse.

"Excuse me, Ms.?" A young Indian male dressed in blue scrubs approached me. "You came in with Ms. Jennifer Foulard, correct?"

"Yes, sir." I said and stood to my feet.

"I'm Dr. Gupta." He held out his hand.

I shook his hand. "Is she OK?"

"Yes, she is going to be fine," he assured me. "The bullet just grazed her. There were no life-threatening injuries."

"Thank god," I said relieved. I hardly knew the girl, but for some reason I felt for her.

"She is requesting to see you." Dr. Gupta continued. "She is in there with the police right now. They should be just about done. Once they are, you can go back."

"Thank you," I nodded.

Dr. Gupta smiled and walked away.

Police? I thought. *Why the hell do the police want to talk to her? I'm pretty sure she didn't have shit to do with what happened at the party.*

Starring at the muted television on the wall, I continued to wait. The time on the cable box hanging underneath the TV read 12:30. It was after midnight and I was ready to lay my head down. Today was definitely one hell of a day. I know one thing; I'm over colleges parties already. You know the saying *it could have been me*? Well this time it was true. I for sure could have gotten shot tonight.

I pulled out my cell phone and thumbed through my contacts searching for my mom's number. Not wanting to alarm her with a call this late, I tapped on her number and sent her a quick text.

I love you, mom.

Tonight's events had me thinking about our last encounter. If something were to have happened to me at the party, I might not have gotten the chance to tell her that. It was the wakeup call I needed. I made a mental note to call and speak with her tomorrow.

After waiting for almost another hour, Jennifer finally came walking through the sliding glass doors. I went to her as soon as she came out.

"How are you feeling?" I asked.

"Like shit." She responded. Her right shoulder had been patched up. "All that fucking pain and I only needed ten stitches. I felt like my arm was going to fall the fuck off."

"Just be glad it wasn't worse than that." I said. "The bullet could have gone into your arm instead of grazing it."

"Yea, you're right." She nodded. "But it still hurt like shit." She managed to let out a light chuckle. "Come on. The nurse said that there are taxi cabs right out front if we didn't have a ride back to school."

We walked out of the hospital and waved for one of the cabs.

"Zayda." Jennifer called. I looked over at her. "Thank you," she smiled. "You know… for staying with me."

"Don't worry about it." I told her.

"No, my own friends didn't come back to check on me." She said as tears began to form in her eyes. "If it were one of them, I would have been right there. We were all right there before the gun went off. If they didn't see me when they got out of the building, why didn't they come back? I would have come back."

I had no response for her. The look on her face was as if it had been on her mind all night. The cab pulled up and we both got in.

"You could have left too," she continued, "but you didn't. Thank you."

"No thanks needed." I said almost to tears myself. I know how it felt to be alone...to have no one in your corner. "Just make sure you are there when I get shot at a party," I joked trying to lighten the mood.

We arrived back on campus and it was as if the party had moved outside. People were still hanging around at 1 AM. A few police cars and ambulance were idling in front of the dining hall. Students lingered around the parking lot, and the sororities and fraternities had made their way to their plots on Greek Row. It wasn't so much of a chaotic scene; people wanted to pretty much find out what was going on more than anything. Campus security and dorm directors tried their best to get everyone to go into their dorms. We walked passed the crowds of people and up to the freshman dorm. A few people were sitting out front discussing what happened. In passing, I overheard one of them say a guy named Ali was the one who shot the gun. There had been an ongoing beef between the bloods and the Muslims on campus. Now Ali, head of the bloods, is on the run.

Gangs? Really? Where the hell did I decide to come to school?

I didn't know how much of that story to believe, but with the way shit spread around these days, the story was bound to get out.

We took the elevator to the fifth floor and headed to our rooms.

"Hey," Jennifer said, "if you feel up to it, how bout we go to the café in the morning. They open for brunch around ten on Saturdays."

"I'm supposed to be riding somewhere with my roommate in the morning, but if we don't go, then sure."

"Okay, just knock on my door and let me know." She said before going into her room.

Once again, I came back to an empty room. I hadn't seen Dani since the party. I'm pretty sure she is Ok. I didn't have her cell number so I couldn't call her. I'll just talk to her whenever she comes to the room.

After changing into a t-shirt and a pair of grey sweatpants, I took two more pills, went to the bathroom, came back and slid in my bed. My crazy day had finally come to an end. If I told anybody what I went through today, they probably would have thought I made it all up. Almost simultaneously, my eyes got heavy when my head hit the pillow. Just as I began drifting off to sleep, I heard rattling at my door. Instantly, I recognized Dani's voice on the other side. I was too tired to get up and open it. Shit, she had a key.

The light from the hall temporarily spilled into the dark room when she opened the door.

"Nigga please, you—" Dani stopped mid-sentence. "Oh, she is here." I heard her say. "No pussy for you tonight." She said, and giggled in a low tone. "You can come in, but keep your voice down. My roommate is trying to sleep."

I didn't feel the need to correct her. I just wanted to get some rest, so I laid there with my eyes closed pretending I was already sleep. Hell, I was going to be asleep soon anyway.

The door closed and the darkness took over the room once again. Her bed squeaked, as if they had sat down on it.

"Ma, thanks again for looking out for me earlier." I heard the guy say. "You always come through for me."

"I keep telling your ass I got you." Dani replied. "You're so used to fucking with them lame ass bitches; you don't know how a real bitch roll."

The room was quiet. Even though they were talking low, I could hear every word clearly.

"I'm going to pay you back, though. You need your money; you got a kid to take care of." He said. "Once basketball season is over and I get back to work, I got you."

"Don't sweat it." she said. "Think of it as a gift." She chuckled. "How are you going to pay the rest of the fine? I know your mom isn't giving you any more cash, especially if she finds out you got caught with alcohol on campus, again."

"I'll figure it out." He told her. "Coach said as long as the fine is paid before our first game I can play. That gives me until the end of the semester. I'll work it out."

Momentarily, the room grew silent.

"Ma, what are you doing?" he asked.

"Shhh. I'm getting you the rest of the money." I heard Dani say. Her voice was closer to me than before.

"Yo, shorty you're crazy." the guy whispered. "Put her shit back."

"Please, she isn't going to miss it." Dani said. "Where do you think I got the first hundred dollars? I told you, *real* bitches do *real* things." She laughed.

My eyes shot open after hearing that confession flowing from her mouth so shamelessly. I threw back my comforter and jumped up out the bed.

Stunned, she stood there with my wallet in her hand. She was caught red-handed. I couldn't control myself. I cocked my fist back and sent a blow to her face. She fell backward down the floor.

Her face was practically hidden behind the darkness, and I'm glad it was.

"You snake ass bitch!" I yelled. I was fuming. The entire time I searched for my missing money she had it all along! She even had the nerve to let me borrow money from *her*.

The guy she was with jumped up and flicked on the lights. There was Dani on the ground holding her nose and mouth. She pulled her hand away from her face and looked at her palm. Her eyes widen when she saw the blood leaking from her bruised nose.

"Oh shit." The guy said. I looked back and recognized him from the party.

"Who the fuck do you think you are stealing from me?" I scolded. I picked my wallet up that had fallen to the ground.

Hastily, Dani jumped up from the ground and came right at me. "I take whatever the hell I want you fat bitch!" I heard her scream as she grabbed hold of my hair. Instantly, we started fighting. Well, I was actually connecting my fist with her face. All Dani seemed to do was pull my hair, in attempt to lower me to the ground.

We tussled all around the room, bumping into dressers, desks, the TV stand…my laptop even fell to the floor from our chaos.

Finally we fell to the floor and I got the upper advantage. I rolled over on top of her and drove my fist into her face once more. She still had a good grip on my hair.

"Get the fuck off of her." the guy said and pulled me off of her. He dragged me by the door, and next thing I knew Dani was on top of me. I fought as hard as I could, but for some reason she was over powering me. I knew she wasn't that strong. There was no way she could ever hurt me with her hits. That's when I realized that the punches were coming from her friend. Yes, they jumped me. I was getting my ass pounded on when my door flew open.

At first, I couldn't see who it was.

"What the fuck!" I heard Jennifer's voice.

I don't know how she did it but she got his ass away from me. By this time, more residents had come into the hall from all the commotion. Karma, the RA, followed by two security officers came into the room. I'm not sure who called them but I'm sure as hell glad they did. One security guy grabbed Dani, while the other cleared the hall. Jennifer helped me off the floor. Everything from my head to my calf hurt like hell. Dani must have fled the scene because I didn't see her anymore.

"What happened?" Karma asked me.

"She's a fucking thief!" I admitted. "Dani better not step foot in this fucking room again. Or better yet, I need to move to a different room before I kill that bitch."

Annoyed, Karma huffed. "I'm going to have to write this up so I need a statement from you." She said. "Ms. Jacob will most likely want to talk to you in the morning. Are you going to be OK for the night?"

I nodded my head.

"OK. Just slide your statement under my door." She said before leaving out of my room.

Jennifer locked the door as soon as Karma left.

"What the fuck happened?" She said with concern in her voice.

I closed my eyes and let out all the emotion I had building up. I couldn't hold it in any longer. I told her everything from Valdis and the abortion I had earlier to the money situation that led to the fight.

With not a single judgmental look or statement, Jennifer listened and consoled me. It was different talking to her about it. If it were either Aja or Jess, their suggestions and opinions would have driven me even crazier. Maybe that's why I didn't tell them. I kind of kept my distance from them as well after my surprise party. I wasn't mad or anything, I just needed space from who ever knew about that situation. She was the friend I needed, and for the first time in a long time, I didn't feel alone.

Chapter Twenty Three

Two Months Later

Dr. Hughes is a Jackass," Jenn spat from my bed. "I spent two whole days studying the chapters he assigned and none of the shit was on the mid-term." She laid on her back starring at the ceiling. I partially listened to her rant while continuing to beat away at the keyboard finishing up my last mid-term paper.

"I mean, who the hell does that?" she resumed. "I've never gotten anything less than a B my entire life. That test better not fuck up my grade in his class."

"Done!" I said as I hit the print button.

Jennifer sat up in the bed. "Luckily for you all of your mid-terms were papers."

"Yea, but my ass won't be so lucky if I don't turn this in on time." I said as I put my sneakers back on. "I need to hurry across campus; I have to have it in by 4:30 pm. You feel like walking me?"

"Nah," she said, "I need to pack some clothes for this weekend and meet up with Terri and Pooda on the second floor. They want to hit the road by five, and I don't want to miss my ride home."

"Oh, yea that's right," I remembered. "You're leaving me up here alone this weekend."

"Yup," she nodded. "I need to handle a few things but I'll be back early Sunday morning. I'm going to bring back some of my mama's home cooked meals too." She hopped off the bed. "I already told her that I needed a feast to come back to school with."

"Sounds good." I put on my grey hoodie with Old Navy written on the front.

"If I were you, I'd push both of these beds together and make one big one." She said starring at Dani's bare mattress.

"Girl, I am not touching anything on that side of the room until she gets the rest of her shit."

"That bitch doesn't want this shit," Jenn laughed as she looked over the few things remaining on Dani's dresser. "She moved to the other dorm two months ago, if she wanted it, she would have taken it when she packed all of her other things. Or better yet, let's deliver them to her."

"Ha. Your ass is always starting trouble."

"No, her and her pussy-ass boyfriend started it." Jenn chuckled. "I just don't like to leave anything unfinished."

"Well she got kicked out of the dorm, and he got kicked off the basketball team so I didn't have to finish it. Shit, I'm not losing any sleep. Besides, if I get into anything else with them, I could get in serious trouble. They are not worth my degree... as long as the bitch stays out of my way."

"Now, that's some real shit." Jennifer said as we shared a laugh.

I picked up my cell phone and glanced at the time. "Oh shit, I have to go." I had to get across campus within the next fifteen minutes. I grabbed the paper from the printer, slid it into a folder and slipped the folder in my shoulder bag. Have a safe trip, and call me when you get home."

"Alright, girl." Jennifer said. We hugged and left the room. I hurried down the steps and out the back door of the building.

I made it to my professor's office just in time. He was locking his door to leave. I was completely out of breath, but I got there. Next, I headed over to the café before they closed for the night. Usually, I would sit in and eat. But I really didn't feel like being there, especially since Jennifer had left for the weekend. It wasn't many students in there anyway. On a Friday, they either ordered out, or if they lived close enough they would go home. I just took my food to-go.

As the cafeteria aid completed my order I felt my cell buzzing in my pocket. I retrieved it without even looking at the caller ID.

"Hello?" I answered.

"Hey sweetie, how are you." I instantly recognize the voice.

"Hey, mom." I replied. "I'm good, just grabbing some dinner."

"What are you doing this weekend?" She asked.

"Nothing." I picked up my food with my free hand and headed out of the cafeteria.

"I was hoping you would come home. Maybe we could get a bite to eat and talk."

"I don't know," I responded. "I was just going to stay up here and relax."

"But Zay, I really need to talk to you." She said with a bit of concern in her voice. "How about next weekend?"

"Is everything alright?"

"I just need to talk to you."

At that moment, a brick of realism smacked me across the face. *Oh my god, she must know about the abortion.* It was a good thing we weren't face to face. My widened, frantic eyes would have been a dead giveaway that I was hiding something. "Why can't you talk to me now?" I asked trying to fish it out of her.

"Because I'm not." she said. "And I want to see my daughter if that's alright with you. I haven't seen you since you left for school, and I really feel like you've been avoiding me."

"I haven't been avoiding you, mom." I rebuked. "We were just texting each other yesterday."

"Zayda, you know what I mean. We haven't talked in a while. Not ever since Val—"

"Mom," I averted. Growing annoyed, I halted my walking and pulled the phone away from my ear. His ass was the last thing I wanted to talk about. Seconds passed as I inhaled and exhaled to gain composure.

"Hello?" I heard her say as I brought the phone back up to my ear.

"Yes—mom."

"Listen Zayda, a lot has happened that affects the both of us. I'm just trying to make sure you're Ok."

It had to be about the abortion. She had been pressing too hard to talk to me face to face. It's been two months since I did it, and honestly I really just wanted to leave the past where it was. I had moved on, and talking to her about it will force me to relive it. But I knew she was never going to drop the issue.

"Mom," I reproached, "I'm fine. You don't have to tip-toe around anything. Whatever it is that you have to talk to me about just say it, because—"

"I'm pregnant."

"What?"

"Yes, Zayda, I am pregnant." She repeated. Almost four months now."

"Let me guess…" I said in a mordant tone.

"Yes, it's Valdis's baby." She confirmed. "I would have told you sooner if you weren't avoiding me."

Fury cultivated me at the thought of her having his baby. Tears filled the brim of my eyes.

"Really, mom?" I hissed. "After what he— after I …" I couldn't get my words out without choking up.

"Zay, you really should come home so we can talk about this. I know that you're upset, but"

"No, there's nothing else for us to talk about."

"Valdis is going to be around, for the baby sake, and I don't want you to feel uncomfortable coming here. This is *your* home Zayda."

My eyes finally drained the tears welled up in them. I was hurt, and this time it was by the one person who I thought would never make me feel this way. Fuming, I muttered, "Mom, I have to go."

"Zayda, please let's just—"

Her plea was silenced by the ending of the call.

Pregnant? I thought as I hustled back to my dorm. I was even more astonished at the fact that she thought I would be OK with it. Like we could all be one big happy family. She must have bumped her fucking head, and hard.

I thought that I was healed— numbed to the pain, but hearing that news just showed me how unhealed I was. I wanted to cry. I wanted to scream. I felt utterly betrayed. It was not supposed to be like this. She was supposed to hate him with me. When I hurt, she hurts. Isn't that how it's supposed to be? A part of me wanted to let her have it. She needed to know that it was not Ok for her to just move on with him after what happened. But the other half wanted to shut the both of them out of my life for good. *Fuck her. I don't need her,* I hissed, *if she needs a man that damn bad then she can live her life without me.*

As soon as I got to my room, I flopped on the bed and laid my head back onto the plush pillow. No matter how hard I tighten my eyes shut, a few tears still seeped through the cracks in the corners. I told myself I wasn't going to cry over this shit anymore. Wiping away the few eloping tears, I kicked off my shoes, and adjusted fully on to the bed. The more I thought about it, the angrier I grew. My mind led me to believe that he was actually excited about the baby and the family they would be starting. Hell, it couldn't be that far from the truth. The way he begged for her the day of my going away party, I wouldn't be surprised. This shit wasn't fair—at all. How come he is the one that gets what he wants? His ass doesn't deserve to be happy.

At that moment, a sudden spiteful urge kicked in. I knew just the right ingredient that would fuck up his perfect recipe. I pulled out my cell to send him a wakeup call, that I, too, am having his baby. Shit, he didn't have to know that I got rid of it. I'll let him just think I'm pregnant. He needs to sweat it out for a while.

Grimacing at the screen, I tapped away on the keys, letting my anger flow through my fingertips. An incoming call interrupted my message. My mom's name flashed across the screen. I stared at it for a second before sending her call to voicemail.

My lips twisted up as my actions momentarily ceased, and the conscious Zayda appeared. I took a deep breath, two, actually. The look I imagine on his face if he reads the message would fulfill my taste for revenge, but it would also let all of my skeletons out the closet. I know for a fact that he would tell her, and it wasn't worth it.

Deleting the message, I tossed my phone next to me, and flicked on the TV. I needed something...anything to take my mind off the both of them.

Movies and snacks kept me occupied for the remainder of the night. It was pushing 11 PM and I was finally being hit with the sleepy bug. A shower was the perfect attribute before a night's rest. I took off my clothes and put on my robe. Just as I opened the door, a guy in a dark blue hoodie straddled passed my room. *These bitches never learn.* I thought shaking my head. *We're on lock down and they still got niggas walking the halls.* The guy walked to the far end of the long hallway, and exited out the stairwell door. I closed my door behind me and headed to the shower room.

It seemed as if I was the only one on the dormitory floor. It was quiet, unusually quiet. There hadn't been a party on campus since the shooting took place. We had been put on a lock down for the rest of the year, but no matter what rules were put in place, the guys always found a way to sneak in the girl's dorm. But tonight it was so quiet you could hear a pin drop.

I was in and out of the shower room in less than ten minutes. As I approached my door, I spotted the same dark blue hoodie standing at the end of the hall. He stood there staring at the ground. I don't know if he was waiting for someone or not but he was definitely creeping me out. I hurried into my room and closed door behind me.

My heart jumped out of my chest when I was greeted by two masked, hooded strangers.

Frightened, I stood there frozen in nothing but my robe and shower shoes. I clenched the collar together as I frowned at the intruders. "Who...what ... What do you want from me?" I asked in between shaky breaths. "I don't have any money so—"

"No money?" one guy said, "Well I guess we're going to have to take something else then." He rubbed his hands together.

Almost instantly, I threw my shower bucket at them and tried to run back out of the room. The tallest one grabbed me, and flung me on to the bed using his muscular frame to pin me down. He clamped my wrist together above my head with one of his enormous mitts. The stench of alcohol immediately pierced my nostrils.

"Somebody help me." I screamed. My squirming wasn't hardly a match for the weight he had on me.

"Shut the fuck up, bitch." he punched me directly in the mouth. The blow sent an awakening shock. I continued to kick and scream trying to break free from his grip.

"Grab her legs," he instructed his accomplice as he covered my mouth with one of his hands. My bare assets were exposed from the robe coming undone.

"I'm going to show this fat bitch how it feels to have shit taken from you." He gritted through the black ski mask. Somehow he managed to pull his sweatpants down and rammed his dick inside of my vagina.

My eyes amplified in fear. His voice was slightly muffled, but I know I've heard it somewhere before. I knew exactly who it was; Dani's coward-ass friend.

Unexpectedly, our eyes locked and the dark soul behind them showed no remorse for what he was doing. I couldn't believe what was happening.

"Yo, man what are you doing?" I heard the other guy ask. "This wasn't the plan."

The door flew open and in walked the blue hooded guy from the hall way.

"We've got to go!" he said in a panic. "Security is in the building."

Dani's friend ignored the warning and continued to pound on my private parts. His crazed eyes never left mine as a tear poured down the side of my face. The louder my cries ascended the more force he applied. It was as if he enjoyed the position of power he had.

"Yo, nigga, come on." The guy said again. Dani's boyfriend turned to look at him. "Wait a fucking min—Ahhhhh."

The opportunity presented itself and I took it the first chance I had. Soon as he turned away, I swiftly slipped one hand free and dug my nails into the skin on his neck. He drove his fist into my face but I kept my grip on him, digging as hard as I could until we both fell onto the floor. He grasped a handful of my hair and slammed my head over and over again on the cold, hard floor, eventually sending me into a black out.

Chapter Twenty-Four

As my eyelids gradually pried open, everything in my vision's path was blurred. My head felt as if it had been stepped on by a herd of elephants. My limbs even felt weighed down. I heard voices but couldn't make any of them out. Where was I? Rapid blinking my eyes, I attempted to clear my view. I could see a little better; however, the bright light caused my head to pound even more.

"Umm" I moaned. My body was covered in pain.

"Zayda?"

Finally, I heard a familiar voice. It was my mom. Was I home? How did I get here? For the life of me I couldn't remember anything.

"Baby, are you awake?"

I felt her grab my hand. She leaned in towards me. The closer she got the more clear her face became.

"Mommy," I droned. "What happened? Where am I?"

"You're in the hospital, honey." She sniffed as tears streamed down her face. "You had a concussion.

Someone found you in your dorm room passed out. Zayda, what happened to you?"

Her words echoed in my mind as I thought back to what happened. Muted images of me being attacked flashed before my eyes.

"Oh my god." I covered my mouth with one hand.

Another nurse walked into the room. "She's awake?"

"What is it, Zay?" my mom asked ignoring the nurse's question.

"He tried to rape me," I cried out. I was slowly starting to remember snippets of what happened.

"Who did this to you Zayda?"

"I— I don't know his name." I thought harder by remembering back to the first time I saw him. "Everything happened so fast."

"I'm going to contact the police." The nurse said before leaving back out of the room.

My cries became hysterical. Could my life get any worse at this point?

My mom climbed on the bed next to me and held me close. "Everything is going to be alright Zay," she soothed, "I promise."

Thirty minutes later the police, my mom and I were the only ones in my room. With the help of raising the head of the bed, I had built up enough strength to sit upright. The police questioned me about the events that lead to my hospital visit. Just like earlier, I didn't know a name to give him. I tried my best to give them the best description of Dani's boyfriend.

"Do you drink, or use any recreational drugs?" the young Caucasian officer asked.

"What!" my mom answered, "No, she doesn't."

"Ma'am I was asking your daughter." He said sarcastically.

"No." I said, "I don't drink and I don't use any drugs."

"Are you sexually active with anyone at your school?" he continued.

"What the fuck does that have to do anything?" My mother grew completely irritated. "Someone attacked my child. Why the hell does her having a sex partner or drinking matter?"

"Ma'am, it's just standard procedure." The older officer informed. "We get cases similar to this from the surrounding colleges, especially on the weekends. A lot of parties, illegal drinking…things could get out of hand. We have to make sure that this attack really did happen, and not some juvenile dispute."

"A juvenile dispute?" She yelled. "She is lying here in the hospital with a concussion. Does this look like a juvenile dispute?"

"Ms. Jones, you'll have to keep your voice down, we have other patients—"

"Y'all asses are supposed to be finding out who did this to her." She continued, disregarding the nurse's request to lower her voice.

"And that's what we are going to do, but first, we need to get all the facts." The officer implied.

My mom paced back and forth in front of my bed. Her obvious annoyance and frustration with this entire situation had begun to take a toll on her. She took deep breaths as she held the back of her neck with one hand. The moment she swiped her free hand over her belly, I remembered. Her pregnancy had completely skipped my mind until now. Her shirt was baggy, so I really couldn't tell at first. But there it was. She rubbed her stomach as she continued to pace the floor.

"If you don't mind, ma'am, we would like to continue." The officer said.

A knock at the door grabbed all of our attention. In walked a middle aged red head, wearing a white coat.

"Hi Zayda," She greeted, "I'm Dr. Logan. How are you feeling?"

"Is that a trick question?" I said slyly.

"I need to speak with you," she looked around the room before looking back at me. "Alone."

"We'll be right out in the hall," one officer said taking the doctor's hint.

Everyone but my mother left the room. She took a seat on one of the chairs next to the bed.

"Zayda," Dr. Logan started, "the results from your CT scan shows no signs of swelling or bleeding. This is a good thing. Now you may continue to have headaches or dizziness for a few days. Judging by the bruises, I'd say you're lucky considering how hard you may have hit your head." She informed. "But you should look forward to a full recovery."

Thank god my injuries weren't too serious.

"However, when you came in we were given the information that you might have been raped." She resumed, "We did a rape kit and pelvic exam. There was a lot of scar tissue on your uterus. Did you by any chance have a recent miscarriage, or termination of a pregnancy?"

I felt a knot in the pit of my stomach soon as those questions fell from her parted lips.

A confused look washed over my mom's face. "What?" she asked with concern in her voice. She stood from her seat once more.

"From the punctures on her uterus your daughter was with-child." She bluntly stated, "Now, we cannot tell if she miscarried or aborted the pregnancy, but there is a small bacterial infection. I'm prescribing you an anti-biotic that will take care of it."

"Zayda?" My mom reared. I just looked away. I couldn't bring myself to look at her. I wasn't at all prepared for this conversation... not at this time.

"Zayda, what is she talking about?" My mom's voice shook.

"Maybe I should leave you two to talk." Dr. Logan insisted. "Your nurse will be around to start the IV antibiotic soon. Any other questions you may have just ask them to page me." She smiled. She collected her chart, left out of the room, and closed the door behind her.

Quivers invaded my achy arms. I felt like I was ten-years-old again. Ashamed, I lowered my head trying to bury it in my chest. My eyes swelled up as the waterworks began.

"Zayda, please— just tell me— what happen." She said calmly and in between deep breaths.

"It doesn't even matter anymore," I whispered. "It's done and over with. I moved on."

"Dammit," she gritted through her teeth. She walked over to the window and stared out at the city's skyline. "Doesn't matter? Over with? Zay, do you hear yourself right now?" She turned to look at me. "You had an abortion. What if something had gone wrong? You heard the doctor. You got a bacterial infection—"

"That's treatable."

"And that's only by the grace of God, Zayda." she scolded. "You could have bled to death. How could you be so dumb and not tell me—"

"Tell you what, ma? Huh?" I snapped. "That I got knocked up by a guy I fell in love with who just happened to be secretly dating my mother? Or that I was pissed at you because you were always his choice."

I folded my arms across my chest. I stared up at the hospital ceiling releasing my frustration. "I thought...I thought he loved me. I thought my life had finally started to make some sense, but then he chose you. It never was about you. It was about me and Valdis, and he chose the other woman. If you hadn't been the other woman and there had been someone else, he probably would have still chosen the other woman." I looked back over to my mom. "Do you even know what it feels like? To be hurt? To have your heart and feelings played with your entire life? Did you even once consider my feelings in all if this? I didn't deserve that...I did nothing wrong to deserve what happened to me."

"And I did?" She said. "You're holding all of this anger in and pissed off at the wrong person Zayda. Now, I know what happened was fucked up. But that doesn't mean I don't care about what happens to you. You are my blood, Zay, my baby. Stop looking at me as if I'm just the *other* woman."

The room fell into a brief silence.

"Before now— before you knew all of this happened. You were moving passed what Valdis did. Mom, you're having his baby! And for some strange reason I feel like you two were working it out. You know what that tells me? Huh? That to you, I was *only* the other woman. Not your daughter." I shook my head with frustration. "Look at yourself. Can you honestly tell me that you're not the slightest bit relieved that I got the abortion? You're having Valdis's baby, mom. He chose you. So everything else doesn't matter anymore."

For the first time, as far as I could remember, my mother had nothing to say. She just stood there marinating in a stew of reality. She wasn't the hard shell I was used to seeing. I was never the one to show anyone any emotion. I had grown immune to the shit life threw my way, but today, after finally releasing my truth, a ton of weight had been lifted from me. I would have screamed it to the world a lot sooner if I had known it would have given me the serenity I longed for. I felt free, sort of.

Twiddling my thumbs, I took a deep breath. "Mom, it's OK, really." I said calmly. "I'm dealing with all of this in my own way. I'm sorry I didn't tell you about the baby, but don't let that stop you from being happy. Do what makes you happy."

"I want you to come home, Zayda." She whispered, "So we can fix this...so we can fix us. Besides, I don't feel safe with you up here after what happened."

"Mom, I'm not leaving school. I'm done running from my problems." I told her.

She planted her bottom on the bed, and wiped away her remaining tears. "I am supposed to protect you." She said. "From the world, and... the –"

"You can't, mom," my voice cracked. "You can't be there to save me all the time. And I get that." I exhaled, deeply. "Let's just start from the beginning. I'll tell you everything, and you do the same."

She smiled and nodded. Her glow was relaxing. We had both gone through so much in such a short time.

We spent the remainder of the evening talking. It was a long awaited conversation. Everything was put out on the table—she even told me the truth of why my dad left. Turns out, Gary wasn't my real father. She had been pregnant before they, but never told him. It came out in spite of him cheating on her and she confessed to get back at him. For ten years, Gary took care of me only to find out that I wasn't his daughter. I wasn't mad at her for that. After all, if he really loved me whether I was blood related or not, Gary would have made a way to still be in my life.

For the rest of the night we talked and cried, and cried and talk. I felt our bond getting stronger than ever.

Chapter Twenty Five

Spring Semester

"Attention ladies of Tubman Hall," A girl with a heavy New York accent chimed in over the loud speaker. *"Please start making your way downstairs to the front lobby for the hall meeting. This is a mandatory meeting, and all must attend, Thank you."*

It was the first week back at school for the spring semester. Since the first semester had unquestionably made a permanent indentation on my mind, you can say I wasn't really looking forward to the second one. However, things were looking up. The Winter break was short... about three weeks. I did go home, but I spent most of the time working at my old job. Not that I really needed the money. I just needed my space. Yes, my mother and I were finally on the same page, but watching her belly grow was still a huge reminder of what happened. Nonetheless, I was going to have a baby brother. Oh, and get this, my mom confirmed that she and Valdis were no longer trying to work things out. In fact, she had a new friend, Ebony. Yes, a fucking woman. You can imagine the expression on my face when she told me about her new lover. Whatever makes you happy, right?

Jennifer and I were now roommates. It's a good thing, too; I don't know if I could take another new situation after Dani's ass. It would be just my luck that I would've ended up with another grimy roommate. When Jenn suggested that we should room together, I couldn't have agreed more. I did, however, find out from Karma, the RA, that Dani wasn't coming back this semester. She didn't know why, but her name wasn't on the returning students list. Good. She was one less thing I had to worry about.

Jennifer and I headed downstairs for the hall meeting. The open lobby area had filled with new and returning students. The stiff, blue lobby couches filled fast, and others got comfortable on the floor along the edge of the room.

Ms. Jacobs, the hall director, appeared through the door at the end of the lobby carrying a bottle of water. The dark tone, short, chubby woman sported a pair of dark blue jeans, a black button down shirt, accessorized with a gold chained belt and matching earrings and bracelets. Her hair was cut short, just about as short as a man's, and she wore an evenly amount of make-up. Yea, she was fly in her own way.

"Ladies," she started, "Most of you already know me, but for those of you who don't, I'm Ms. Jacobs." She slowly paced the center of the floor. "I am not your mother, your friend, your babysitter, your maid, your sister, your baby's god mother, not even a girl you would come across on the street. Each of you has your own responsibility and will be held accountable for your own actions. Each semester I stand here, in this very spot and warn each group of young women about what happens in the real world. Amongst this group, some of you are thieves, some are liars, and believe it or not, most of you may very well be a walking sexually transmitted disease."

A few of the girls chuckled.

"Yea, you're laughing," She continued, "but I am serious. This is not the perfect little home you are used to, and I guarantee you that one of every five girls here will be knocking on my door by the end of this semester, crying to me about the mess you got yourself in. I don't say this to scare you. I say this because you all need to wake up. We have rules in place for a reason. Ladies, stop sneaking these guys in the building through your windows. Stop propping open the back doors. Every time you do, you are putting the lives of everybody here in jeopardy. There is a prison down the road. Anybody could get in here. And if I catch one of you doing it, there are no second chances." She twisted the cap off the water, took a sip, and cleared her throat before continuing her thoughts. "The tragic events that happened last semester will not, and I repeat, will not happen again. It's heartbreaking when I think about the lack of care and the negligence that goes on. You are all young women, and should stick together as such."

Just about everyone who was there last semester knew about my attack. Words travel faster than a speed racer. I could feel the stares from a few of the girls when she brought it up. I felt transparent—exposed to the world. Everyone knew my business, and most had already formed their own opinion about it. One rumor was that I invited the guys to run a train on me. Another was that I was being paid for my services, and when the guys didn't want to pay up, things had gotten out of hand.

People really amazed me. It's crazy how easy it is for some people to find entertainment on another person's tragedy. The *old* Zayda would have let the assumptions eat her alive. Now, I pretty much didn't give a fuck what anyone thought about me. I'll tell you one thing, no matter how many stares or rumors that transpired, no one ever said it to my face.

That day was still a huge blur, but the good thing was that Dani's boyfriend was caught. The description I gave the police helped them pick out suspects, and the rape kit that was done at the hospital confirmed who it was. Needless to say, he was put behind bars.

The cheering in the room broke my thoughts. "What happened?" I leaned over to Jennifer and asked.

"The building is off of lockdown," she whispered back.

"Ladies, ladies," Ms. Jacobs said as she held up one finger. The room was once again silent and she had our attention. "We are starting this semester off with trust. I am leading by example by trusting you to do the right thing. But I'm telling you now, if one messes up, you all mess up. The first time I get a report of a propped door, alcohol, after hour guest—anything, Tubman Hall will be on lockdown for the rest of the year, including May Weekend. Your friends will not be able to stay for the concert and step shows. If you ask me, you all are lucky to be having an end of the year festival, especially after the last party." The tone in her voice indicated that she was getting winded. She paused for a second. "Excuse me," she cleared her throat and took another sip of water before continuing. "I am counting on all of you, ladies. Have a good weekend, and an even better semester."

The meeting was over. The room disbursed into different directions; some headed to the stairs and elevators while others to the front doors. It was almost 11:30 AM, and the dining hall would be opening soon for lunch. We went back to our room, grabbed our coats, and headed out to the dining hall.

The January's winter chill filtered the air. The light coat of snow that covered the ground and bare trees brightened up the scenery. My face and ears were freezing. You can say that I was not a fan of snow. If it weren't for Jennifer, I would have just stayed in my room and ordered out.

We arrived at the dining hall and swiped our IDs at the front. I didn't expect for there to be a lot of people there yet because it had just opened up. I was wrong. It was jammed packed. Every food line had at least twenty people waiting.

"I'm going to grab us a table," I told Jenn. "There might not be any by the time we get our food."

She nodded her head. "You want me to get you something?"

"Just some fish, rice, and corn."

"OK."

I stopped at the condiment stand and grabbed us some forks, cups and napkins before finding us a table. There were some empty spots in the middle of the room. I placed the items on the tabletop and sat down.

You know that feeling you get when you can feel someone's eyes on you? Well, I felt that ten times over. I looked behind me and met eyes with a brown skin guy with braids. He had a light faded beard and mustache, and his individually braided hair hung passed his shoulders.

I frowned as to say *'what are you looking at'* but he didn't budge. An eerie feeling crept over me. I had never seen him before, and the fact that he blatantly stared at me with his cold emotionless eyes had my guard completely up. I didn't trust anyone, or give them a chance to fuck with me. My radar was always on. I kept my eyes on him painting a picture of him in my mind. I wasn't going to forget his face. He was up to something, I just had that feeling.

"Zayda?" A male's voice called.

Startled, I looked up. I couldn't believe my eyes.

"Tony?" I said, surprised. "What are you doing here?"

"I go here now." He told me.

"Oh," I ignorantly said and turned back around. I looked back over to the creepy guy's table but he was gone.

"Can I sit down?" Tony asked.

"There are plenty of seats at another table." I spat without even looking at him.

"But I was hoping we could talk."

"Why?" I questioned. "You like talking to *grizzly bears* now?"

Just then, Jennifer arrived at the table, placed the plates of food down, and took a seat. "Hello," she said to Tony. "Who are you?"

"Nobody," I answered before he could.

"I'm Tony," he extended his hand to her.

"Jenn," she said as she shook his hand.

"Tony was just leaving," I said with an obvious attitude.

An awkward pause briefly lingered.

"Yea, I was just leaving." Tony said. "I'll catch up with you some other time, Zay. You ladies enjoy your meals."

Tony walked away from the table and headed towards the front door. I slowly rolled my eyes to the side and watched him walk away. He had a slight limp in his saunter. Just as he reached the door he turned back to look at me, and we caught eyes for a brief moment one last time before his exit.

A host of different emotions came rushing at me. I haven't spoken to Tony in over four years. Even attending the same high school wasn't enough to draw us together. Now all of a sudden, he sees me?

"What was that about?" Jennifer asked as she began to stuff her face.

"I don't know," I said softly as I shook my head. "But it's not important."

"Humph," she shrugged. Knowing I was full of shit, she said, "I guess you'll tell me when you're ready."

"Really, it's nothing." I assured her, knowing she didn't believe me one bit. But, she was right. When I get ready to talk about it, she'd be the ear to take it all in.

As soon as we were done eating lunch, we went back to the dorm. The winter's cold called for a hot, steamy shower. Then, I was going to ball up in my bed and watch movies for the rest of the day. For some people, this was the perfect weather. There were even some guys in front of the dorms playing football, full teams and all.

Just as we came within reach of the elevators, Jenn's phone rang.

"Who is this?" she asked with her face turned up as she looked at the unsaved number on the screen. "Hello," she cautiously answered. "Oh," she laughed. "I forgot I gave you my number. I thought you were a bill collector or some shit." She joked. "When? Right now? Uh, ok. What's your room number? Aight, me and my girl Zayda are about to walk over there now."

I looked at her sideways.

"Ok, see you in a few." She said before hanging up.

"Zayda is about to take her ass upstairs." I said as a matter of factly.

"Girl that was this nigga Brian from the basketball team." She said, "Come on, walk me over there."

"Now?"

"Yea."

"Why?"

"Why not?"

"I'm not going over there to be a third wheel." I laughed. "While y'all loving it up, I'll be there looking stupid.

"Girl, please." She laughed. "Ain't no loving going on tonight."

I twisted my lips up as if to say *Yea right.*

"On second thought, maybe you're right." She said, "Cuz' that nigga is fine."

We both shared a laugh.

"Well, I'll be back later, Ok?" She said.

"Aight, see you." I told her. She walked back out of the front door. The elevator still hadn't come yet. I jabbed at the button a few more times. Finally, the doors opened up. I stepped aside to let the few people off before getting on.

"You can't speak?" I heard someone say.

I looked up and there was Carl, the Kappa, smiling.

"Oh, hey," I said, "I didn't see you."

He stepped back onto the elevator before the door closed. "How are you feeling?" he asked.

"I'm good." I nodded.

"I mean, I heard about what happened." He sincerely said. "I really haven't seen you after—"

"I'm fine, really. How was your break?" I asked changing the subject.

He nodded his head and dropped the other issue. "It was OK, I guess."

"Just OK?" I said as I pushed for the fifth floor.

He shrugged, "I mean it was the same ole, same ole. I went back home to Texas to visit my peoples."

"Texas? Really?" I said, "Shit, its warm there. I probably wouldn't have wanted to come back." I smiled.

"Well, maybe the next time I go, you could come with me."

"Yea, whatever?" I sucked my teeth.

"I'm serious."

"Seriously crazy." I said.

The elevator stopped, and the doors slid opened on my floor.

"I'm crazy to invite you to Texas?" He smiled.

"Uh yea," I responded as I stepped off, "You don't even know me."

"You're right," he replied, "You could be one of those stalker chicks." He quickly stopped the door as they were about to close. "I can't have all that. My mama don't like no crazy chicks."

"Yea, you wish." I laughed. "I see you got jokes, huh?"

"I got a lot more. How about I tell them to you on our first date." He suggested, "Dinner first, then the trip to Texas."

"How about you let the elevator go before you break it?"

"I will when you say yes." He winked. "Saturday around seven?"

I hesitated to answer.

"I promised to be a gentleman." He added. "I'll have you home by nine. I wouldn't want to get you in trouble or anything."

"Ha, I'm grown." I smiled.

"So that's a yes?"

Biting my bottom lip to fight back from blushing, I shrugged. "Ok—I guess."

"Girl, you just made my day." He smiled and let the elevator go.

I wasn't really sure of his motive. He was just too damn friendly. But this time around, I wouldn't fall so easily.

As I turned the bend from the elevators to head to my room, I stopped dead in my tracks when I saw Tony standing by my door.

"Zayda, wait," he said as I turned to go in the opposite direction. He limped as fast as he could to catch up to me. "Hold up."

"What!" Annoyed, I turned back around.

"I just want to talk to you."

"Tony what the fuck could you possibly have to talk to me about?" I hissed.

"Zayda, I know you're pissed." He said, "I know you hate me, but I just needed to tell you that I'm sorry."

"Tony, sorry should have come a long time ago." I said trying to walk passed him.

He grabbed my arm. "I know. And trust me, Zay, I felt bad for what I did to you. You were my friend—my best friend. It's just that—"

"What!" I snapped. "It's just that you were embarrassed of me once you got your little *girlfriend*?"

"Zayda, it wasn't like that."

"No, Tony, it was *exactly* like that." I sighed deeply, and almost in tears. Damn, I didn't realize how much anger I still had inside. It was like I buried it in a volcano and seeing Tony caused it to erupt. "You were ashamed of me, and you chose your side. Do you know how much that hurt me? And for what, to be popular? To have a girlfriend? Tony, me and you were like family. I would have never turned on you. I hope that bitch was worth it."

The elevator door opened and a few girls walked off briefly silencing our conversation.

"Zay," he continued when the girls were far enough down the hall. "What I did was wrong. I was young and immature, and honestly, the look on your face that you had that day haunted me. I knew you were hurt because of me. If I could take it all back, I would in a heartbeat. I loved you Zayda. I've always loved you and I still do."

"Oh please, Tony—"

"Zayda, I'm serious." He sternly said. "I love you."

"Just like you love Tiffany, right?"

"Tiffany?" He frowned up his face. "Tiffany is a gold digging bitch looking for a meal ticket." He said. "Soon as I hurt my ankle she bounced on me."

"Oh," I nodded. "Now I see what this is about. You and your little girlfriend broke up, and now you think you can just pick up our friendship where it left off."

"Zayda, me and Tiffany haven't been right since junior year." He admitted. "She followed me to college when she heard about my ball scholarship. I was the only starting freshman. She played my arm like a trophy wife until one practice I took a fall and busted my ankle. I told her that I may never play again."

"Never play again? Are you serious?" I asked. Even though I hated him, I still knew how much he loved the game. And he was one of the best players in high school.

"No, my injury wasn't that bad." He said, "But she didn't know that. After that, she told me I was worthless, and she couldn't use me anymore."

"So now you see how it feels." I said.

"Truthfully, I wasn't hurt." He shook his head. "I was more pissed at myself for letting this charade go on for so long. None of them were my real friends; not her or my teammates. If I didn't have a nice jump shot they wouldn't give a fuck about me. The only real friend I had was you, Zay. And I know things will never be the same between us, but I promise I'll make it up to you."

I really didn't want to let go of my attitude. I wasn't done being mad at him, but I knew he was sincere about what he said. He was right, things was never going to be the same between us again. But I had to forgive Tony. Not for him, but for me. Hearing him finally admit that was sort of a closure point for me.

"Tony," I said as I looked him in the eyes, "Take care of yourself." I walked around him, headed to my room.

"Zayda," he called after me. "I want to give you something."

I stopped in my tracks but never turned around.

"Just one more thing," he continued, "And I promise to leave you alone."

I turned to look at him.

"Will you please just walk me to my car?"

I took a deep breath, and slowly nodded my head yes. "Fine."

Shivering, I stood at Tony's car in the parking lot behind the dorm. He rumbled through his trunk in search of something.

"Are you almost done?" I complained, "It's cold as shit out here."

Without saying a word, he closed his trunk with a book in his hand, and stood directly in front of me. "Zayda, a few months ago my grandmother passed away."

My jaw instantly dropped. "What?" I wasn't expecting to hear that. His grandmother was practically his mom. She meant so much to him, and by the water building up in his eyes I knew that it was still hurting him.

"About a week before she died, I went to visit her in the hospital." He continued. "She started telling me things about life, and making the right decisions. She's done that before, but this time it was different. It was like she was preparing me to live without her. Giving me advice for the future when she would no longer be around. Then out of nowhere she says, call her...call Zayda and tell her how you feel. It shocked the hell out of me because I never told her about what happened." A single tear slipped from his eye and slowly rolled down his face. "After she died, I was packing up a few of her things and I came across this." He held the book out to me.

I took it from his hands and opened to the first page.

"Oh my god!" There was a picture of me and Tony as young kids. I laughed as the memory of that day came back to me. We were about eleven- years-old. That was the day we found out that Tony was afraid cats. We were at the pool with my mom, and someone decided to throw a stuffed cat in the water. Well, Tony thought it was real, he fought like hell to get out. He was knocking over smaller kids, and everything trying to get out the water. He didn't care who was in his way.

I turned to the next page and there were more photos. "Wow, she kept all of this?"

"Yea," he said softly. "And I'd like you to hold on to it."

"Why?" I questioned. "How come you can't hold on to it?"

"Because," he said, "I hope that one day you look at this and… you'll want your friend back."

Shit, now he got me about to cry. I thought. "Thanks, Tony, but I can't keep this." I gave him the book back. "I'll see you around, OK?" Just as I turned to leave, I spotted that creepy guy from the dining hall easing up in a black Chevy Impala. He gawked at me, this time much more intently. His arm slowly eased out of the window holding a black handgun. My life flashed before my eyes when I saw the weapon. I froze in fear.

With the gun pointing directly at me, he yelled, "This is what happens when you snitch on my big brother!"

The gun sounded off as he released bullets from his chamber one by one. All I can remember was Tony grabbing me and throwing me to the ground. A few more shots sounded before I heard the tires screeching.

Fearfully, my body trembled, and my heart raced a mile a minute. I didn't know if I was shot; I didn't feel any pain. Frantically, I screamed. Tony's body was slumped on top of me. "Tony?" I called out, but he didn't answer.

I sat up and rolled his body on to his back. "Tony!" I cried again, "Tony, wake up. Please, wake up."

That's when I saw the blood seeping from behind him pooling on the ground. "No. No. No." I cried. "Come on, Tony. Somebody help me!" I yelled out.

I looked up and a few students were running out the back door and toward me and Tony.

"Security is on the way," a girl informed me with a cell phone pressed against her ear.

I hovered over Tony's body, in disbelief of what was happening. I felt weak; I felt defeated by life. What did I do to deserve all of this? Life wasn't supposed to be this hard, or was it?

That day was an eye opener for me. I was going to live each day like it was my last. No more grudges, no more living in fear, no more holding on to the things I cannot control.

"I forgive you, Tony." I whispered. I closed my eyes and waited for help to arrive.

Chapter Twenty Six

Present day

The moment Jennifer stepped over the threshold to her house, she paused.

"What's the matter?" I asked her.

"It feels different in here," she mumbled. "Sort of cold. I know I haven't been here in over a week, but I was expecting that homey feeling."

"It's all in your mind," I assured her. "This is the same home that you and Neil built together, and one day, it will get back to the way it was."

"Yea…I hope so."

"How about you go take a shower, and I'll see what you have in the refrigerator that is good to cook."

She nodded her head yes and headed upstairs. Taking a seat on her couch, I pulled out my phone and ordered Chinese food take out. Because I had already been at Jennifer's earlier in the week to clean her place, and to get away from Carl, I knew there wasn't any food in the kitchen. I disposed of the leftovers that had gone bad, and bleached the entire refrigerator. I also took care of the mess left behind from the crime scene investigators, and I even scrubbed her carpet of Neil's blood. If she was going to get out on bail, she wouldn't want to come home to some mess. I didn't want her to see anything that was going to remind her of that day.

The food was delivered about twenty minutes later, but Jennifer still hadn't come downstairs. Wondering what was taking her so long; I went up to her room to find out.

"Jennifer, honey, are you okay up here?" I shouted as I walked up the steps. "You get lost or something?"

Jennifer didn't respond. Complete silence lingered in the hallway. I didn't hear the shower running from the bathroom, so I cracked open the door and poked my head in. The bathroom was empty.

"Jennifer?" I called again walking to the master bedroom.

When I opened the door, Jennifer was sitting on the floor beside her bed with her head lowered and her knees pulled into her chest wearing the same clothes she'd came home in.

"I thought you were getting cleaned up."

She lifted her head and revealed to me her glassy eyes and face full of tears.

"Jenn, what's the matter?" I took a seat on the edge of her bed and slid down to the floor beside her.

"My life is so fucked up," she began. "I mean, even if Neil does still love me, there is no way he and I could work things out. I tried to kill him for Christ sakes. How can anyone come up from that? He thinks I'm crazy and maybe I am," she looked over to me, "I love him, Zay. But even now, I was sitting up here getting ready to get in the shower when I came across his T-shirt. Just a little T-shirt made my mind go into a trance. First, I thought about when we first got the T-shirt on a cruise a year ago. Then, I thought about how the shirt looked all good on him, and how other women would see him attractive, too. Then, I started thinking about him given into the other women's attention, and somehow they ended up fucking, and those urges to hurt him came rushing back."

"All that from a T-shirt…"

"I'm crazy," she nodded, "I know I am. I've got to be. Loving Neil has changed me. It's like I would do anything he asked me to do even if I knew it went against all laws. If he wanted my last breath, he got it. I will run down the street butt ass naked if he'd asked me to, just because. I never said no to him, and maybe that's the problem."

"I think sometimes we love so hard, and so much that we forget we have to love ourselves first." I shifted on to one side, "It sucks, but we as women get stupid in love. It's blinding, and that's when it becomes dangerous."

"Yes," She agreed, "It's like you're standing outside of your own body watching what you're doing, but you can't stop it. Even when you know what you are doing is wrong, you just can't stop. How do you deal with what Carl has done? You don't get that urge to make him hurt the way he hurt you?"

"I do," I admitted, "but thinking about Cherish brings me back to the level of sanity. As much as I want to snap out, break shit, blow up the fucking house… I can't. I just think of my daughter."

"Neil never wanted kids." Jennifer confessed.

"Really? I thought *you* didn't want them."

She shook her head, no. "That was my cover up. I didn't want to tell anyone my husband didn't want kids.

I was ashamed, and jealous. He told me before we even married that he didn't want any children, but I thought I could change that. That man went as far as having himself fixed because I wouldn't agree to take birth control. Now, he can never have any."

"Damn," I exhaled. She never told me that. I thought I knew everything about her. You never know what is going on inside someone's home. Once the doors are closed, it's like an entirely different world.

"I thought Neil was the family type." I added, "He'd always seem so open and friendly…and father figure-ish, even."

"After last year, I knew something changed. He was just too different… so harsh. Every little thing I did annoyed him. He wasn't happy with what I wore, my hair, what I cooked—one time he actually got mad at me because I bought a different brand of toothpaste. How he was talking to me was as if I was just an average Joe on the street. That's when I first suspected him of having an affair. There wasn't any evidence to prove anything, so I ignored it…until I found the condoms, just recently. That explained it all. Some other woman had taken my place; snatched my husband from right under my nose." A few more tears fell from her eyes, but she just wiped them away.

"I know Neil still loves me, but he's gone. I don't have his heart, anymore, and that hurts me to the core."

"Well… maybe it's not like that. He's had time to think, so…"

"No," she said, "It is like that. I just wish I can tell him how I feel, and then I can leave with closure."

"Leave?" shocked by her statement, my head snapped back in her direction. "Leave where?"

"I was thinking I'd just move back to Maryland with my dad. I can start a new life there; away from Neil, and away from all of this. I won't be able to do that knowing he's still reachable. I don't want to be able to just get in the car and drive to him. I need to go as far away as possible."

"I definitely understand that—even though I don't agree with you leaving. You have to do what you have to do. And who knows, maybe me and Cherish could come out there with you."

A smile spread across her face, "You know you're always welcomed."

Leaning in toward her, I gave her a hug. Sadly, this is the life God gave her, and she had to walk the path. I'm just glad she's making the decision to better herself instead of sticking around in an unhappy marriage. As her friend, there was one more thing that I knew I could do for her. Tomorrow, I was going to talk to Neil. He needs to reach out to his wife; at least for closure if not anything else.

Chapter Twenty Seven

The next morning when I woke up, I couldn't get Jennifer off of my mind. I shot her a motivational text along with a strengthening prayer. She didn't respond right away. She was probably still asleep. It *was* eight o'clock in the morning. The only reason I was up was because we had to go meet with Carl's lawyer, Ronald, and his legal team. Yes, he was still under investigation, but Ronald said that he had some good news to share. He requested that I come along because this decision would require both of our inputs. I guess Carl never mentioned to him that we weren't on level grounds, but anyway, I'm going as a supportive wife, once again.

Our meeting wasn't until 1 PM, but I wanted to stop by the hospital to see Neil beforehand. Ronald's office was only five minutes away from where Neil was.

After getting myself and Cherish ready, we headed downstairs. Carl was sitting in the living room when I came down.

"Good morning," I said as I passed him and went into the kitchen carrying our daughter in one arm.

"Good morning," I heard him say back. That was the most we really said to each other in the past week or so.

Opening the refrigerator, I grabbed the premade breast milk bottle from the shelf. When I closed the door, Carl had come into the kitchen.

"You want me to cook breakfast or something?" He asked.

I was a little taken aback by the question. *Why is he being so nice all of a sudden?*

"No, thank you. I'm just going to grab something on the way to my mom's. She's waiting for Cherish, now. They're going to the flea market in Jersey today."

"Well how about dinner? I can make us that for later."

"Umm, okay, I guess. I mean, it's only dinner right." *What else was I supposed to say?* The days that he ate my cooking, I never asked— I just made it. He must have something up his sleeve, and beating around it, once again.

This time, I wasn't going to force him to tell me. I stood quietly, momentarily, giving him the opportunity to take the initiative. He didn't. So, I continued on with what I had planned.

"I'll meet you down at Ron's firm... at 1 o'clock, right?"

"Yeah," he nodded, "1 o'clock."

"Great," I said before leaving out of the kitchen. After fastening Cherish into her car seat, we headed out of the front door and to my car. I didn't have much time, so I needed to hurry before I was late to our meeting later.

"It's about time you got here with my grandbaby!" my mama shouted from her car.

My windows were all the way up, and my air-conditioning was on full blast, but I still heard her loud mouth as I parked my car on the opposite side of the street from where she was. I got out of the car and unlocked the car seat from the back.

"Mom, you said to be here about 9:30."

"I know what the hell I said," she twisted her neck, "It is 9:38. You were supposed to be here eight minutes ago. I would have left if you didn't have my baby in the car with you."

Rolling my eyes, I chuckled. "Oh mom, whatever."

"Yo, Zay!" Zaire shouted with excitement from the backseat of the car.

"Hey Za Za, what's going on?" Opening the car door, I leaned in and kissed him on the cheek before strapping Cherish in beside him.

"Where you headed to now?" my mom asked me.

Leaning inside her window, I kissed her on the cheek as well. "I got to make a few runs, and then me and Carl are supposed to meet with the lawyer later on. Hey Thea," I said to my mother's girlfriend sitting in the passenger side.

"You look like you slimming down there, Zay." she told me.

"Shit, I wish. With all of the stress I've been under, I probably gained a few pounds. It must be just my outfit," I said referring to the teal-colored maxi dress I had on.

"Well, listen; don't wait up for us because we are going out to have some fun." My mother interrupted,

"And don't be calling my phone asking me where your baby is."

"Yeah, I know mom." I smiled, "Thanks again for taking her."

"Yea, yea, yea. Now move away from my car so we can leave." she winked.

My mother was a hoot; but that was the way she showed her love. When she ignores you— that's the time to worry. It meant she didn't give two shits about you. I watched her drive off before getting back into my own vehicle, to make my way to my next destination.

Traffic wasn't too bad. I got to the hospital in about twenty minutes. There was just enough time to try and talk some sense into Neil, and find out what his plans were. I already knew his room number from the times Carl visited. He came home a few times still wearing his guest pass that had the room number on it. I headed straight to the room without bothering to check in. I did, however, stop at the gift shop to buy a teddy bear and a get well balloon, trusting my gesture would show that I'm coming in peace.

When I got to the floor, a nurse walking by kindly pointed me into the direction of Neil's room. The door was shut when I approached, so, lightly, I knocked.

"Come in," a deep voice yelled from the other side. Even through the heavy hospital door, I could tell it was Neil.

"Hope you don't mind visitors today," I said as I opened the door, "You know I had to—Carl?" My husband was the first person I saw when I walked in the room. "What are you doing here?"

"I was just about to ask you the same question." He responded.

I came all the way in and shut the door.

Neil looked up at me and smiled. "Hey! Who is this beautiful lady coming in here?"

"Hey Neil," leaning over to him, I pecked a kiss on his forehead. How are you feeling?"

"I've been worse. It's going to take a lot more than a knife to stop me."

From the corner of my eye, I could see the unpleasant look on Carl's face. He wasn't too happy with me coming down there… oh well.

"Mr. Harris!"

Our attention diverted back to the door, and in walked a tall, gray-haired man wearing a white coat and black framed glasses.

"I'm sorry, I didn't realize you had visitors." he said when he looked up at me and Carl.

"It's fine. You can come on in doc," Neil informed.

Carl stood from his seat, "Maybe we should step outside, Zayda."

"Oh, you don't have to," the doctor flagged his hand, "I'm not here for any exams. I just wanted to come by and shake Mr. Harris's hand. I won't be here when he is discharged tomorrow, but everything is all taken care of."

"Tomorrow? Really?" I looked at Carl and then down to Neil.

"You didn't tell her?" Neil asked Carl.

"Tell me what?"

"We'll talk about it later, honey." Carl said brushing me off, "You were saying doc?"

No he did not just hush me up. If Neil wasn't a recovering patient, I would have cussed Carl's ass out in front of the doctor.

"Well, the in-laws are coming in town tonight," the doctor continued, "so I've got to play the best son-in-law role, again."

"Ha! You are crazy." Neil said.

"No, my mother-in-law, that bitch is crazy. But anyways, it was good to meet you, and I'll see you for a follow-up on the wounds in about a month."

"Cool, doc," Neil held out his hand.

The two of them shook hands before the doctor looked over at Carl and me. "You two have a good evening."

A fake smile was all he'd gotten out of me. I was still stuck on whatever it was Carl neglected to tell me. The second the doctor stepped out of the room and closed the door, I brought the conversation right back up.

"So, what didn't you tell me this time, Carl?"

"They are letting me go home tomorrow," Neil interjected.

"Obviously. Why is that such a secret?"

"Zayda, Neil is going to be staying with us for a while."

"Is that so?" I looked at Carl.

"Since Jennifer made bail, Neil can't go home. Not until after the trial." Carl added, "I personally told him since it was his house he could legally make her leave."

"Carl, I'm not going to do that. Where else is she going to go?"

"Yo dawg, why do you even care? The bitch tried to kill you."

"Don't call her a bitch, Carl." I defended.

"Excuse me… the witch tried to kill you."

Neil burst into laughter.

"There isn't anything funny about what happened." rolling my eyes at my husband I turned completely around and gave him my backside to look at. "I think it's very mature of you to let her have the house, Neil."

"Oh, she can't have my house," he shook his head, "but she can borrow it for right now. When this is all over with, I'm keeping my house and she will have to find somewhere to go."

"Neil, listen—"

"Zayda, I think it's time for us to go." Carl cut me off, again. "We should start making our way to the lawyer's office."

"We still have about an hour and a half before our meeting."

"Well if we get there early maybe he can fit us in now, and get it over with."

"Whatever," I knew exactly what he was trying to do—avoid me bringing up Jennifer, again. I didn't feel like the *tit-for-tat* with him today, so I dropped the issue…for now.

"Neil, you are always welcomed to stay at my house," I smiled.

Truth be told, Jennifer was my friend, but so was Neil. Yes, I was pissed at him for cheating on her, but who was I to judge. I couldn't turn my back on him, either. Remaining mutual between the two was the lane I was going to stay in; at least until they were officially separated. But if Neil and Jennifer *did* split up, you better believe he can kiss my ass too.

"I'll be back tomorrow to pick you up." Carl told Neil as the two of them slapped hands.

"Aight, cool." Neil responded.

Carl went ahead of me out of the door. Just as I turned to leave, Neil grabbed my arm.

"How is Jennifer doing, anyway?"

"Why do you care?"

"I'm not a monster, Zayda."

My eyes shot over to the door to make sure Carl wasn't looking.

"Well, what you did to her sure made her feel like you are one. You need to call your wife, and stop hiding like some little ass boy."

My words must've struck his heart. Guilt covered his face just that quickly and serves him right. I gave him one final look before following my husband out of the door.

"So let me get this straight, you want me to give up Cartman?" Carl clarified for the third time as if Mr. King, one of Ronald's associates, would change his answer. The FBI had been on him for quite some time, but had never been able to link any of the crimes to him until now.

Carl took a deep breath. "Snitching? That's the best you can come up with? What the hell am I paying you for?"

Mr. King opened the folder lying on his desk in front of him. He pulled out a few large photos and placed them in front of us. Carl and I both sat up in our seats and peered at the photos.

"Marcy?" Carl whispered with his brows furrowed.

"Why is she riding shotgun with Agent Bennet?" I asked as my eyes traveled to another picture. Oh shit!" She the fucking feds?"

"I told you, they been on Cartman for a while."

"Dammit!" Carl sat back in his chair.

"At this point, there is no telling what information she was able to dig up; for as long as she's been undercover, she probably got dirt on all of you."

"Obviously, not enough." Carl interjected. "If she did, I wouldn't be sitting here right now."

"But you better believe they are damn close." King corrected. "But that's not the question. It will happen. The question is when and to whom."

Carl looked at me and then back at Mr. King.

"What's the big deal?" I blurted out, "Just tell them his affiliation with the whole thing."

"Zayda, it's not that simple. He didn't put a gun to my head and make me do anything. I can't just snitch?"

"You can't? Not for us... for me... for Cherish? You could go to jail for a really long time, and you still won't put us first?"

Carl didn't say anything.

"Oh. I bet if Marcy asked you would—"

"Zayda, please don't start this right now." Frustration was evident in Carl's voice, "For the last time I am not fucking her. She's a fed for god sakes."

"But your ass didn't know that then!"

"Listen," Carl took a deep breath. "If they want to build a case against Cartman then they will have to do it on their own. I'm not just going to hand over any information *and* still do a bid. It's not like snitching is going to get me off completely."

"You're looking at fifteen years, Mr. Kinsley, fif—teen—years. Now I can probably get them to shave off about eight...maybe even ten. But you have to be willing to cooperate."

Mr. King briefly waited for a response, but Carl didn't even look up at either one of us.

"You do know if anyone testifies against you, that's it. It's also whoever gets the deal first." Mr. King added.

"I'll have to think about it." Carl mumbled.

"Well, think fast." Mr. King grabbed the photos and placed them back into the folder. "Who knows what kind of shit they are waiting to drop."

Snatching my bag from the floor, I huffed. "We're done here, right?" I asked. Without waiting for an answer, I got up and left. I cannot believe Carl is making this a hard decision. If it were up to me to save my family, I'd sing like a bird. I couldn't even stand to look his way right now.

I couldn't help the tears filling my eyes as I rushed out of the building and to my car. Since Carl had his own car already down there, I didn't even wait for him. I needed some time to myself; even though it appears that I'm about to have fifteen years' worth of alone time. *Why is he being so stupid? Maybe he should go to jail. That will give him time to think about what he did. He not only fucked up his life, but my life as well.*

Chapter Twenty Eight

I couldn't sleep all night. It wouldn't be the first time. When the night transitioned into day light I knew there was no use in still trying. I was up and dressed early. Since Carl had to pick up Neil from the hospital, today, I decided to take Cherish and go hang out with Jennifer. I didn't tell her the news of Neil staying with us just yet—over the phone would not have been good. But I have to tell her, because if she finds out, and I didn't mention it to her, she'd be pissed... I know I would if it were me.

I agreed that Neil could stay only if he sleeps in the basement. It was like a miniature apartment down there anyway; a full kitchen, a lounge area with a pull-out sofa bed...the only thing it's missing is a bathroom. That was on Carl's to-do list. However, there was one on the first level of the house he could use.

Yesterday, I set up the basement and made sure there were enough blankets and pillows for Neil to be comfortable. He was only going to be with us for a couple of weeks. Hey, and if Jennifer is planning on really moving to Maryland, he might be able to move back to his house even sooner.

Carl had already left to meet Neil at the hospital, and Jennifer was meeting me downtown at our favorite cheap restaurant... TGI Fridays. That was the only place in Philadelphia that served half-price alcohol during lunch hours, and their Jack Daniel's steak and shrimp is the best.

My princess was already to go with the dress her auntie, Jenn, brought her for the baby shower. It was way too big for her when she was born, but she's just now filling it out. Jennifer is going to fall out when she sees her in it; a pink sundress with a matching head bow and pink sandals. What the hell, since she was pinked out, I might as well throw on pink too.

The cool summer's breeze hit against my face as I drove through the city with my windows down, and K Michelle CD gracing my speakers. I swear, every time I'm in my emotions, or something crazy is taking place in my life, K Michelle and Keisha Cole's music stay in heavy rotation. It's like they are talking directly to me. Sometimes when I'm driving, I find myself acting as if I'm in the music video. The people in the other cars probably get a good laugh when they pass by me.

I just love being outdoors. The fresh air does wonders for my stress level, and helps me think about the good things happening. I just thank God I am able to take care of my daughter, she is healthy, and I have a strong support system. If it weren't for my mother, I'd be an emotional wreck right now. Maybe I need to get back into the church. That's probably why I've been dealt such a bad hand lately. This is God's punishment for neglecting him. First thing Sunday morning, I will be sitting front row of the congregation.

When I arrived at the restaurant, Jennifer had already reserved the table. It wasn't packed at all due to the fact that it was only 11:30 in the morning, and they had just opened up.

"Hey Divas!" Jennifer greeted us with a smiling face and opened arms, as usual. If I was a stranger, I wouldn't be able to tell that she just got out of jail and fighting an attempted murder charge. She was hiding it very well. I gave her a hug, and she took Cherish from my arm.

"I'm glad to see the old *you,* again." I told her as I admired her get up. She sported a pair of white high-waist shorts, a loose yellow backless tank that draped over her hips, and a pair of six-inch yellow sandals that showed off her freshly done pedicure.

"Shit, I feel like the old me, again." she took a seat. "Being in there with those crazies had me feeling some type of way. I was at Unique Appeal Hair Salon first thing in the morning yesterday." She rubbed her fingers through the bob-cut she loved to sport.

"I already ordered you a drink," she continued.

"Good, I could use a drink, but only one. Girl you know I don't like to drink a lot when I have the baby with me."

"Hey, that's fine with me. Shit, all I need is one. I'm taking Brandy's advice. That one drink a day will keep the stress away."

"And turn you into an alcoholic." I added just as the waiter approached our table with the beverages. We both shared a laugh.

"Parrot Bay and pineapple?" The young, brace-faced waiter asked.

"My fav!" I nodded at Jen and gave my approval. The waiter sat the drink in front of me. "And a double shot of Hennessey on the rocks."

"Henny?" I asked with one eyebrow raised at her.

"Don't judge me…judge your mama." She chuckled as she took a sip of the dark cognac.

"Are you ladies ready to order?"

"Could you give us a few more minutes?" I asked, even though I always ordered the same thing.

"Certainly," he replied, "Just wave me over when you are ready."

"So, how did things go at the therapist?" Jennifer asked when the waiter left our table.

For a second I had forgotten I told her that. I still hadn't said a word about the trouble Carl was in.

"Ok, I guess. I just don't think his head is in it anymore."

Jennifer shook her head. "Carl needs to get it together while he still has a chance. You are too good of a woman, Zay; a better one than me. Shit, if I rolled that way, ya ass would be mines."

"Cheers to that." I laughed, raising my drink in the air.

After lunch, we drove to the King of Prussia Mall about thirty minutes outside of Philadelphia. There, we spent the day shopping and loose talking about any but our husbands. I was able to get Cherish's fall clothing wardrobe out of the way. The girl's section in the children's clothing stores is always filled with a variety. It's like playing dress-up with a doll baby— that, I can't get enough of. I also picked out a few items for myself. Ashley Stewarts had their annual *buy one get one half off* sale. I racked up on a few pairs of jeans, a few blazers, and some lightweight shirts for the fall.

Jennifer didn't buy any clothes; however, she bought damn near the entire shoe section at Macy's. Shoes were her drug. I'd be surprised if she didn't already own every pair she just bought.

Before I knew it, hours had passed and it was almost 7 PM when we arrived back at Jennifer's house.

"I needed today," Jennifer said as I put the car in park. "It took my mind off of all the bullshit going on. I felt like we were in college again. Thank you, Zay."

Damn! I thought. Little did she know, I was about to cast a shadow over her parade. There was one more thing that I needed to tell her, and hopefully it would only cause light showers instead of a tidal wave.

"Jenn, I went to see Neil yesterday."

"You did?"

I nodded, "He was discharged today."

"Already? Are you serious?"

"Yes."

She looked up at her front door. "Is he here?"

"He's staying with us... at my house. Carl suggested it. He said that he shouldn't go home since you made bail."

"So... he knows that I'm out, and he didn't even call me?" Her voice lowered.

"But he did ask about you." I said, hoping that would make her feel better. "I told him he needed to call you and stop acting so fucking childish."

"He's not going to call." Jennifer shook her head, "I'm over it."

As much as she wanted to believe the lie that just flowed from her lips, she couldn't—and neither did I. Either way, I left it alone. She knows about Neil now, and that is all that mattered.

"How about Cherish and I stay with you tonight?" I suggested. "We could have our own little girly slumber party."

"Sure. Why not." Jennifer shrugged. "It is pretty boring in here by myself."

"I just have to go home and grab a few things for us."

"Okay, well you can leave her here with me while you run over there."

I looked in the back seat, and my baby was rocked out; head leaning off the side of her car seat, and all.

"Yeah, maybe you should take her in and lay her down. She looks pretty uncomfortable."

Jennifer got out of the car, unstrapped the seatbelt and lifted Cherish into her arms."

"I should be back in about a half an hour... forty-five minutes, tops."

"We'll be here," she said before walking up her pathway and into her house.

As I pulled off, I grabbed my phone from my bag. I haven't spoken to Carl all day, and he didn't even bother to call me. Swiping my thumb across the screen to unlock my phone, I dialed his number.

"Hello?" He answered.

"Hey, it's me. I was just calling to let you know that me and the baby will be spending the night at Jennifer's." Just as I finished my sentence, my cell's battery died. "Fuck," I said tossing it to the passenger seat. I really need to get a car charger; especially since I hate driving without a phone. Anything could happen, and I wouldn't be able to call anyone for help.

Before I went home, I made a quick stop at the only liquor store that was open this late. Since Jenn and I were taking it in for the night, and my daughter was already sound asleep, I planned on drinking. I made it just in time before they locked the doors. We didn't need anything heavy—just a bottle of wine. After paying for my bottle, I headed home.

When I arrived, both Carl and Neil's cars were parked in the driveway taking up my spot. Carl must've taken Neil by his house to get it. At least Carl was thinking on his feet. They went while Jennifer and I were out shopping so they didn't run into one another.

I pulled alongside the curb and hopped out. I hated parking on the street, but since I was only going to grab a few items there was no sense of me asking them to move a car. As I neared the front door, I saw the basement light on and could hear T.I's verse in *Swagga Like Us* blaring.

"Where the hell does he think he is?" I said out loud shaking my head. "I know he's a guest and all, but he is gonna have to follow the house rule. I don't even blast music *that* loud."

I entered the house and closed the door behind me. The music was even louder inside. Shaking my head, I headed upstairs to my bedroom to pack an overnight bag.

"Carl?" I called out but didn't get a response. When I opened the door to my bedroom, I was pissed. Livid. Both lamps and the television were on. The bed wasn't made, and Carl's towel hung off the side of it. He also left a pair of sweatpants, black t-shirt, socks and boxers scattered about the floor.

Shaking my head, I huffed. He knows how much I hate when he leaves his clothes lying around. Carl had a habit of not cleaning behind himself right away. Maybe I'm partly to blame, because I've allow it for so long. I always took care of keeping things tidy, but this didn't make any god damn sense. "His ass is too old for this shit." I hissed. I wasn't about to let him ruin my day. I hurried up and packed a bag for me and Cherish, and headed back down the steps.

After sitting our things by the front door, I went to the basement to let them know I was staying at Jenn's. Opening the door, I yelled down. "Carl!"

Since the music was so loud, I know I couldn't be heard so I walked down. "If y'all turn down this god damn stereo I wouldn't have to be scre—Oh my God!"

My heart jumped out of my chest, and almost suffocated me when I saw what was taking place in my house. My husband and Neil were all over one another. Their nude bodies clung like magnets, as their hands explored each other's masculine frames.

My jaw dropped opened. I couldn't believe my own eyes. I was in so much of a shock that I couldn't force myself to move. My stomach curled over and I wanted to vomit. It was the most disturbing thing I'd ever witnessed. My husband is gay. Carl kissed down Neil's chest until he reached his hardened manhood. When Neil laid his head back on the headrest of the couch, his eyes locked with mine. Like a deer caught in headlights, he stared back at me in terror. The way Carl bobbed his head up and down on him; he didn't even notice Neil's body stiffen. Even I could see his tremors. It wasn't until Neil tapped Carl on the shoulder and pointed in my direction that Carl took his mouth off of Neil's dick and turned around. It was at that moment my heart literally shredded into dust particles. I was wrong this entire time. I hadn't lost my husband to another woman, but to his best friend... a fucking man. Tears danced on the brims of my eyelids until they could no longer hold them in. My bottom lip quivered, uncontrollably, and my body had begun to take on a numbing feeling.

Carl quickly grabbed the sheet lying on the floor and wrapped it around him. The second he began to approach me, I ran back up the steps. I needed to get far away from there, and fast.

"Zay, wait!" he yelled. "I can explain."

I didn't speak. I didn't scream, talk, hell I don't remembering breathing as I picked up my bags and ran out to my car. My face was covered in tears by the time I got behind the wheel and started it up. Carl came running out of the house gripping the sheet covering his nude body. I didn't give him a chance to reach my car. My tires screeched against the tarred street as I sped off into the darkness.

Where was I going? I didn't know, and I honestly didn't care. Anywhere was better than being at my house right now.

My first instinct was to call Jennifer. Snatching up my phone from the seat with one hand, while keeping the other on the wheel, I tapped my screen. Nothing happened. That was when I remembered my battery had died. "Ughh!!" Forcefully throwing my cell, it hit the windshield and dropped to the floor.

My mind was racing faster than my driving. About fifteen minutes away from my house, I pulled over alongside a playground and put my car in park. Across the street were a row of residential homes. A few folks sat on their porches taking in the cool air. Leaning my head back on the headrest, I closed my eyes. The first image that popped into my mind was Neil and Carl's sexual interaction.

"Ahhhhhhhhhhhh!" I let my frustration out on my steering wheel as my fist drove into the center. I punched it—hard. I punched and I punched and I punched as if it were Carl's face. The car horn honked with each hit. By now, I probably had the residents eyeing my car wondering who the hell I was.

"He's a faggot!" I yelled and punched the horn once more, this time cracking something inside my hand. "A fucking faggot!"

I grabbed my hand and squeezed when I felt the sharpening pain. When I looked down at it, that quickly, I noticed it started to swell.

Another woman I could understand, but a man? Why did he marry me? Why would he do this? Carl had to have known he was into men long before he met me.

"I kiss the same lips he sucks his best friend's dick with." I hissed out loud, "He kisses our daughter."

This all had to be one big nightmare because my life can't be this pathetic. What did I do to deserve all of this? My chest began to tighten up—something that happened whenever I got too overly excited.

I reached down to the floor for the bottle of wine I just purchased. Popping open the top, I raised it to my lips, and took the entire bottle straight to the head. It was late, but I didn't care. I popped in my K Michelle CD and turned my music on full blast. As the words flowed from the speakers, I drank my way out of the despicable ditch Carl had pushed me in.

Chapter Twenty Nine

By the end of the CD, I had gone through the entire bottle wine. I was hoping that the liquor would numb my pain, but the only thing it did was increase it. Plus now, I was drunk. My limbs felt heavy like I was fighting against gravity, and my vision doubled…sometimes even tripled. I needed my bed. I was only minutes away from my house, so I figured if I went slow and took my time, I could make it home.

Reaching up to turned on the ignition was hard to do at this moment.

"Come on, bitch, you got this shit." I mumbled. My pep talk was the only motivation I had to complete this task. I pepped my way in to switching the gear into drive, and lifting my foot off of the brake pedal. When the car eased up, slowly, I tightly gripped both hands to the steering wheel.

"This isn't so bad," I convinced myself. Moving my foot slightly over to the right, I gave it a little gas—well… at least I thought it was only a little bit. My car took off as if it was the time machine in the movie *Back to the Future,* and swerved all over the road. I felt the pressure from my gut move up to my chest like I was on a rollercoaster.

"Holy shit," I screamed and tried to regain control of the car. As the car drove on to the sidewalk, I quickly turned the wheel to get back on the street; doing that only made me dip into the opposing traffic's lane. Luckily for me, there weren't any oncoming cars.

I hurried up and turned down a small block only to sideswipe an SUV parked on the corner.

"Fuck!" The alarm from the SUV echoed into the opened sky, but I didn't stop. I continued down to the next block. Finally, I felt in control…somewhat. I was able to level out the wheel until a random car came out of nowhere when I sped across the intersection. I looked down to the floor for the brake pedal because my foot couldn't find it. When I located it, I pressed it down hard, causing my tires to screech, and stopping just in time before I ran into someone's house.

"What the fuck are you doing!" the driver in the other car yelled, "You ran the stop sign, ass hole."

My heart nearly exploded from it beating so fast. Deep and heavy pants filled my car.

"Oh my God," turning my head, I looked back to see where the other car was. They had already taken off in the opposite direction.

I felt crazy, weird almost. I mean, I've been drunk before, but this was different. It was as if I knew exactly what was going on, but at the same time, I had no clue. I couldn't feel parts of my body, and my tongue was so dry, it kept sticking to the roof of my mouth.

Taking a deep breath, I closed my eyes, briefly, to get myself together before attempting to get home. I lifted my foot off the brake pedal, again. This time I was staying away from the gas. It took a while, but thank God, I was able to coast the car until I reached my house.

Carl and Neil's cars were still parked in my driveway. I didn't expect Neil to still be here. Seeing his car sparked the flare to the anger inside of me. I had every intention of ramming my car into the back of his. I pressed on the gas pedal once again, but my arms, somehow, didn't agree with my mind. The wheel pulled to the right causing me to diverge. Just missing Carl's Buick, I ended up on my lawn slamming down on the brakes just before I crashed into a tree.

"Fuck it." I said as I put the car in park. I stumbled out of the driver's seat, and left everything in there; my purse, my cell phone—I even left my keys in the ignition. That car was going to have to stay there until morning.

My front door was unlocked when I turned the knob. The alarm sounded off the moment I opened it. I walked in and closed the door unbothered by the sound. Carl came rushing down the steps. He stopped mid-way when he saw me standing there. I didn't say a single word to him. I didn't even look his way. When he came down the rest of the steps to cut off the alarm, I bypassed him and went up in the direction he had just come from.

"Bed," I mumbled, "All I want is my bed."

Managing to make it all the way up to my room, the moment I got close enough to my bed, I plopped down on the soft mattress. My head was spinning, and I felt like I could bring up all the food I had eaten today.

"Zayda, we need to talk." Carl had come into the room.

I didn't budge. I just laid there with my eyes closed.

"I didn't want you to find out this way," he continued.

"All I want to do right now… is— get— some– sleep." I said slow and stern. He was trying my patience. "I do not feel like talking, arguing, or crying. That is what will happen if you try to explain yourself to me right now. So, please Carl, just leave me *the fuck* alone."

At this moment, I just wanted to soak in my drunkenness and get away from my reality.

"We're going to have to talk about this sooner or later, Zayda." He said as he took a few steps closer to me. Carl just wasn't getting the hint.

"What the fuck are you not understanding?" I scowled maliciously. "I said I don't want to talk about it right now."

"I didn't know how to tell you," he continued, "or if I should tell you, but this is who am. Now that you know, I guess— well, I'm hoping, that you'll accept it."

My eyes shot open and over at him, "Accept what? That you're gay. A down low dirty, trifling, conniving, lying, manipulating— "

"Zayda, I don't want to lose you as a wife." Carl finished with a sad ass puppy dog look as if I really gave a fuck.

"You've got to be fucking kidding me!" I pulled myself up off the bed. "You fuck men in the ass, Carl. You get on your knees and suck another man's dick like a bitch. What makes you think I want to still be married to you?" Even through my drunken slur my words came across clear as day. "I was trying to avoid this conversation, but since you wanted to be a jackass about it, I can play this game, too."

"So it's that easy for you to stop loving me because I have a preference in men?"

I jumped up from the bed. "Preference?" I repeated. "You act like were talking about a box of cereal, or a vacation spot. What? You were too ashamed of your little *preference?* Didn't want to put a ring on your little boyfriend, huh?" I moved in closer toward him. "I wonder if Jennifer knows of your faggot fuck sessions. You're not a man, Carl. A real man would have accepted who he was a long time ago. Instead, you pulled me into you're fucked up fantasy world living a double life." My face was so close to Carl's he could probably taste the alcohol I drank. "Tell me something, Carl, are you the bitch in the relationship?" I taunted, "You're probably going to make a pretty lil' mama in prison, too." I could see the temper rising in Carl's face. His thick neck was now covered in veins. He tightened his lips, and gritted his top row of teeth against the bottom. Yes, my words were deadly, and I intended for the kill. "At least I can respect the openly gay man." I edged on, "But you... you're a coward; a down low living mutha fucka. And don't expect me to keep your little secret under wraps, fag boy."

"Listen, Zayda, you're drunk, alright. There is no reason to act lik—"

"Like what? Like I just saw my husband sucking on a man? If Neil hadn't of seen me watching, you would have gone all the way, wouldn't you? You look like you swallow that shit too. Probably got a million of Neil's babies pumped in ya gut. Did I ruin your night, husband dearest? You wanted your ass packed too, didn't you?"

"Zayda, enough!"

"Oh no, Mr. *take-it-in-the-ass*, we are just getting started. This *is* what you wanted, right…to talk? Well I'm calling it how I see it. And you deserve everything I'm saying, right now, for what you did to me. You made me fall in love with you." I growled, and vehemently poked him in the chest emphasizing on each word. I looked at him with the most wicked, revolted glare that I had ever looked at anyone in my life. Carl was worse than a cheating husband. "How would your daughter feel if she knew her daddy was on his knees pleasing another man?"

Before I knew what happened, Carl cocked his hand back and sent a loud, hard, painful smack across my face; a smack so rigid that my neck twisted causing me to lose my balance and fall down to the floor.

"I said that's enough, Zayda!" He spat as his huge frame towered over me appearing even more beastly.

"Don't you ever think you can disrespect me like that." He threatened. "I am still the *man* of this house. I am still your husband, and you will not talk to me that way."

His chest heaved up and down, and his muscles protruded through the black tank top that he had on as if he just went five rounds in a boxing match.

Shocked by his reaction, I quickly grabbed my face. It stung, badly. That was the first time Carl had ever done anything like this. He never put his hands on me. This was a completely different side of him. He was in full bitch mode, and I wasn't having it.

Glowering at him, I went from anger to rage. My teeth clenched tightly together as my stare locked on him like a lioness about to attack her prey. The moisture in my mouth seemed to increase. I wiped my lips with my hand and looked at it. This motherfucker hit me so hard that my mouth was now full of blood.

With my eyes still trained on him, I eased my way back up to my feet. Carl didn't move. He kept his masculine demeanor stance with his feet slightly ajar, his hands planted firmly on his waist, and his chin held high as if he had done something to prove a point. The only thing he did was further piss me off.

Mustering up all the saliva I could, I spit one giant glob of blood in his face, "Don't you ever fucking put your hands on me again!"

I pushed him, but he grabbed my arms and swung my body over to the dresser knocking over whatever sat neatly on top of it. Deodorant sticks, lotion containers, perfume bottles, you name it...everything went crashing to the floor. Grabbing hold to the dresser, I was able to catch my balance.

"I'm not going to tell you again," he wheezed, "Calm the fuck down!"

My eyes quickly scanned the dresser for the closest thing within my reach. An autographed baseball from the team members of the Philadelphia Phillies sat on its display.

Without any hesitation, I grabbed the ball, turned around, and threw it at him as hard as I could.

"Fuck you," I screamed. The ball hit him directly in his face snapping his head backward. He hit his head on the doorframe behind him. I heard the loud thump when it connected.

"Ahhh!" He screamed as he grabbed the back of his head and winced in pain. He hurled over, and his body dropped to the floor. I just stood there and watched as he squirmed around like a fish out of water.

"Fuck you and this life!" I screamed with my eyebrows dipped low, and my nostrils flared, "I'm leaving you."

Carl didn't respond. He continued to breathe heavily holding onto his head, but I knew he heard every word I said. Call me cruel, but it actually felt good seeing him in pain. I didn't feel one bit of regret for hitting him with the baseball.

Stepping over his body, I left out of my bedroom and closed the door.

This night just went from bad to fucking worse, I thought as I limped over to the bathroom to check the damage he did. I could feel welts forming on my face already. As I stared at my reflection in the mirror, I began to hate the sight. The old Zayda was starting to surface.

Why me? Why is the bullshit always following me? As I examined my face, I noticed the dark area forming under my eye. He hit me harder that I thought. Had I not been drinking, it probably would have felt much worse.

Grabbing a clean washcloth from the closet, I held it under the warm water to saturate it. In time, my bruises will heal, but what Carl did to me plagued my heart, and there was nothing he could say or do to mend it. I wanted out of this contract, and by any means, I was going to do just that.

I went downstairs pressing the warm rag against my skin. Just as I got to the living room, Neil's ass was coming up from the basement. He looked at me as if he didn't know what to say. Guilt filled his eyes and like a nervous little boy, his lips shuddered as he searched for the right words.

"Zayda, I—"

"Get the fuck out of my house." I spat in a low, ominous tone. "Don't even fix your lips to try to explain shit."

Unlike Carl, it didn't take much for Neil to get the hint.

"Okay. I'll just grab my keys." He said with shame lacing his voice. He made his way back down to the basement.

Moments later, the house alarm sounded off indicating a door had opened. To avoid seeing me, again, Neil left out of the back door. After silencing the alarm, I walked over to the window and watched as he backed his car out of the driveway.

My head was spinning, and my hand still throbbed from earlier when I hit it in the car. My knees felt as if they were going to give away at any second. My body felt as if I had been hit by an eighteen-wheeler truck. I guess my buzz was starting to wear off because I was feeling every bit of pain from my arms to my lower back.

Using the back of the couch as a crutch, I held on as I made my way around to the front. I laid face-up on the sofa staring at the ceiling fan. My tears now slid down the sides of my face and dropped onto the armrest. Closing my eyes, I took deep breaths in and out attempting to still my adrenaline.

Everything is going to be okay, Zay, I thought, *you don't need him. You deserve better. Remember, when one door closes another one opens.*

Raising my left hand, I looked at the stunning princess-cut diamond ring that represented my marriage. It sure was a beauty. But like most things, when the meaning changes, it loses its value. I slid off my wedding ring and tossed it on the coffee table. The ring landed in the empty ashtray. I guess that was God telling me that's where it needed to be…this marriage had burned to the ground. The process of self-comforting begins now.

"I—just—can't—give up now." I began singing the words slowly ridding my mind of all the agony. "I've come too far from where I started from." With each word that flowed out of my mouth, more tears streamed down my face. "Nobody told me, that the road—" I paused as emotion literally jammed in my throat. "Would—be easy…Mmmm mmm." My verbalization turned to hums for the remainder of the song, but before I could make it to the end, I drifted off to a peaceful sleep.

I woke up the next morning by the horrific cries of my daughter.

"Cherish!" I yelled out. Sitting upright on the sofa, I looked around. The crying was coming from upstairs.

"Baby, here I come!"

Just as fast as I stood up, I fell back down on my behind. I had to get my pounding head together before I could do anything. Needless to say, after last night's lonesome drinking, I had a major hangover. Cherish's hollers only added to my excruciating headache, but I still needed to go to her aid. I got up once more, this time a bit slower. The sun was bright, and shining through my white sheer curtains causing me to squint my eyes.

"Oh God," I mumbled. "I feel horrible."

Just barely making it up the steps, I went into the baby's nursery. The moment I opened the door, the crying stopped. Cherish wasn't even in there. I paused just as I felt myself about to go into panic mode, it hit me.

"Jennifer," I sighed in relief. I completely forgot that I left Cherish with her last night before returning home to all the chaos. Her cries must have been a dream, but it sounded so real.

Blowing out the air that had built up in my lungs, I took a seat in the rocking chair. The events of last night slowly crept into my mind replaying the scenes as if they were a movie. I couldn't believe Carl acted that way. He doesn't ever have to worry about me again. He can forget about seeing his daughter as well. If I told my mother that he put his hands on me, she would flip. I would probably have to spend my last on her bail money. I'm just glad things are now out in the open, and I'm no longer living a lie. I'll just start my life over. No… it will not be easy. Carl made all of the household's money, but I can get a job; anything to take care of my daughter. Plus, the money I'd been putting away over the past few years should be just enough for a startup fund.

"I guess I *should* call Jennifer to let her know I'm okay," I said to myself, "she's probably worried sick."

My tender fist pulsated as I pushed against the arms of the chair to stand to my feet. Gently rubbing it, I walked across the hall to my bedroom. *I guess he decided to sleep where I knocked his ass out at,* I thought referring to Carl lying in the same position that I left him last night. One side of his face was swollen from the baseball I threw at him. *When he wakes up, I hope his headache is a hundred times worse than mines was.*

I stepped over him and went to get a pair of fresh clothing to change in to. I feel asleep in the same navy blue, knee-length capris with the white pin stripes, and white sleeveless tiered top that I had on the day before. My navy blue Michael Kors flats were also still on my feet.

Accidentally kicking Carl's leg trying to step over him, I almost tripped and fell onto the floor myself. Luckily, I was able to catch my balance.

I looked down at Carl. When he didn't budge from my clumsiness, I proceeded to my dresser and pulled out a fresh pair of underwear. After another glance at Carl, I noticed he still hadn't moved, and from where I was standing it looked as if he wasn't even breathing.

"Carl?" I called his name as I stared at his still body. Again, he just laid there. The harder I looked, the more anxiety grew in my stomach. I still didn't see his stomach rising, and come to think of it, Carl wasn't wailing out his usual loud snores.

I stood for a second waiting to see if it was just me; maybe I was going crazy, again. "Carl?" I called, again, this time much louder. I walked over to him and stood directly over his body.

"Oh my God!" I shrieked. His eyes had rolled to the back of his head. The only thing I could see was the bottom of his sclera.

"Carl! Carl, wake up!" I yelled as I dropped down to my knees and shook his body, jaggedly. I even pulled on the straps of his tank top...Carl was nothing but heavy, deadweight.

Frantically, I pressed my finger to his neck to check his pulse. I didn't feel anything. His skin was cool and clammy like I was touching the skin of a rotten apple.

"No!" I cried falling on to my bottom, "Nooooooo! What have I done?" With a high-pitched squeal, I hunched over Carl's dead body clinging tightly to his shirt. "What have I done?"

This couldn't be real. Never in my life have I been that close to a dead body, and not to mention, be the cause of why he no longer breathing.

"I didn't mean to, Carl." I cried. The air in the room was thinning by the second. Gasping hard, I took deep breaths to try and breathe what little air was left.

"How did this happen? It was only a baseball. He was breathing before I went to sleep. Baby!" I whined looking into his face. "Baby, I'm sorry. I didn't mean it. You have to believe me."

At the moment, everything Carl had done to me was a non-factor. I still loved him, and just because I was going to leave him didn't mean that I wanted him dead.

Sniffing in the oncoming flow of snot dripping down my nose, I looked up at the door frame and noticed a smudge of blood. It must have been where Carl hit his head. Last night, I wouldn't have thought the impact was hard enough to draw blood. I screamed, over and over for my husband to wake up, but my cries literally fell upon deaf ears. I was in shock—drowning in disbelief. There was nothing I could do to bring him back. My husband, Carl Kinsley, was gone.

Ripping the comforter from my bed, I hurried and laid it out on top of Carl covering his body, completely. I was a murderer. The walls were closing in, and I needed to get out of the house. I couldn't stay here much longer or else I'd lose what was left of my mind. Rushing out of the room and down the stairs, I nearly broke my neck descending them two at a time.

"I've got to go," I rushed over to the sofa and searched the area. "I've got to get out of here." Freaked-out was an understatement. My heart beat so loudly in my ears that, at one point, the cardiac rhythm was all I heard. "Where the hell are my keys?" I said searching the entire area. They were nowhere to be found. I checked under the sofa, the table, and in between the cushions of the seat.

Shit, I thought, *I must have dropped them outside.*

When I opened the door, my car was parked exactly the way I left it...on my lawn. I went to check the car for my keys and found them hanging in the ignition. I jumped in the seat, turned the key and backed out of my grass.

I couldn't think. My mind was scrambled like an egg. Carl's distorted face kept appearing in my visual as I drove straight to Jennifer's.

As soon as I reached her house, frantically, I jumped out of the car, rushed to her front door, and speedily jabbed at the doorbell.

"What the hell is wrong—" Jennifer said snatching the door open. She paused mid-sentence when she saw me standing there. "Girl, why are you ringing my bell like some mad woman? And why haven't you been answering your phone? I was just about to put Cherish in my car and head over there to check on you."

My eyes zoned in on hers. In my mind, I was telling her everything that happened. But nothing came out of my mouth.

"Zay? Are you okay?" She asked with a concerned look. "What's the matter? What happened to your face?"

Again, I just stood there breathing deeply trying to get the words that jammed in the depths of my throat.

Jennifer gawked at me, strangely. "Maybe you should come in and sit down."

"No!" I finally spoke. My eyes nervously shifted between the floor, Jennifer, and then back over to my car. "I need you to keep Cherish for a couple of days."

At the last minute, I decided not to tell her what happened. I didn't want to tell anyone until I knew what my plan was. Telling her may only complicate things. I trusted Jennifer— more than my own husband, but she was already going through her own attempted murder investigation and didn't need the double worry.

"I can't explain now. Just please keep Cherish and, I'll call you in a few days."

"Wait, where are you going?" she asked as I turned to leave.

Without looking back, I kept moving full speed to my car. If anything happens to me there is no doubt in my mind Jennifer will take care of my daughter. I jumped back into my car and sped off.

"Zayda, how could you be so fucking stupid?" I reprimanded myself in the car. "I should've just left it alone. I shouldn't have said anything to him."

My sporadic outbursts were all gibberish. How was I supposed to explain this shit? One minute I wanted to call the police, and the next minute, I wanted to drive far away from Philadelphia. I can't tell anyone he's dead. I was drunk, and even though it was an accident, no one will see it that way.

Carl shouldn't have put his hands on me. I would have never thrown that damn ball. The police should understand if I explain it, right? I pondered for a moment on doing the right thing. But who was I kidding? A dead body and a deranged wife didn't mix.

"I can't go to prison. I wasn't made for prison. My daughter needs me out here. Carl knew I didn't mean to kill him— that wasn't my intention. Ugh, why did it have to happen to me?"

Back at my house, I parked my car, correctly, in the driveway, grabbed my phone from the passenger seat, and my purse from the floor…all the things that I left in there the previous night. Before getting out of the car, I checked my surroundings. My block was quiet as usual. Even though I was the only one who knew what happened, paranoia was high and lively. A crazy potent odor invaded my nostrils the moment I stepped through the door. It smelled like a mixture of rotten trash that has been left out in the sun for a few days, and the butcher's shop. It was heavily concentrated as if it was being pumped through the heating vents. Covering my nose with my hand wasn't enough. The stench was now on the inside of my palm. Quickly, I pulled my hand away from my face and looked at it. It was now covered in blood.

"What the fuck is happening?" I whispered as I wiped the blood away with my other hand, but it didn't come off. Uncontrollably, I shook my hand until instantly, the blood disappeared, and the odor had left as well. I kept staring at my hand and taking in long whiffs waiting to see if the blood and odor would come back. When it didn't, I knew I was going crazy. It was all a hallucination. Knowing that Carl's body was lying in its temporary grave right above my head cast an eerie feeling over me; as if a dark cloud hovered over my head.

As long as my husband's corpse was still in this house, I wasn't going to be able to think clearly. I had to move his body; at least put him in the trunk until I can figure out what to do.

Chapter Thirty

Dear God, please forgive me for what I have done, and what I am about to do. Amen

When I opened my eyes, I looked down at Carl's body. I managed to roll him up in the comforter like a Caterpillar in its cocoon. It was the only way I'd be able to drag his body down the steps, through the living room, the dining room, the kitchen, and then out to the garage. I had already backed in his car in front of the garage door, so I wouldn't have to drag him far from the house and risk anyone seeing me.

It was a little after 8PM, and the sun was setting for the night. I tried to put Carl in the trunk, but his body was so heavy that I couldn't lift him high enough. The backseat was the next option. It was still tough, but I did it. I made sure to put the alarm on the car before going back into the house.

Maybe I could drop his body off at the hospital, I thought as I made my way back into the living room. *Someone there will know what to do.* I eased down on the sofa while my mind contemplated my first plan. *But, there is no way I'll get the body out of the car without anyone seeing me. Maybe I could—*

A sudden beeping noise faded into my hearing and interrupted my thoughts. Swiftly, I jumped up to see what it was. Following the sound, it led me over to the basement. As I got closer, the beeping sounded more like a ringing phone.

"What the hell is that?" Cautiously, I descended the steps down to the basement. The ringing got louder. When I reached the bottom of the step, I looked around the large empty room. My scanning stopped at the bar, and there was Carl's cell phone lighting up. I went over and looked at the screen. It was Neil calling him. I stared at the phone until it stopped ringing. Carl had twenty-five missed calls and fourteen missed text messages— all from Neil.

Snatching the phone up in my hand, I began to thumb through the messages. Neil has been trying to get in contact with Carl since last night. One message even read, *Now is the time to pack up your shit and leave. Run away with me like we planned.*

Another read, *Zayda knows about us now. You know she will tell my wife. This is our chance to be together.*

The texts got me furious all over again. It burned my eyes to even read the messages. Neil and Carl were two sick mutha fuckas. Just as I closed his message box, another text came through.

I'm on my way! You haven't been answering your phone, and I need to see you. We need to talk about this.

"Dammit," I hissed with widened eyes. "What makes you think you have any right to just pop up? He's not your fucking husband!" I screamed at the phone as if Neil could hear me. The last thing I needed was for him to come here. "Shit!" I grasped my hair in frustration and nervously began to pace the floor. "If I tell Neil that Carl hasn't been here, he will definitely ask why his car is still parked in the driveway. Or better yet, what if he looks inside Carl's car and sees the body."

I had to get Carl out of here. Quickly, I stuffed the phone in my pocket and rushed back up the steps. Knowing Neil, he was probably already somewhere close if he threatened to come by, so I didn't have much time. Without thinking, I hustled back out to the garage and hopped in the driver's seat of Carl's car, started the engine, and sped out of my driveway.

I left just in time, because no sooner than I gotten minutes away from my house, I felt Carl's phone buzzing against my thigh. I already knew who it was. I kept my eyes focused on the road ahead of me as I pulled his phone from my pocket.

I'm out front, the text message read.

Neil just wasn't giving up. If he could have his way, he'd probably fight me over Carl like a bitch in high school. The phone vibrated again, and rang several times afterwards.

Finally, I pulled over by the waterfront on Kelly's drive. It was a nice quiet spot where bikers and joggers go to get their morning, midday, and sometimes, for the daring ones, an evening exercise. There were hardly any street lights that lit the area. The moon always acted as the lamp casting a glowing tint in the night's sky over the river. Tonight, I seemed to be the only one out there.

This was also the same place Carl brought me to on one of our many dates. We sat in this very spot and talked for hours upon hours. I think that was the day he made me fall in love with him. It was only about a month after we first started talking, heavily. That night was also when he and I made love for the first time. Yes, right in his car. We'd been out all night, and as the early morning's sun arose, he blessed me with the best sex I've ever had. I remembered that night like it just happened. I was nervous, especially since I had just gone through a crazy freshman year. Sophomore year had just started, and I was skeptical about dating a college senior. Unsure of what his intentions were, I didn't want to get my feelings too caught up. Well, Carl kicked down the door to my heart and claimed it. He's had it ever since. About two years after that, in my senior year, Carl brought me back to this same spot, and proposed marriage.

Tears formed in my eyes as I reminisced back to that day. It's funny how life takes a turn. Now, here we are… sitting in the same spot that held so many meaningful moments in our lives. Everything had finally come full circle, and my purpose on this road was a murderer. Had I known what I was signing up for back then, I would have run down another path without looking back. My life was ruined, and even if I get away with Carl's death, I will be forever imprisoned in my mind. Every time I looked into my little girl's eyes, I'll be reminded of not only what her father has done to me, but what I did in return. Slowly, I looked over my shoulder and back at him lying in the backseat. A sudden wave of guilt hit me, hard.

This isn't right. He doesn't deserve this. In spite of him being gay, and the infidelity, he's Cherish's father. Our marriage wasn't all bad. The Carl I knew was my best friend, my consoler, my guidance. That man I've been living with this past few weeks was none other than a demon.

The calm river waters ahead of me helped bring my mind back to ease. I got out of the car and leaned up against the hood. A brisk air blew brushing up against my face. I took a deep breath inhaling nature and exhaling the anger.

Whatever punishment is waiting for me, I'll have to face it, I thought. I didn't want to be this mad person, anymore. My mind was in a bad place, and if it weren't for this moment of peace and reflection, I wouldn't have found my way back. Closing my eyes, I tried hard to rid myself of the demons that had a hold on me, until…

Baby, I love you!

That was what Neil sent to Carl's phone; the four short words that sent me over the edge; the four words that lit the wick to a colossal C4 bomb. My blood felt like it was on fire as it ripped through my veins and aimed directly to my heart. At that moment, I felt it. I felt the darkness invade my body and took over the ship. I wasn't in control. I saw everything that was happening, yet I couldn't stop it.

Leaning into the car, I used one hand to press the brake pedal, while switching the gear from Park to Drive. After one last glance to the back seat, I let go of the brake and stood back as the car coasted its way into the Schuylkill River. A normal person would've run away. A normal person would've heard the loud splash when the car impacted the water. A normal person would've felt bad. But I didn't. I just stood, heartless and emotionless, and watched as the front of the car dipped downward into the water causing the tail to lift up. Bubbles filled the area around the car as it began to fill with water. Gradually, the smooth flowing current drifted it further and further away.

About a mile down the river, someone spotted my mess. Pedestrians passing by in their own vehicles stopped, abruptly, when they saw it. A man and a woman got out of the car. Her piercing shrieks echoed into the air.

"Oh my God! Someone might be in there. Call the police." I heard her say. They didn't see me standing down the road hiding in the darkness. They were too focused on the car in the river, anyhow. I turned and walked in the opposite direction. By foot, it was going to take at least an hour to get home.

It didn't take any time for the car in the river to make the top story on the morning news. By 7 AM, the media had footage of the car being airlifted from the water. I lay on my bed, detached, as I watched the muted television mounted to the wall in front of me. I hadn't been to sleep yet. Even if I wanted to, I couldn't. My eyes just refused to close. My senses also seemed to be on their own little high. A salty taste lingered in my mouth. My limbs were tender, mainly from my long walk home last night. Every noise outside from birds to streetcars, every tap at the windows whenever the wind blew, even my neighbor's voices, were all amplified. Our homes weren't even connected to one another, but I heard the faint argument between her and her boyfriend; something about him forgetting to take the trash out the previous day. If only what I was going through was that simple— taking out the trash.

My buzzing cell phone broke my attention. I looked over at it connected to the charger on my nightstand. I'm pretty sure everyone who knew Carl and I closely saw the news, and recognized his car. So either my mom or Jennifer was calling to confirm. Too bad I had no explanation for them, or anyone else. I didn't move an inch. I let the call go straight to voicemail every time. I'll just send Jennifer a text later on and let her know that I am okay. I needed these next few days to withdraw all the cash I could. By the end of the week I planned to be on the road heading out of town. I wish I could leave now, but once the police find Carl's body, it would be too suspicious of me to happen to leave town the same time my husband turns up dead.

For the past few hours, I've come up with a plan that would secure me a spot on the innocent bench for sure. Who better to take the fall other than Carl's jealous, homosexual, secret lover? Thanks to Neil, I have the stalking text to prove it. Carl was ending their little affair, and Neil didn't take the rejection too well. He called my husband all night. He even sent text messages begging Carl to leave me. My husband confessed his affair to me and asked for my forgiveness. We were going to work on our marriage, but last night he didn't come home. He forgot to take his cell, so I didn't have a way to contact him. When I woke up this morning, I saw his car on the news.

That was my side of the story. Neil was going to be my scapegoat. Why not? He had his share in fucking up my life, so why not return the favor and see how he likes getting fucked in the ass...oh wait, he likes that type of shit.

I had no remorse for putting Carl's death on Neil. Maybe next time he'll know not to fuck with an angry black woman's husband. This payback was for Jennifer, too. From him cheating on her, hurting her, and probably gave her the same STD he gave my husband who, in turn, gave it to me. Yea, he deserves what is coming to him.

Turning onto my stomach, I stretched my arms and legs outwards releasing all the tension cradled in my bones. Glancing at the television, an alert at the bottom of the screen that read *Sinking Car Empty* caught my attention. Confused, I felt the bed for my remote and turned up the volume.

Investigators say that after recovering The 2015 Buick Enclave from the Schuylkill River just a little while ago, there was no pedestrian in it. Now, they're not saying if, in fact, this was intentional or just an accident. The police diving team has already begun searching the river for any other clues that could lead to answers of why this car was in the river. However, police are running the tags to see if they can find out exactly who the vehicle belongs to. Witnesses who reported to the authorities say that they did not see anyone around at the time of spotting the car. We will keep you updated on this story as we get the information. Reporting live from Kelly Drive, Sterling Howard, Channel 6 action news. Back to you, Tom.

I pressed the mute button on the remote silencing the television once again. Tapping the remote against my chin, I thought. *It's only a matter of time before they find out Carl's name and address. They'll want to come here and question why I haven't come forth about it.*

"I think now is a good time to recognize the car on the news." I said to myself. Sitting up on the edge of the bed, I reached over and grabbed my cell phone. The game was about to begin, and there was no turning back. I was already in too deep. Now, it's every man for them self. Neil had no idea what was about to hit him, and I was swinging with a spiked, thick metal bat.

"Hello, 911?" I said with apprehension driving my tone. You know, to make it more believable. "I think... I think I just saw my husband's car on the news."

Chapter Thirty One

NEIL & JENNIFER

Neil was abruptly awakened by the sound of a car alarm nearby. He sat completely up in the driver's seat and looked around with his heart thumping hard and fast. He had been in the car for nearly five hours, just a few houses down from the home he shared with Jennifer. Neil contemplated on whether or not he'd go inside. After having no luck with reaching Carl, he gave up...at least for the night. His mind was boggled. Carl never ignored him. Even if he and Neil were in the middle of an argument, mainly about them being together, Carl would still, at least, reply to a text message.

Neil knew that Carl was embarrassed the night Zayda caught them, but honestly, he was relieved. Their secret was finally out. Neil loved his wife, but Carl gave him life...a reason to live. When he was with Carl, Neil knew that it was okay to be who he couldn't be with the rest of the world. He wanted to come out a long time ago, even before either of them was married, but Carl wasn't ready. Neil wasn't sure if he'd ever be ready. But he dealt with it, and hung around because of his undying love for Carl.

Sitting back in his chair, Neil took a deep breath when he remembered where he was. Biting the bottom of his lip, he stared at the beautiful landscaping in front of the place that housed his many secrets. Neil and Jennifer were friends before anything. He never intended to be married to her, but when his career began to take off, and when he got more involved within his fraternity and community, having a wife was more acceptable than tagging a man along on his arm. It was the way society trained people to think, and Neil became a victim of it. In result of it, he kept his homosexuality under wraps.

Since the day Jennifer stabbed him, he realized that life was, indeed, too short to live unhappily. So whether or not Carl would continue their relationship, Neil was coming out to his wife. He owed that to her, at least.

For the first time, ever, Neil rang the doorbell to his own home. After a few moments, Jennifer opened the door with baby Cherish in one arm. Her smile quickly faded when she laid eyes on her husband for the first time since their altercation.

"Can we talk?" Neil asked.

Hesitantly, Jennifer nodded her head and moved to the side to allow him by. Neil stepped into the house and waited as if he were a guest in someone else's home. By her convivial demeanor, he knew that Zayda hadn't told her about him and Carl yet. Jennifer would have flipped the moment she saw him. That put him a little at simplicity. That news should come directly from him so she doesn't have to hear it anywhere else, and making it seemed a hundred times worse.

Jennifer felt uneasy. She didn't know why he, all of a sudden, came to the house. He hadn't even so much as reached out to her. She closed the door and locked it back.

"I was just going to put her down for a nap," Jennifer said, "Let me take her upstairs first and then we can talk."

"I'll be in the dining room," Neil told her. He watched her walk up the stairs and momentarily disappeared on the level above him. Neil looked around the living room. Everything was exactly the same way he remembered. Their house was beautiful— fit for a king and queen. Unfortunately, the person he wanted to share it with didn't want him. Shortly after Neil took a seat at the dining room table, Jennifer joined him sitting in the seat directly across from him.

"How are you feeling?" Neil eased in to start the conversation off.

"I've seen better days." Jennifer replied. She couldn't help but to notice how good he looked sitting across from her. She always thought he resembled the actor and singer, Tyrese. His chocolate skin was glistening with sweat as if he just came from the gym. Little did she know, it was from sleeping in a hot car all night.

"How are you?" she asked.

"Better."

"Listen, Neil I—"

"Jennifer wait," Neil cut her off. "Please, just let me tell you this first. I know things have been rocky between us these past few months, and I'm not sure why we let things go on the way they have been. I should have been the man of the house and taken control of the situation. I just got so caught up in everything else... Jennifer I never meant to hurt you. I love you."

"Neil…" Jennifer said, "It's not all your fault. I should've been the woman of the household and made sure you held true to who you are…your word. Marriage is a team effort. So, I won't let you take the blame all alone. And I love you too." Jennifer reached up and touched the back of Neil's hand. "I honestly don't know what I would've done if you would've died."

Neil gazed at his wife. He wanted so badly to remove his hand but opted against it. He didn't want her to take his rejection the wrong way. He needed her to be settled because what he planned to tell her next was going to destroy her entire world.

"Jenn, I think you may be misunderstanding the meaning behind what I'm saying."

"Okay, well what are you saying?"

Neil froze with hesitation. *Tell her. Just say it. You need to let her know,* he coached himself internally as he searched for the right words to break the news.

"Jennifer, I—"

Loud banging at the door caused both of them to shoot their eyes to the front of the house.

"Who the fuck is that?" Jennifer jumped up from her seat and headed to the door. Neil followed directly behind her.

Two police officers were waiting on the other side of the door when Jennifer answered.

"Mr. Harris?" One cop asked as he looked passed her and at Neil.

"Yes?" Neil answered with furrowed brows.

"We need you to come with us down to the station for questioning."

"What is this about?" he stepped in front of Jennifer.

"Do you know Carl Kinsley?" the officer proceeded.

"Yes. Why? Did something happen to him?" Neil's heart began to race at the thought of Carl possibly being hurt.

"We were hoping you would be able to tell us." The taller of the officers said.

"Tell you what?"

"We can talk about that once we get to the station."

Jennifer's eyes traveled between the officers and then up at her husband. Nothing about them was welcoming, which sent red flags up in her head.

"Should I call our attorney?" Jennifer asked with a worried look in her eyes.

"No," Neil told her and looked back at the cops, "Unless I'm under arrest."

"It's just questioning for now." The officer informed, yet still, that didn't settle Jennifer's concerns.

Neil took another brief moment of silence. He didn't know what was going on. He hadn't seen Carl since the night before last, and now the police are showing up wanting to question him.

"Okay." Neil finally agreed.

"Should I come down there with—"

"No. I'll be back soon." He told Jennifer.

Following the police officers to the car, they opened the back door for Neil to get in. Jennifer watched from the door as they pulled away from the curb. The moment they were out of sight, Jennifer closed the door and rushed to her phone. She called Zayda's cell phone but got no answer.

"Zay, I need to bring Cherish home," She said on the voicemail. "Neil is at the police station, and I have to get down there. Call me back, or I'll just drop her off on my way out."

A few minutes later, Zayda replied with a text message.

Drop her off at my moms, please.

It was the first communication Zayda had with her since she frantically showed up at her door.

Are you okay? Jennifer messaged back.

Zayda instantly replied, *Yes, I'm fine. I will call you later.*

She was acting strange. Jennifer didn't know what was going on with her best friend, but whatever it was she was surely going to find out.

I'm here if you need to talk... you know, about anything. Jennifer responded.

Thanks...

This wasn't like Zayda. Jennifer made a mental note to stop by her house later on. Once she finds out why the police wanted to question Neil, she would check on her friend, regardless of how Zayda felt about it.

"It's too much shit going on right now." Jennifer took a deep breath. She had been stressing for the past few weeks, however, she was glad that Neil finally came to the house. Jennifer had prepared what she would say to her husband if he ever reached out to her. But all the preparation she did went out of the window. None of the words came out once she laid eyes on him. It wasn't how she expected. Once she saw that Neil was calm, her attitude took a detour in a different direction. She knew sooner or later that the man she married would eventually come around and fix things between them.

Her heart smiled at the thought of them actually repairing their union and moving on with a happy life. The fixing part, however, was what she was worried about.

"If you are giving us another chance, God," She said as she made her way back upstairs to get the baby ready, "Thank you."

Chapter Thirty Two

NEIL

"For the last time, I haven't seen him." Neil repeated to Detective Hagans sitting on a stool across from him. They had been in the small conference room for only fifteen minutes, and he was already asked the same questions three times.

"Mr. Harris, the last time you spoke with Mr. Kinsley, you said that y'all had a disagreement. What was that disagreement about?"

Neil looked to his right at Jeffrey, his lawyer and uncle. With uncertainty glistening in his eyes, he shook his head and looked back at Hagans.

"I'd rather not say."

"Why not? You've got something to hide?" Hagans insisted.

"I ain't got shit to hide."

"It's kind of funny to me that your friend turns up missing right after y'all have an argument."

"Disagreement." Neil corrected.

"Ok, a disagreement," she continued, "and you don't want to tell me what it was about."

Hagans knew more than what she led on. The police had already gotten Zayda's statements, and she informed them that Carl and Neil were having an affair.

"You know what that sounds like to me?" Hagans stood from the stool, and leaned on the table closer to Neil, "Sounds like you might know exactly what is going on. It would be in your best interest to tell me. Maybe I can help you."

Neil looked at his uncle, again, "Could you give us a few minutes please?"

Both Hagans and Jeffrey were shocked by his question.

"You want me to step out?"

Neil nodded his head, yes.

"I don't think that's a good idea for you to answer questions without me in here. You may stand the chance of incriminating yourself."

"It's cool, Jeff." Neil assured him.

Hagans patiently waited for the two to make a decision.

"Ok." Jeffrey stood from his seat. "I'll be in the hallway."

When the door closed, Hagans sat back on the stool and folded her arms on the table in front of her waiting for Neil to continue.

"Look, I haven't done anything. I love Carl. I will never do anything to put him in harm's way," Neil attested, "We are… were lovers."

"Were?"

"That was what our last disagreement was about. His wife, Zayda Kinsley, caught us having sex."

"And what did she do?"

"She didn't do anything." Neil shrugged, "She left. She was gone for a couple of hours after she saw us."

"What did Carl say?" Hagans asked.

"Carl was pissed. He didn't mind living on the down low. He didn't want anyone to know about our secret attraction to men...or each other."

"Well, apparently, neither do you." Hagans held her hand up towards the door. "Is that why you made your lawyer leave?"

"Detective, I've known Carl for a long time. An image can mean a lot to men like us. Jeffrey doesn't know about what we do, but if Carl told me that he wanted to be with me, and only me, I would scream it to the world. I'd come out in a heartbeat. I love him more than some damn image. But I'm not about to expose his secret in front of my uncle even if he is representing me."

"Sounds like you really do love him," Hagans added, "I bet you were angry when he wasn't willing to leave his wife, and just be with you."

Neil crumpled his face at her, "If you are thinking I would hurt him over it... don't. I don't know where Carl is. I've been trying to reach him myself. Did you ask his wife?"

"We did."

"And?"

"Well, she hasn't seen him either."

"Carl has gone away for days upon days before. Why is this time any different?"

Hagans reached for a folder sitting at the end of the table and slid it in front of her. She opened it, and pulled out a few photos.

"Do you recognize this car," she held up one of the photos.

"That looks like Carl's vehicle." Neil grabbed the picture from her hand. "What happened to it?"

"We retrieved that vehicle from the river this morning. It does belong to Carl Kinsley, but we haven't been able to find him."

A sudden wave of sadness combined with fear hit Neil as he examined the photo of the damaged vehicle.

"Mr. Harris, is there any other place you could think of that Carl could be? Any enemies?"

Tears filled his eyes as the worst thoughts came to mind, "No." he mumbled and handed her back the photo. Clearing his throat, he wiped the few falling tears from his face, "I can make a few calls and ask around."

Detective Hagans nodded, as she put the pictures back into the folder.

"Are we done here?" Neil asked.

"Yea, we are done."

Hagans could tell Neil was shocked to see the photos. His reaction couldn't be staged. It was too pure and genuine. Neil stared at the photo as if he lost his best friend for good. Hagans sort of felt bad for him.

She watched as he got up from the table and left out the door. A tap on the two-way mirror broke her gaze. Hagans got up, left out the room and walked to the next room where Lieutenant Parker and Agent Bennett stood watching the questioning session.

"Good job, Hagans," Lieutenant Parker said as she entered the room. "Come in, and have a seat."

"What's going on?" Her hazel eyes traveled between the two gentlemen.

"Hagans, this is Agent Bennett." Parker introduced.

"Agent?" She raised her eyebrows. "With Internal Affairs? Am I under investigation?"

"No," Parker said. "He's not here for you. But you are being taken off of the Kinsley case. The FBI will be taking over from here."

"Why?"

"Carl Kinsley has been involved in corporate fraud and corruption." Agent Bennett stepped in. "We don't believe that this is a case of a missing person. He was under federal investigation. This entire bid may all be just an escape route."

"With all due respect, Agent Bennett, I don't think Mr. Harris would lie about being homosexual just for a scheme. I mean, I know when someone is lying, and that man in there didn't know what was going on."

"Ma'am, I'm pretty sure you are good at what you do, but I've been in this field for twenty-four years. Underestimating a person can be deadly. I've seen it happen more than I can count."

"Sir, I don't think he ran," Hagans turned back to Parker, "If that was the case, why would Kinsley leave his wife. Don't you think she would have gone with him? And they have a daughter. I think we should look deeper into this."

"Oh, and we will," Agent Bennett assured her. "*We* plan to get to the bottom of it all."

Chapter Thirty Three

For two whole days I was secluded from the world. No television, phone, nor visitors. When I wasn't being the worried, innocent wife who was so willing to give up whatever information the police asked for, I cleaned. Everything was under control… my story was so rock solid that a jack hammer couldn't break through it. Neil had been taken in for questioning the same day I put the bug in the police officer's ear. Jennifer had been blowing my phone up left and right, especially since I'd been avoiding her calls.

When she texted me about Neil being taken in for questioning, I was pleased at the quick response of the Philadelphia police department. However, I was shocked when she followed up with informing me he was with her at the time the police came.

The nerve of his fake ass to go back home to her after what just went down. I wish I could tell her what happened that night, but I couldn't risk her creating loopholes in my story. In due time, Neil will be behind bars, and she won't have to worry about him playing with her heart any longer.

Yes, everything and everyone was handled... except for me. On the outside, I appeared calm, cool and collected. But internally, I was losing it. Some days, I would hear footsteps in my house, and when I'd go to investigate the noise, nothing was there. That funky strong stench would come and go, and no matter how much I cleaned up, a red shaded tint reappeared over various areas of the house where Carl's blood smeared from me dragging his body.

To keep from conceding to my illusions, I kept busy by cleaning. I cleaned every inch of my house from top to bottom. No matter how much bleach or carpet cleanser I used, the blood kept reappearing. A few times I even saw blood coming from the drains in the tub and sink.

Every room I went into I felt like someone was watching me. The sight of Carl's face haunted me, and his voice spoke to me in my sleep. I just couldn't get away from him.

It was going on 4 PM, and like a slave, I was on my hands and knees scrubbing the living room carpet when I heard the doorbell ringing. I ceased, and shot my eyes over at the front door. It was so quiet in my house you can hear a pin drop, so whoever was at the door couldn't tell if anyone was home or not. Eventually, whoever it was will go away.

Again, my bell rung, this time the person banged on my door as well. Deliberately, I got up from the floor and eased my way over to the window. I slightly pulled back the curtain and saw Agent Bennett standing there along with two other men dressed in a similar get-up as Bennett; slacks and a dress shirt. Their car idled in my driveway with the siren lights flickering.

As I made my way to the door, he banged on it once more.

"Who is it?" I yelled as if I didn't already know.

"Mrs. Kinsley, its Agent Bennett. I need to speak with you about your husband. It's very important."

Cracking open the door just enough so he could see me, I asked, "Yes?"

"Mrs. Kinsley," he started "we have been trying to reach your husband. There has been a warrant issued for his arrest. We also have a warrant to search your property. When was the last time you saw or spoke to Carl Kinsley?"

"What? Why would you need to search my house? My husband has been missing for the past two and a half days." I informed him.

He raised his eyebrows. "Is that so?"

"I would also like to know where he is." I lied.

"Well, if you don't mind stepping aside for us to check inside the house," he held up a piece of paper and exposed the warrant.

I don't need you snooping around my goddamn house. Stepping to the side, I mouth the word 'OK' and nodded my head.

The men that were with him headed in different directions to begin their search.

"Is anyone else in the house?" Agent Bennett asked me.

"No. Just me."

At this point I didn't trust anyone. Even if he was the investigator for Cartman's office, he had to know something about the local police finding Carl's car. I saw right through the fake shocked expression he offered when I told him Carl was missing. Something about this just didn't feel right. I couldn't resist the urge. I had to ask.

"Agent Bennett?"

"Yes?"

"What exactly are you searching for?"

"Clues."

"What kind of clues?"

"Ones that would help us find your husband."

"He's going to jail, isn't he?" I asked. That's the only reason I could think of that he would need a warrant. "Marcy took a deal, right?"

The way he avoided eye contact, I could tell he didn't want to answer my question.

"You don't seem too mad about it," he folded his arms across his chest, "Why is that, Mrs. Kinsley."

Offering a sly smile, I turned on my feet, "Enjoy your search, Agent Bennett."

If you think I'm that fucking stupid, you need to shoot yourself, I thought as I walked into my kitchen. Him being here only means one thing...I need to start putting my move in motion. Even though I had an air tight plan, who knows what they will dig up. Whatever it is, I will be long gone when they do.

The agents took about twenty minutes to do what they came to do. I sat on my sofa the entire time sipping Moscato and waiting for them to get the fuck out of my house. When I overheard one of the guys telling Agent Bennett that the house was all clear, I was satisfied, but he wasn't pleased with that information.

"We're all done here," he shouted to me.

I got up and escorted them to the front door with my wine in hand, of course. When I opened the door to let them out, I saw Jennifer walking up my driveway.

"We'll be in touch," Agent Bennett told me before leaving.

"Thank you." I responded.

In passing, Jennifer greeted the unfamiliar men and joined me at the door.

"Who was that?" She asked me. My eyes were still pinned on the agents.

"FBI." I nonchalantly answered.

"Are you serious? What did they want?"

"Carl." I leaned up against the door frame, "you know my husband is a criminal now."

"About the job thing?"

I shrugged my shoulders, "I guess."

"Where is Carl, anyway? Neil told me about his car being found in the river. Is Carl OK?"

When the cars finally turned off my street, I looked at Jennifer.

"I have to go to the bank, you feel like riding?" I asked without acknowledging her question.

"You sure you want me to go? You haven't been fucking with me for the past few days." Jennifer joked.

"Too much shit has been going on." I told her, "I needed time, and honestly I still don't think I got it all together. You understand that, right?"

"By all means, take all the time you need." She agreed.

"Well, right now I need to go to the bank. Hang on a sec; I'll grab my bag."

"Seized?" I yelled at the bank teller when she informed me of my account. My commotion drew the attention of the other few people waiting to be serviced. Lowering my voice to its original state, I asked, "Seized by whom? This must be a mistake."

"Ma'am, I am unable to see why," the young, burgundy haired teller told her. "The account has been blocked. You will have to speak with the branch manager. You can have a seat-"

Before she could finish her sentence, I stormed away from the counter and out of the building.

My accounts were separate, I thought, *I didn't even use my married name. How the hell can they just take all of my money?*

Jennifer was in the car blasting Lauren Hill when I returned to her.

"That was fast." She said as she turned down her music.

I hopped back in the front seat, "I just had to make a deposit," I lied. "It was hardly anyone in there."

She started the car back up and pulled into traffic.

My fucking money is gone! All of it. Damn you Carl! I was enraged, but I had to keep cool in front of Jennifer.

"So what's the deal with you and Carl?" her question ripped through my thoughts, "He just left with no explanation?"

"Me and Carl are no longer an item." I said staring out the window. My mind was on getting the hell out of dodge. I had a feeling shit was about to hit the fan. Why the hell didn't I know about the accounts? Every penny I had was gone…vanished. I was counting on that money to get out of Philadelphia.

"What do you mean by that?" Jennifer swiped her hair behind her ear.

"I mean, that it's. Now maybe me and Cherish really can move to Maryland with you?" I wasn't really considering it at first, but now, I really didn't have a choice. I was broke. Leaving with

Jenn would be a huge help until I got back on my feet.

"Uh, Maryland... of course." I sensed much uncertainty in her hesitant response.

"Why does that sound like a *but* is about to come up?"

"But... I need to think about leaving before I actually do."

"Why? You were just all *I got to get out of here* and *I can't be next to Neil* a few days ago. What changed?"

"Well, Neil and I finally got the chance to talk."

I looked over at her, "Let me guess... y'all are going to work things out?"

"No, I didn't say all of that." She defended.

"You're saying something like that. I mean first you were ready to start your life over, and now that you've talked to him, you're not. What does he have to hold you here besides love...if he even has that? Y'all ain't got no kids together."

"Damn girl," Jennifer's voice squealed. "I just said I talked to him, nothing more. You jumping down my fucking throat like I did something wrong."

"Trust me; talking to him again is wrong. You don't need him in your life."

"Wait a minute," She pulled the car over and put the gear in park, "you were the one who told him to fix it, if I remember correctly."

"Yea well, at the time I didn't know then what I know now. Neil ain't shit, him or Carl."

"So that's where this attitude is coming from," she nodded, "You and Carl are separating, so you got to reflect it on my marriage."

"Carl is dead. Neil is gay...they both were," My harsh delivery briefly terminated all conversation. "I saw the two of them, my husband and yours fucking, in my god damn house. Now you tell me he's still the man for you."

"Zayda, what the fuck are you talking about?"

"Exactly what I just said."

"Carl's dead?" She asked with her head slanted to one side.

"And...They were fucking."

"Zayda....What did you do?" A scared expression etched across her face.

I thought I was over it. I was good at hiding my pain, but seeing the look on Jennifer's face sparked my flow of tears.

"It was an accident," I finally admitted. She was the only person I spoke those words out loud to.

Jennifer sat with her jaw hanging low as I told her everything that happened from the fight to dumping his car in the river, and the text messages Neil sent to him. I even told her about the STD he gave me. Come to find out, she had it too, just the week before I found out that I had it. Carl made me think I was crazy. I don't know how he got the negative results on paper, but I know now it was him.

"They have been playing us…all this time." I concluded as I wiped away the tears that trickled down my face.

I looked over at Jennifer, and she was in shock. I wasn't going to tell her, but I couldn't let her make the mistake of going back to Neil. Truthfully, I felt like a huge weight was lifted off of me when I finally opened up to someone.

Without another word to me, Jennifer started her car and drove off. We rode the rest of the way to my house in silence.

When we arrived, she didn't say so much as goodbye when I got out. The car door was barely shut before she sped off, leaving me standing there on the curb. She was hurt. But I'd rather have her hurt at me telling her the truth instead of living this lie.

Chapter Thirty-Four

NEIL & JENNIFER

"…Yes, that'll be perfect," Jennifer heard Neil saying into the phone when she opened the front door, "Thank you, so much. I owe you for this one." He ended the call and shot his eyes at the door, "Hey."

"Who was that?" Jennifer asked as she walked over to the sofa where Neil sat.

"That was Ronald," Neil said. "He is going to pull a few strings and get Carl's missing story in the news; the more people keeping an eye out, the better."

Emotionless, Jennifer leaned on the arm of the chair as she watched him mark something down on a piece of paper. Since the day he was taken down for questioning, Neil devoted all of his time in finding Carl. At first, Jennifer just assumed that he was only being a good friend. After what Zayda told her today, it all makes sense as to why he was going so hard.

"Neil?"

"Yeah, what's up?" he answered as he continued to write.

"If I were missing, would you go this far to find me?"

"What you mean?" he replied clearly unaware of her current state. Had he looked at her, Neil would have been able to tell she had the eyes of a crying woman.

"All of this is what I mean...the news reports, countless hours spent trying to find Carl; I don't even think you've eaten in the past two days."

"He's my friend," Neil explained, "And I know he would do it for me if the shoe was on the other foot."

"But if it were me...would you take the same measures?"

Neil finally stopped what he was doing, "Where is all of this coming from?"

"I just need some clarity... that's all. I don't feel that if I was in the same predicament you would react the same way." She honestly answered.

"Jennifer, don't be silly. I mean, we had our differences, and we've been through our shit, but you are still my friend. Of course I would react the same way. We were friends first, remember?"

"Friends?" she repeated. A small tear escaped from the corner of her eye.

"Jennifer, what is this about? Why do you look so sad? Did something happen today?"

"You tell me?"

"Tell you what?" Neil turned completely toward her.

More tears came down Jennifer's face as she could no longer hold in her emotions.

"Do you love him?" she asked although she already had the answer.

"Love who?" Neil raised his eyebrows, "Jennifer, what are you talking about?"

"Carl." she sternly replied, "Do you love Carl?"

Neil paused when he began to realize what his wife was referring to.

"I was with Zayda today." Jennifer said just above a whisper. Her voice had become choked with emotion. "Why didn't you tell me, Neil?"

"Jennifer, I'm sorry. I, honestly, did want to tell you when I came over here. I told you we had something to talk about, but then the whole thing with the police happened and Carl missing...I just put it on the back burner for now."

"No...it's been on your back burner this entire time we've been married?"

"Jennifer, it wasn't like that."

"Then what was it like, huh?" her sudden change of tone was evident of how she felt...livid. "Was this all just one sick ass game for you?"

"Jennifer, please—"

"Fuck your *pleases*!" She stood up from the armrest, "You cannot give me back what you've stolen from me. While I was loving your gay ass, you were jumping on my heart like a kid at the playground. Were you even in love with me?"

Neil stood to his feet and approached her, "Jennifer, of course—"

"No," she backed away shaking her head robustly, "Do not come near me."

Neil exhaled deeply, "Jennifer, I'm sorry."

She put up her hand not wanting to hear anything he had to say. With a face full of tears, Jennifer slowly backed away until she reached the steps, "I'm leaving."

As she began up to her room, Neil hurried over to the stair case, "Jennifer, we need to talk about this."

"You made your choice a long time ago, Neil; I'm the one just finding out. There is nothing else to discuss."

"But there is..."

Jennifer stopped and turned to him, "Why?" she asked, "why are you fighting so hard when you just said you planned to tell me anyway. You were always going to end things with me, so why are you trying so hard now?"

Dumbfounded, Neil stood at the bottom of the steps, lost.

"To make yourself feel better." She answered for him, "You need to hear yourself apologize, and justify so that you can sleep comfortable at night. Well, guess what? You don't get to explain to me. Our past is irrelevant."

At this point, Neil couldn't even look Jennifer in the eye. He hung his head low as he drowned in his own shame. Neil knew how badly this news would hurt her, and even though he was never in love with Jennifer, he still had love for her—a lot of love. He even felt bad when he had to make her think he was sleeping around with other women just to cover up his relationship with Carl. There were never any other women, or men for that matter. It was always

Carl. Neil battled with his secret day in and day out. There wasn't a clear road for him to take. He didn't want to end things with Jennifer unless Carl was ready, but he always knew in the back of his mind, that Carl's talks of being with him was all bullshit.

Neil couldn't help but to hope that one day it would happen, and allowed himself to entertain the thought in the first place. Carl was never going to be ready, but Neil couldn't stay away from him either. The only person who won in this love square was Carl. He had both his wife and his lover submissive to his every beck and call.

Moments later, Jennifer returned to the living room carrying a large suitcase in one hand. Just as she suspected, Neil had returned to the sofa doing whatever it was he was doing when she came in.

He turned around and looked back at her, "Jennifer, you don't have to leave. I will leave. You can keep the house."

"I think you and your man will enjoy it more," she said, "Assuming that you'll find him alive...good luck with that."

She left out of the door and threw her bag in the trunk. When Jennifer hopped in the driver's seat, she pulled out her cell and sent Zayda a text.

Maryland seems good right about now. Pack your things; I'll be there in a few hours.

There was one stop Jennifer had to make. If she and Zayda were really going to leave, that meant she was going to be on the run. She hadn't had her court appearance yet for stabbing Neil, and was warned not to leave the state. At this point, none of that mattered, and with Zayda admitting to her that she killed her husband, it was time they both ran.

After a twenty minute drive, Jennifer arrived at her boutique. She hadn't opened it since before she was arrested. This was the last time she'd come here, so there were a few things she needed before they left. Jennifer kept a small stash of money in a safe located in the back office. It was too late to withdraw money from her account. The amount she would need exceeded the max amount at an ATM. Once she left the city, all credit and bank cards would be trashed so that she wouldn't leave a trail behind her.

Inside the safe, she had well over fifteen grand. It was inventory money she hadn't deposited into the bank yet. She grabbed that, along with the pistol she kept in the store for security reason. Heading out of the office, she noticed a few of Neil's clothing she picked up from the drycleaner's. It was five of his favorite suits; two of which she purchased for him.

As she passed through the main part of the store, memories of Neil making love to her overran her mind; mainly because they had blessed each part of the store with their bodily fluids when she first opened it.

Back then, she was so in love with him, she couldn't see the now obvious signs of his feminine ways. Neil preferred his pubic hair shaved, got more pedicures that she did, and the nigga was stylish from head to toe. He even pushed Jennifer to hire her trainer to keep her fit, and when her muscles started cutting through her skin, it seems as though their sex life increased. Jennifer thought it was because she looked finer without clothes, but it probably made him feel as though he were fucking a man.

Now, as she stood in the middle of her boutique, the value of the business wasn't worth living the lie she was. Jennifer went behind the counter and searched the shelves. She found exactly what she was looking for...a can of hairspray and a lighter.

She flicked the lighter once, making sure it worked, and headed back to the office.

"I'll see you in hell," she hissed over Neil's suits as if she were talking directly to him. Jennifer flicked the lighter in one hand, and sprayed the flammable fumes from the can onto his clothes. In seconds the material was consumed with fire, and she left the office to burn.

Chapter Thirty-Five

Whether or not I have the money, I'm leaving; especially after reading Jennifer's text. I'm just going to have to do with whatever I have in my wallet.

Maybe my mom can give me a few more bucks, I thought to myself as I moved around my room collecting my most needed items to pack, *I'll ask her when I pick up the baby.*

Quickly, I stuffed whatever could fit inside my two duffel bags, and zipped them shut. Next, was Cherish's bag. I went into her nursery and pulled down the *Dora the Explorer* suitcase from her closet. Just as I began packing her things, I heard someone banging at my door.

They were banging so hard I thought my door would come off the hinges. I rushed down the stairs and open it.

"Alright, alright...I'm coming, sheesh." I said knowing exactly who it was.

Snatching the door open, I came face-to-face with an unexpected guest. Neil stood there with a mischievous look on his face. He was the last person I'd expected to see...ever.

"What the fuck do you want?" I hissed. He had no right to come to my house after he violated it.

Without warning or welcome, he barged into my house, "Where is he, Zayda?"

"I didn't say you could come in."

"I know you know where Carl is." He ignored me, "Tell me where he is right now, and why the hell was his car in the river? And furthermore, why were they questioning me about him?"

"I don't know what the fuck you're talking about."

"Oh no?" he said, "well, let me refresh your memory. I was fucking your husband. And let me tell you, it was good. I was giving him the best sex of his life. That night you saw him sucking my dick was only the beginning of what I was about to do to him. But your fat ass had to come and ruin it—you ruined us."

"Fuck you!" I spat at him, "you need to get the fuck out of my house."

"Look at you, you're pathetic. He didn't want you. He never wanted your funky ass pussy."

"But I wasn't his secret, was I?" I shot back, "I was the one living the life with him that you wanted, while he hid you like an ugly child. The sex was all you could offer...and all he wanted. You were his little bitch."

Neil's chest heaved up and down as I could see my words eating through his heart.

"Yea," I continued to taunt, "The truth hurts, don't it."

"I am only going to ask you this one last time, what did you do to Carl? I'm not going anywhere until you tell me what happened."

"I don't have to do a god damn thing," I stormed up on him, "Now I'm only going to tell you this one last time…get out of my fucking house before I send you with his ass."

His eyes widened from my threat, "Bitch, what the fuck…did you do?" he gritted through his teeth.

"I did what I had to," I smirked, knowing that it would piss him off…Good. "You want to find your little boyfriend put your swim gear on, ass hole. By now, the sharks probably ripped his body to shreds."

Before I knew it, Neil grabbed me by the neck and forced me down on the glass coffee table causing it to shatter. Glass particles broke through my back as he pinned me to the floor. He had a firm grip on my neck cutting off my air supply.

I kicked and punched at him in an effort to get him off of me.

"What did you do to him, you crazy bitch!" he cried out. Neil lifted my head and slammed me against the floor, repeatedly.

Gasping for air, I tried to pry his hands off of me. A sharp pain shot up my chest…I was choking, and that's when I realized Neil was going to kill me.

"Let me go," I mouthed, but he didn't stop. I felt around the floor by my side and came across a large piece of broken glass. I grabbed it, and rammed it into his side. I held it so tightly; my own blood drew in my palms.

"Ahh!" he screamed in pain. That was enough for him to get off of me.

Neil fell over and grabbed his side. I got up as fast as I could, and headed for the door. Before I could get to it, the door swung open.

"Freeze!" I heard. A swarm of police had entered my home.

Agent Bennett was the first face I recognized. Along with the others, he had his gun pointing directly at me.

"Zayda Kinsley, you are under arrest for the murder of Carl Kinsley."

Chapter Thirty Six

My stomach growled like a lion as I lay on my back and stared at the ceiling. I was in the middle of yet another deep talk with God when it kept interrupting me. Sitting up on my bed, I rubbed my stomach and looked across the room at the empty bunk. Just a day ago another body slept there…another bunkie transferred. I've been in prison for five months now and already went through four roommates.

Yep! They got me. I found out that the warrant Agent Bennett had to search my house was just a ploy… they bugged it. They heard my confession to Neil of dumping Carl's body in the river.

"Kinsley!" Shelton, the on duty correctional officer, yelled out as he approached my bunk space. "You have a visitor."

"Today is not my visitation day." I glanced up at him.

"I don't make the rules," he uttered, "I just follow them. I was told to come get you, so let's go."

Nodding my head, I got up from the bed and follow behind him bypassing the many women wearing the same tan prison outfit as me.

The moment I walked into the visitation area and saw my daughter's smiling face, my heart fluttered. It was the first time I'd seen her since my trial. My mom held her up on the table waving to me.

"Oh my God, you've gotten so big." I was amazed at her growth in such a short time. I walked over to the table and picked her up.

Filling her chubby cheeks with kisses, I held her, tightly. I didn't want to let go. She smelled so good…as if she had been bathed in Johnson and Johnson's baby lotion. Her soft skin was so warm and cuddly. I had to quickly make a mental note of everything to get me through hard times while I'm in here. I pulled her face away so that I could get a good look at her once more.

"You're getting teeth too, huh, mama?"

"Yes," my mother contested, "and she is eating everything in sight."

"That's my girl." I took a seat on the empty chair across from my mother and sat Cherish on my lap.

"How are you holding up in here, sweetie?"

Leisurely, I shrugged one shoulder and replied, "I'm holding, I guess. It isn't as bad as I thought it would be. Watching a bunch of prison movies scared me at first. But I just stay to myself, mainly. I read…a lot, and talk to God. I was also thinking of writing a book.

"Well that'll be interesting." My mom nodded her head.

"How are you?" I asked. I could already tell she was fighting back her tears.

My mother sat back in her seat and folded her arms across her chest. The look on her face saddened me.

"Worried." she answered, honestly. "I can't stop thinking about you being in here. I mean…" she began to choke up, "I never thought my daughter would ever be in prison.

"Mom, I never meant to disappoint you. If I could take it all back, I would… in a heartbeat."

"And Zaire keeps asking about you, and when you are coming over to see him. I don't—" she paused to clear her throat. "I don't even know how to tell him. That's why I haven't bought him up here yet."

"Mom, you have to tell him. You have to let him know that his big sister did something wrong and it'll be a long time before he gets to see me again."

"I know I have to, but it will hurt him. And to see him that hurt will hurt me too. I feel like a failure. I was supposed to protect my children from all of this. I can't protect you from being in here, and I can't protect Zaire from being hurt."

"You're not a failure, mom. Don't let the mistakes that I made weigh heavy on you, because I made them."

I got up to go to the next table for the box of tissues sitting there. I slid them down in front of her. She grabbed one from the box and wiped her tearful eyes.

"But just know that I never stop praying for you, Zayda. Praying that your situation changes. You are just a baby, and you had your whole life ahead of you."

I looked down at my baby playing with my fingers on one hand and stroked her jet black hair with the other.

"And so does Cherish." I said softly. "Mom, I need you to do me a favor."

"Anything."

"I need you to not bring her here ever again... and stop your visits as well."

"What? Zayda why?"

"It's not fair to her to have a mommy in prison. She'll always wonder what it would be like to be with a mommy. While she is still young, I want her to forget about me. I'm going to be here for the rest of my life and I want her to be able to enjoy hers."

"Zayda, I won't do that. She needs to know who her mother is."

"You might not understand right now, mom, but trust me this is for the better. Give her a life that I can't give her. Let her be happy. She shouldn't have to grow up knowing that her dad died at the hands of her mother who is now rotting in prison. Do you know what psychological damage that will do to her? I don't want that for her. So I need you to stop the visits. I'll have them remove you from the visitors list."

"Zay, No! Please don't do this."

"Mom, I love you." I began to choke up, "And I love her. As much as this is going to hurt me, it's something that I have to do."

I turned my daughter around to face me. I wanted to get one last look before I never saw her again. Her eyes, so pure and innocent, held not a bit of fear or terror behind them. This is how I always wanted to remember my only daughter. I gave her one last kiss and stood from the table. My mother stood up, as well. I handed Cherish back to my mom, and gave her, too, one last hug.

"Promise me you'll make her happy." I whispered in her ear.

My mother couldn't bring herself to say the words; she just nodded her head.

"I love you," I told her. My words only made her breakdown even more. I couldn't stand to see her this way, so I turned on my feet and headed back over to the correctional officer.

"I'm ready." I said.

Today was the last day I vowed for my loved ones ever to see me this way, again. I want my mother to remember the woman I used to be. I had everybody fooled about my life. Well, except myself, I guess. I have issues that only God, himself, can fix. I lie to cover up my ugly truths, and I allowed myself to believe that the immoral revenge I got on my dead husband, and his lover, was okay. I belong in here with the rest of the caged animals. Society was no place for us. I may seem normal, but the fact that I would do it all over again, the exact same way, tells me that I haven't changed from all of this. And for that, I am where I belong.

The guard escorted me back to the bunking area. As we walked past a female correctional officer, she yelled out to me, "Kinsley, you've got a new bunkie. I just dropped her off in your room."

My eyes traveled ahead to my area, and I saw another woman standing there.

As I neared my assigned spot, my eyes widened with disbelief. "Jennifer?"

She lifted her head and looked at me. Her eyes lit up with relief.

"What are you doing here?" I asked her.

Jennifer sat down on her bunk and folded her arms across her chest. "Someone had to finish what you started… right?"